My Own Worst Frenemy

A LANGDON PREP NOVEL

Kimberly Reid

KOREMATSU CAMPUS

Teen

Dafina KTeen Books
KENSINGTON PUBLISHING CORP.
www.kensingtonbooks.com/KTeen

DAFINA KTEEN BOOKS are published by

Kensington Publishing Corp.
119 West 40th Street
New York, NY 10018

ISBN-13: 978-0-7582-6740-5
ISBN-10: 0-7582-6740-1

First Printing: September 2011
10 9 8 7 6 5 4 3 2 1

Printed in the United States of America

For Aunt Marsha,
who tried to teach me life is an adventure.

I finally get it.

ACKNOWLEDGMENTS

Writing a book is solitary work, but publishing a book takes many talented and dedicated people, not to mention friends and family who don't disown you even when making deadlines means you haven't said boo to them in forever.

So I want to thank those people, starting with my editor, Selena James. Thank you for totally getting what I wanted to do with Chanti's story, helping me make it better, and giving me the opportunity to let her story grow beyond this novel. Kristine Mills-Noble and her design team gave this book a fabulous cover—I still keep it on my desk and stare at it regularly. I also appreciate the effort of all the people at Kensington I don't know the names of who helped in the process of getting this book into the hands of readers.

Kristin Nelson, literary agent extraordinaire, told me years ago that my voice and writing style would be a good match for young adult novels. It took me a while to see the possibility in my writing that she did, but now I get to work on a series and in a world that I absolutely love. Thanks Kristin for being able to see both the forest *and* the trees when I can't see either one.

A writer can have all kinds of support systems, but only other writers can understand the very special madness—and the joy—that we go through in turning blank paper and a random idea into seventy thousand words other people might pay to read. Thank you to all the writers in the Literary Ladies Luncheon of Denver for camaraderie and commiseration over really good dim sum. Special thanks to Elise Singleton, J.D. Mason, and Carleen Brice who have buoyed me during low points and helped me celebrate the good times.

Chanti's story isn't autobiographical, but I'd be lying if I said I didn't get a lot of inspiration from my actual life. It's hard not to when you write crime stories and your mom was a police detective, your stepdad is a criminal lawyer, and your husband has made a career working for both the police and the court system. Thank you to my family for raising and training me to think like a cop, and occasionally like a criminal. You probably didn't realize you were doing that, but it worked out great!

I am lucky to have family and friends who have always been there for me—much love to all of you.

Finally, many thanks to you readers—writers do what we do hoping one day you'll read and enjoy our stories. It wouldn't be nearly as much fun without you.

Chapter 1

I'm eating Coco Puffs on my last day of summer vacation and watching the news because there's nothing else on but Sunday-morning church shows and infomercials. The reporter is on location, telling me how the police finally closed down a prostitution ring. I'd rather not share my breakfast with hookers or the helmet-haired reporter who's way too happy reporting their arrest, so I reach for the remote. That's when I recognize one of the women being loaded into the police truck. In case I'm not sure what I'm seeing, the reporter steps to the side and passes her arm through the air, Vanna White–style, so I can get a better look. The woman is trying to hide her face, and doing a good job, but I'd know that outfit anywhere.

It's definitely Lana, in her favorite wig, the platinum-blond one with the bangs. She's wearing a baby tee that reads YOUNG, WILLING, AND ABLE, with the neckline cut wide so one side slips off her shoulders to reveal a red bra strap. The T-shirt is cut so short that if not for the bra, all her business would be peaking out from the curled edges of cotton. If the shirt isn't bad enough, the Daisy Duke shorts are. And God, please don't let her bend over to duck into the truck like the other hookers are doing. Too late.

But that isn't the worst of it. People I know might be watching this. I might have to explain to them that my mother is not really a crack ho. Come to think of it, I'd be better off letting them think she *is* a crack ho since her real job is ten times worse. In my neighborhood, you can't get much lower than a vice cop.

A few hours later, no one has mentioned Lana or the fact that her butt cheeks were all over the news. It makes sense—none of my friends would be up that early on a Sunday, especially when it's our last day of freedom. We're spending it on my front porch doing what we've done pretty much all summer. Talking about being broke, gossiping about who hooked up and who broke up over the break, and trying to figure out what's going on at Ada Crawford's house across the street.

Ada's house doesn't fit in with the rest of the street. It was built in the fifties like the others, but her house is prettier, what real estate agents would call a *real cream puff* if anyone was actually interested in buying in our neighborhood. It's freshly painted and newly landscaped with the greenest grass that Ada has to water practically 24-7, which is no problem since she also has a new sprinkler system. Everybody else's house appears to have the original 1950s paint job, new landscaping is limited to plastic flowers on the porch, and we have to water our half-green, half-brown grass with a garden hose. What makes Ada a mystery is that she's got the nicest house on the block and no job. I know people can make a food stamp stretch, but not that much.

"It has something to do with all the men coming and going," I speculate. "There goes one now."

"Maybe she's a romantic and has lots of generous boyfriends, Chanti," Michelle offers.

"Riiight, she's a romantic. And please pronounce my name right—*Shawnty*, not *Shanty* like the towns where poor people live in a Steinbeck book."

"Who?" Michelle asks.

Maybe if she stopped calling me a book geek and picked one up herself, she'd find out. I know I sound a little testy, but Michelle annoys me. She's taken my best friend since third grade away from me, which is funny because Tasha and I never hung out with her before this summer. We even called her Squeak when she first moved on the block—not to her face or anything—because her voice reminded us of Minnie Mouse. Now they're almost besties. It isn't all Michelle's fault since I've been somewhat negligent in my best-friend duties and I suppose Tasha had to find someone to hang with all summer, but I'm still a little peeved.

"Well, she can't be dealing, because someone else has cornered that market, right, Michelle?" Tasha says as she glues a track onto Michelle's scalp. Tasha's mom can't stand the smell of the glue, so she has to do all her weaving outside. Most people would be afraid to get their weave done on somebody's porch by a girl with no professional training, but Tasha is a lot cheaper than the salon and really has a way with hair. She's like the weave whisperer or something.

There's a loud bang and Michelle jumps out of her chair and ducks behind the glider swing, ripping the newly glued track right off her head because Tasha is still holding it.

"What is your problem?" Tasha asks.

"I thought I heard a gunshot."

"I know this isn't the farm, but it's not *that* bad, Michelle," I say. "Mr. Harrison is trying to get his lawnmower started. It always sounds like that."

Michelle comes out from behind the glider and returns to her chair. "Now it's my turn to correct you—I lived on a ranch, not a farm."

"Close enough," I say.

"Michelle isn't too far off the mark," Tasha defends her. "Isn't that why you aren't working at Tastee Treets anymore?"

"My mother made me quit because a meth-head held us

up, even though I was in the back walk-in freezer sneaking some Rocky Road during the whole thing," I say. "Besides, that guy pulled a gun—he didn't shoot it."

"Well, I heard somebody did get shot last weekend, a couple blocks over," Tasha says.

Tasha knows everything about our neighborhood, but I know there wasn't a shooting two blocks over because Lana would have been talking about it for days. It would have been another justification for making me change schools, which she decided to do when my school announced it was closing. After years of people leaving for the suburbs, our school was down to five hundred students so the city merged it into our rival, North High. Lana won't move because she says if we wait a minute, it won't be long before someone opens an Asian bistro, a yoga studio, and a Starbucks on Center Street and we'll be all gentrified, like what happened in some other Denver neighborhoods. Then she plans to sell for a lot of money. Lana is more optimistic than I am. I think we'll be waiting longer than a minute for that to happen.

"Chanti, you can't convince your mother to let you go with us to North?" Tasha says. She knows me so well, it's like she can read my mind. I bet she can't do that with Squeak.

"It's the day before school starts. What do *you* think?"

I've been telling her all summer that nothing I say will make Lana change her mind about forcing me to go to some stuck-up rich school across town just because I made one little mistake. She thinks I'll get into more trouble if I stay in Denver Heights and go to North.

"Don't get attudinal on me, Chanti. I'm not the one who screwed up my life."

I ignore Tasha and do the only thing I can given the situation: I lie.

"The only thing worse than going to a school you hate is starting a new school after everyone else. Even if Lana lets me go to North, by the time the transfer paperwork happened,

I'd be starting three weeks late. By then, everyone will have staked out their tables in the cafeteria. All the back seats in class will be taken. I'd rather go to the new school on day one than start North late and be the new girl."

"That would be tragic," says Michelle in the only tone she seems to know—sarcastic. "Ow, Tasha. Stop pulling!"

"At least I didn't choose my school based on a boy," I say to Michelle, who gives me the finger. "A boy so sorry he gets kicked out of school before he even started it, and in the meantime spends the summer cheating on me with Rhonda Hodges so I have to break up with him anyway."

Michelle looks sincerely wounded now, not just from the way Tasha is handling her head, and I feel bad for adding on that last part. But not as bad as I feel about her messing up me and Tasha's perfectly good friendship. Although I'm sure Tasha would say I was the one who messed things up.

"You wouldn't be new," Tasha says. "You'd know me and Michelle, and a bunch of other people from the old school. Not to mention kids from around the way, like . . ."

"Speaking of kids from The Ave," I say, cutting her off because there's no chance of me going to North and it bums me out talking about it. "Did y'all hear about Donnell Down-the-Street?"

"What about him?"

"He got picked up." I say this as though it's old news, knowing that neither of them have heard a thing about Donnell Down-the-Street. We call him that because there are two Donnells on Aurora Avenue, where I live. The one closest to Center Street got to keep his name without anything added on. The other one got arrested yesterday. I only know this because Lana told me during this morning's tirade entitled *Chanti, You're Going to That School and Donnell Is Just Another Example Why—As If We Need More Examples—and You Better Not Ask Me Again Because You're Going and That's All There Is to It.*

"No he didn't!" Michelle says without a hint of sarcasm.

Until recently (well, until Rhonda Hodges), she had a serious thing for Donnell DTS. "For what? How do you know?"

"I just do."

Tasha vouches for me. "Chanti always knows this stuff before everyone else. She just does."

My friends can never know Lana is my source. They think she's a paralegal in an office downtown. That's because when you're Vice and all the undercover cases you work are related to drugs, prostitution, or gambling, it's all about the down low. The minute anyone figures out she's a cop, she'll have to leave Vice and go back to the burglary division, which she says is nowhere near as exciting. Lana guards her secret like Michelle guards the fact she is no longer a virgin (thanks to Donnell DTS) from her preacher daddy. But I know all about Michelle because Tasha can't keep her mouth shut. I keep it to myself because that's one of the things I do well, hold on to other people's business. You never know when you might need it.

Information is negotiable, like currency. I learned that from Lana. Not information like her identity, of course. That secret keeps us both safe. It's the reason I call her Lana instead of Mom, even though everyone knows her by a totally different name on the street. Thanks to great genes and the fact that she had me when she was just sixteen, Lana looks too young to be my mother, which is kind of helpful. The fewer people who know I'm her kid, the better. Some of her more vindictive perps would be happy to know she has a kid. Except for my grandparents in Atlanta, I'm the only one outside the department who knows what she really does—we don't have family in town and Lana's closest friends are cops. So keeping Lana's secret sort of makes me her partner. It's like I'm kind of a cop, and it doesn't matter that I'm way too scared to actually ever *be* a cop.

Just as I'm about to tell them what I know—which is nothing, but I'm very good at embellishing—we see MJ

Cooper walking toward us, on the other side of the street. Tasha and Michelle go quiet because they're too busy trying to watch MJ without actually looking at her. Well, I'm not afraid to look at her, and I do. That's why I notice that she stops for just a second, like she might consider crossing the street, but she gives me a look that almost strikes me down where I'm standing, then keeps walking.

Michelle speaks first, but only when she's certain MJ is halfway down the block. "What's *she* looking at?"

"Seems like she's still mad at you, Chanti," Tasha says. "What did you do to her, anyway? Whatever it was, I think you best watch your back."

"Please. She's just been watching too many reruns of *The Wire*. Thinks she's Snoop Pearson or somebody," Michelle says. "Nobody's scared of her."

"Chanti's mother is. That's why she's sending her away to school."

Tasha thinks she knows everything.

"It isn't *away*. It's like ten miles from here, and I'll be taking the bus there and back every day."

"Well, MJ's still the reason," Tasha says, smug in being right.

"I wonder if she had anything to do with the police harassing Donnell," Michelle says.

My natural instinct is about to kick in, the one that makes me angry whenever anyone acts like the cops are the bad guys, but I let it go. Because around here, where profiling was probably invented, sometimes they *are* the bad guys. Still, if anyone on The Ave is prime for getting picked up, it's Donnell DTS, if not for whatever he did last night, then surely for something else.

"Donnell doesn't need to be harassed," I remind Michelle.

"It isn't his fault he's like that."

"Whose fault is it?" Tasha asks.

"My daddy says it's because he doesn't have a father figure. He sees that a lot in his congregation."

"You mean his church of twenty that he holds in your basement?" Tasha asks.

"It'll be a big church one day and you won't be talking smack then," Michelle says. "He used to have a good-size congregation when we lived in Texas."

"My father skipped out before I was born and you don't see me going to jail," I say. "It's Donnell's third time in. Don't make like he's a choirboy."

"It's only his second time," Michelle says, as if it still makes him eligible for that choirboy job. "Not that I'm defending him or anything."

"Yeah, you are, and you need to give it up." Tasha adds. "Donnell ain't thinking about you, especially if he's in jail. If he's thinking about anything other than how his public defender is going to get him off, it's going to be how he can get even with Chanti."

Uh, what?

"Why does he care anything about her?" Michelle asks, looking at me suspiciously.

"I heard he knows it was Chanti who told you about Rhonda Hodges."

"How would he know that unless you told?" I ask Michelle.

"Because I told," she says, seeming not to care one bit that I now have an ex-con gunning for me. That'll be the last time I mind someone else's business.

"I also heard MJ isn't talking to Chanti because she double-crossed her."

"Tasha, how come half your sentences start with 'I heard'?" I say, angry not so much with Tasha's gossiping than with the fact that she's probably right on both counts.

"You used to ask me for the scoop all the time, Chanti. Now that it's about you, suddenly you don't want to hear it."

Tasha doesn't understand. I'm starting eleventh grade and never had a real boyfriend, I have to keep my mother's job a secret on a block where the truth would get us run out at gunpoint, and I have to start a new school tomorrow. With all that going on, I really don't need to hear two crazy ex-cons might have it in for me.

Chapter 2

Okay, so Donnell DTS truly is a crazy ex-con. But MJ is a true friend, or was. Right now, she probably wants to kill me. I can see how Tasha and Michelle might be skeptical. They never got to know MJ like I did, even though I was hanging out with them when I first met her a couple of months ago. I was at a party Tasha and Michelle talked me into driving them to. They couldn't get the keys from their parents and didn't want their hair to get messed up on the walk over even though it was less than a mile away. That was the only reason I agreed—if it was the pure torture I expected it to be and I had to leave, they could always walk back or find another ride. Parties are so not my scene. I'd rather be home with a good book, but my friends act like reading is the death knell of a social life, so I went and regretted it immediately.

It almost never rains in Colorado, and since it's practically the desert, we have single-digit humidity in summer. It's probably the only place on the planet where nearly every day is a good hair day. So that was a completely bogus excuse to ask me to drive them. When they got to my house, I saw the real reason was on their feet—platform stilettos so high that they could barely walk down the driveway to the car, much less seven city blocks. And even if they could manage seven blocks in Denver Heights on a Friday night in those shoes (Michelle in leopard print and Tasha in hot-pink patent leather), people would mistake them for *being* the party, if you know what I mean.

"Chanti, I cannot believe you're wearing high-top tennis shoes," said Michelle, apparently forgetting who her transportation was.

"Why?" I asked, looking down at my black Converse All Stars. "They look good with skinny jeans."

"Yeah, if you were going to a basketball game, and even then they'd be questionable. We're going to a *par-ty*." I was half expecting her to spell it out for me as though I'd never heard the word before. Just because I never go to any doesn't mean I don't know what they are.

"Sorry, I didn't get the memo that I was supposed to shop at Sluts 'R' Us."

"Don't even. We look good," Tasha said as she and Michelle got into the car, convinced it was true.

The party was in a house on the last block of the Heights on the south end, so it looked a lot like Aurora Avenue. When we got there, I expected music blaring and people out in the yard dancing (okay, so my experience with house parties is mostly old movies from back in Lana's day), but we could have been pulling up to an empty house from the looks of it. The only indication there was a party in there was all the cars out front. But you see lots of cars outside a wake, too.

We went inside and someone immediately shoved plastic cups of something into our hands. A good dance beat was playing, just not loud enough to hear it from the street. One girl demanded that our host, whoever that was, turn up the music, but her request was denied since the neighbors had already threatened to call the cops. People danced to it anyway, but most of the kids were just talking in small groups. There was a couple making out in the darkest corner, on the verge of needing to get a room. I recognized a lot of people from school—no one I hung out with and a few who actually made me glad I wouldn't be going to North High in the fall.

"This party is tired. I don't know why I let you talk me into coming."

"If anyone knows tired, it's you, Chanti," Michelle said. "All you ever do is sit at home with your books and TV. And when you really want to live on the edge, maybe an On Demand movie. I'm sorry, but anybody who opens a book that isn't part of a homework assignment is seriously tired."

"Leave her alone. There's nothing wrong with being different. It's okay if Chanti likes to read," Tasha said.

"Or watch cop shows. What is your obsession with cops, anyway? Unless he's exceptionally hot, I got no love for a cop, in real life or on TV."

"Michelle, lay off. Chanti's here to have fun, not have her social life critiqued."

I was thinking there was nothing more sad than having Michelle's pity, except for needing Tasha to defend me, when I noticed Robert Tice, one of the cutest boys at school and way outside my realm of possibility, checking me out from across the room. At least that's what I thought he was doing. It may have something to do with what Michelle said about me not having a life, but I'm pretty clueless about boys—what they want (okay, I know at least one thing they want), or what it means when they look at you the way Robert was looking at me right then. Since I didn't know the proper response to his flirting, if that's what he was even doing, I looked away. I've always found that in the face of danger, the best thing to do is run. So not only did I look away, I turned my back to him and pretended I was suddenly interested in whatever had torn Michelle and Tasha away from critiquing my lame life.

"I can't believe *she* showed up here," Michelle was saying. "Do you think she was invited?"

"From what I've heard, she doesn't need an invitation.

She can crash whatever party she wants. Who's going to stop her?"

People stopped dancing, talking, and making out to watch the new girl's entrance at the front door, but only for a second. Conversations started up again and people went back to dancing. Not a single person greeted her or stuck a plastic cup of Red Bull and I-don't-know-what in her hand like they had when Tasha, Michelle, and I showed up.

"Who is she?" I asked Tasha, since she seemed to know so much.

"She just moved to Aurora Ave. She was in a gang in Los Angeles."

"The Bloods," Michelle offered.

"You don't know anything. It was the Crips."

"Why can't they ever be from something other than the Bloods or the Crips?" I asked. The new girl's alleged gang affiliation just made all of Tasha's information suspect to me. Because to hear the world tell it, either there really are no other gangs in the universe, or the Bloods and Crips have some serious marketing skills.

"She did some time," Tasha continued, "and had to move out here to stay with her grandmother. Like that's supposed to keep her out of trouble."

"What did she go to jail for?" I asked.

"That's the part nobody knows. But I have my theories," Michelle said.

I wasn't interested in Michelle's theories so I told them I needed to find the bathroom. Really I just wanted to be home, sitting on my bed and reading one of the books I'd checked out of the library. Maybe I *was* lame, but Robert Tice must not have known it because he was still scoping me out. So I escaped all of them by going out the back door and into the yard of whoever's house it was. I didn't even know. My circle of friends is pretty small—Tasha. And now Michelle, thanks to Tasha.

So I was standing with my back to the party and the noise, considering whether to drink my Red Bull and Whatever to dull the pain of being at the party, when someone pushed me from behind. A four-finger push can really send you flying when the perpetrator sneaks up behind you and you never see it coming. Now I had Red Bull down the front of my shirt, and I was thoroughly pissed. I'd hoped that by the time I turned around, either the pusher would be gone or I'd have found some unknown courage with which to kick his or her butt. But neither thing happened.

"I saw you in there checking out Robert. That's *my* man. You must not know who I am."

She was right, I had no idea. But I do know she was a whole lot more pissed off with me for looking at Robert than I was about her ruining my shirt. So I was willing to forget about the shirt and go back inside before anyone got hurt. Like me. Unfortunately, she wasn't so forgiving, and stepped right up in my face. The top of my head came to her chin. This was truly a big girl, like a pro linebacker, and just as intimidating. Though I was scared out of my mind, I couldn't help feeling sorry for Robert Tice.

"Do you know who I am?"

I wanted to tell her that I didn't, but I did know from her breath that she'd had a lot more from the plastic cup than I had. From the looks of her bloodshot eyes, her cup hadn't contained much Red Bull, either. It must have been all Whatever. But I didn't say any of this because she had her hand on my throat by then, and I couldn't talk, anyway.

"I don't know who you are and could not care less, but I do know you'd better let that girl go."

This voice came from behind the girl pressing her hand against my larynx. My assailant looked a little confused, and a lotta angry. She let go of my neck and turned to whoever had just threatened her. I stepped away to see who it was I'd be forever grateful to, and found it was the Blood/Crip girl. I must have been the only person at the party who didn't know who *she* was because the girl willing to kill for Robert Tice's love seconds earlier just walked back to the party without another word.

That's how I met MJ Cooper, former BFF and now my sworn enemy.

Chapter 3

My mother also missed out on knowing the real MJ and agrees with Tasha that she's bad news. Lana figures the only way to keep me out of trouble is to keep me away from The Ave and MJ Cooper. Her solution? Langdon Preparatory School. They don't usually let new kids enroll past ninth grade, but they were doing some community outreach to give poor kids a chance not to be poor, and opened up three scholarships into the eleventh grade. Lana called in a favor and got me one of the scholarships. She didn't tell me what the favor was, but all the favors anyone ever owes Lana have something to do with crime. Something going down at Langdon Prep bad enough for someone to owe Lana a favor sort of defeats the whole point of sending me there to keep me out of trouble. When I pointed this out to Lana, she wasn't interested in the irony.

After I walk the mile from the nearest bus stop, and I swear half of that is the long winding driveway, I see that everything about the school involves money. There's grass everywhere, not something you see a lot of in Colorado, and it's as green as Ada Crawford's lawn. They must spend tall dollars on their water bills. All the buildings look like they were built a couple centuries earlier than 1957. That's the year

etched into the marble sign, along with LANGDON PREPARATORY
SCHOOL, planted in a round of grass and flowers inside the
circular driveway. There are three castle-looking buildings
made from huge gray stones, built around a big stretch of the
unnaturally green grass. They look like they should be somewhere in New England, not where the buffalo used to roam.
And, of course, the walls are covered in ivy—new money trying too hard to look old.

I see a woman at the front entrance holding a sign with
my name on it, like they do at the airport.

"You must be Chantal Evans. Let me introduce you to
our other scholarship winners . . ."

Before she can finish, the girl beside her makes her own
introduction. "I'm Bethanie, with an *i-e*, not a *y*," she says,
without bothering to look at me.

She's more interested in checking out the driver of the
Escalade that just pulled up. Someone has gotten it into her
head that she's too good for the rest of us, which is a little
misguided considering she's here on the same scholarship I
am. But later for her. I'm more interested in the guy standing
next to her, who is *most* hot. Way too hot for me to think I
have a chance, but a girl needs a fantasy to get her through
the day, right? Lucky for me, I've found mine as soon as I hit
the school grounds.

"Marco Ruiz," he says, holding out his hand.

Sadly, it takes me more than a second to realize he wants
me to shake it, so I leave his hand hanging in midair before I
reach out to grab it, but only for a moment. Even if he thinks
I'm lacking social skills, I've already touched my fantasy guy. I
never get to touch my fantasy guy on the first date. Well, to be
accurate, I *never* get to touch my fantasy guy, so already I'm
ahead in the boy department. Maybe Langdon Prep won't be
so bad, after all.

A bell starts clanging somewhere on the campus.

"Time to get moving. We're going to start with a tour of

the school and grounds," the woman says. "Oh, and I'm Headmistress Smythe. You can call me Headmistress Smythe."

She pronounces it with a long *I*, and already I know she's a fraud. Especially with that fake accent. I watch a lot of detective shows on the BBC, and she's about as British as I am. I roll my eyes at her, thinking there is no way I'm calling anyone headmistress anything, like I'm in a Dickens novel or something. Marco catches me giving her the eye roll and smiles. Nice smile. I wish I could make up another reason for him to shake my hand.

"All the academic buildings are here, built around the quad," Smythe says, starting the tour. "Your classes will be in these three buildings."

"It's a beautiful campus, especially the botanical garden," Bethanie says, already kissing up to Smythe. The plaque in front of the garden shows it's named after our tour guide.

"I designed it myself, ordered all the flowers, even helped plant it," Smythe says, all smiles and sunshine. Two seconds later, she's scowling. "Unfortunately, our new science teacher convinced the board that the garden requires too much water and sets the wrong environmental example for our students. Soon my garden will become a xeriscape of rock and cacti, or something equally horrid."

"That's too bad," Bethanie commiserates.

"It truly is. But what's done is done. Let's get on with our tour."

We're about to go inside Main Hall when I remember the manicure set I have stashed in my bag. I just know the cuticle scissors will set off the metal detector, so before we get to the door, I stop to fish them out.

"Ms. Evans, have you lost something?"

"No, I need to get something out of my bag. I don't want to set off the detectors."

"The *what?*"

"You know, the metal detectors at the entrance."

"I can assure you there are no metal detectors anywhere on the Langdon campus. There's no need for them. At least not until you arrived. Pray tell *what* is in your bag?"

After that comment, I consider giving her a heart attack by telling her it's a Glock, which she clearly expects, but I show her the manicure set instead.

"Well, that's a relief. Please, let's move on. We're already two minutes behind schedule."

Bethanie with an *i-e* gives me a look like she's taken a whiff and thinks I stepped in something, but Marco leans in and whispers, "I'm used to metal detectors, too. I guess rich kids don't commit crimes."

And if they did, they could afford to get someone else to do it for them. Based on the Jags and Benzes we saw rolling up, the Kate Spade bags on the shoulders of girls getting out of them, and the swagger of boys who have never been pulled over for Driving While Impoverished, I bet Langdon's budget can cover paper and whiteboard erasers without having to pimp out students to sell overpriced candy bars and stale popcorn in Christmas tins. The "nonessential" classes they cut at my old school—like PE and art—not only exist at this school, they come in assorted flavors. There's fine art, musical arts, and theater; team sports, recreational sports, and dance classes. Instead of half lockers, we each get a full-sized locker, and none of them squeak the need for WD-40 when opened. An hour later, I'm relieved when the tour of tennis courts, soccer fields, and libraries (two!) finally ends, until Smythe announces we'll be attending an immersion workshop for the rest of the day.

"What's an immersion workshop?" Bethanie asks.

"We realize you come from a different background, and we thought it might aid in your success if we helped you understand *our* history and culture here at Langdon."

Oh, I get it. She means we're all broke and not used to the bling lifestyle at old Langdon Prep.

Marco leans in again and whispers, "This is bull."

See how he wants to get near me all the time? He smells good. So good that I'm caught off guard, and all I can whisper back is, "Yeah, this is bull."

He probably thinks I'm an idiot. Right then it hits me that he is more than hot. He is beautiful, and I can't stop making a fool of myself in front of him. Brown eyes framed by lashes so long I'd normally say they were wasted on a boy, but look perfect on him. They don't look girly on his otherwise straight-up masculine face. And how sexy is that name? Like a character from the soaps. I say it in my head several times, rolling the *R* in a way I could never pull off if I said his name out loud.

Smythe leads us to a classroom where we find a woman vacuuming. She looks up at us for just a second before she goes back to pushing the Hoover.

"Mildred, why are you still running the vacuum when classes have begun?"

"I'm a little behind schedule this morning. This is the last room, and I'm just about done."

"You'll have to finish it later. And perhaps you need to work on your time-management skills."

"My skills are just fine," Mildred says in a tone that suggests it's about to be on between her and the headmistress. "The only reason I'm off-schedule is because you told me to repot that ficus tree in your office and clean out the ashtrays in your car before I started my rounds."

"I do *not* smoke," Smythe says, looking busted. "Just say no to tobacco, right, children?"

"Well, someone broke into your car and filled the trays with cigarette butts."

"Now you look here . . ." Smythe steps to Mildred, hand

on hip and minus the accent. I see now she's what Lana would call a BFH sister—Bourgie From the Hood. Everyone knows a BFH chick, maybe an aunt or a neighbor who tries to fool people into thinking they're all high-society but could jack somebody up if necessary. Smythe remembers we're all watching her, takes a step back, and suddenly sounds like Mary Poppins again. "If you must know, my husband smokes. Now, please get that thing out of here so we can conduct class."

I was hoping for a showdown, but I guess Mildred remembers Smythe is her boss and she leaves without another word. But if looks could kill, Smythe would be laid out.

For the first two hours we listen to Smythe drone on about the history of the school, with a rundown of all the "luminaries" who have attended, including two U.S. senators, one governor, and the CEO of a major fast-food chain. There's also a Miss Colorado in the group, but Smythe mentions this as an afterthought, like a lesson in what we should not aspire to. Her tone is more like, "We also have an alum who was a pole dancer." I want to remind her that those pageant winners do good stuff like raise money for orphanages, but I'm only basing that on what I remember seeing on *Entertainment Tonight*, so I keep my mouth shut.

I'm fighting off sleep and Marco is too—I catch him in a myoclonic jerk a couple of times—but Bethanie is really into it. I think Smythe could have read the school charter (again) and kept Bethanie's attention. Clearly she isn't here because her mother forced her to leave everything she knows to avoid Armageddon, also known as Aurora Ave. Then Smythe announces we have a special guest arriving any minute. I doubt it's the former Miss Colorado, and I'm hoping it's the fast-food CEO with show-and-tell because I could use a burger right about now. But no, in walks this girl wearing the same uniform I am, which means she's just some student and won't be passing out any burgers.

"Students, I'd like to introduce you to Melissa Mitchell, our student body president."

"Everyone calls me Lissa." She gives the whole room a wave like European princesses do in the movies.

"Lissa took time away from her rigorous studies to spend an hour sharing with you the merits of a Langdon education from the perspective of one who has certainly made the most of her experience here."

From what I can see, Bethanie is instantly charmed. No doubt she'll be interested in getting all she can from the Langdon experience. When I turn to see what Marco thinks of all this, to my horror, I'm pretty sure he's thinking about an experience that has nothing to do with Langdon and everything to do with Lissa Mitchell. He stands up to shake her hand—what is with that anyway? Who under the age of thirty shakes hands when they're introduced? Madame president nearly knocks me over to get to him.

"I'm Marco."

"Nice to meet you Marco. Such a gentleman. That's so refreshing."

To Bethanie and me, she barely manages a "Hey." Her weave slaps me in the face when she turns away from us. It's a nice weave, I have to admit. She must have the best stylist in town—no porch beauty shops for her—and the money to pay for real hair. Anyone else would think it was hers, and not just because she has the receipt to prove it. But that's my thing, my superpower if you will. I notice everything. Lana says I'd make an excellent cop. Which would probably be true if not for my fear of guns, confrontation, or strenuous activity of any kind.

"Oh, I just realized I didn't have you sign off that you have read and understood the Langdon honor code. Please come up to my desk and sign, and then we can listen to all the lovely things Ms. Mitchell has to share with us."

Bethanie can't wait to sign her life away to Langdon,

Marco is busy flashing *my* smile to Lissa, and I'm at the back of the line working up the nerve to give her the evil eye that says, "He's mine, and you'd be wise to back up." Some women can do that. Lana could. MJ could. But they're both scary, and scary won't work for me. I could probably do crazy. Just as I get my crazy look going, Lissa looks down at the notes she's about to bore us with. Smythe looks up at me then, and I'm pretty sure *she* thinks I'm crazy.

"Is there anything wrong, Chantal?"

"No, um . . . it's just that I don't have a pen."

"Well, that's the first thing you'll learn at Langdon Prep. Always be prepared. A student without a writing instrument may as well not be in school. Am I right?"

I think she'd rather *I* not be in this school, specifically. I just ignore her question.

"Here, you may use mine to sign the sheet. I suggest during the lunch break you go to the bookstore and purchase one."

I sign her stupid honor code and start walking back to my desk.

"Excuse me, Miss Evans," Smythe says.

"Yes?"

"My pen? I'd like that back."

I didn't even realize I was still holding it. I hand it over to her. "Sorry about that."

"Careful with other people's belongings. That's not just any pen. It's a Montblanc." Then she puts her cheery face back on and adds, "But you probably didn't know that. No harm done. Now Lissa, are you ready?"

"I think so. That's lovely, Headmistress Smythe."

"Isn't it? Would you like to use it?"

"Oh no, I have one. Three years at Langdon, you know. Always prepared."

I don't know what makes me more ill—knowing I have

to listen to madame president for the next hour, or Smythe being right. I wouldn't know a Montblanc from a Paper Mate. And up until five minutes ago, I wouldn't have cared.

In the cafeteria, all eyes are on us. Everyone is checking out the scholarship kids. At least the food is good. I'm pretty sure they don't have a choice of chicken picatta or pork tenderloin on the menu at North High. I'm already thinking about what I'll choose from the dessert bar when I notice Lissa sitting a few tables away, staring harder than anyone else in the cafeteria. She's sitting with two girls who might be clones of her. From the neck down, every girl in the place looks pretty much the same thanks to the uniform— Burberry-looking plaid skirt, white button-down shirt, and a crested tan blazer. But the girls in Lissa's entourage are wearing the same hairstyle right down to the headband and the size of their waves. Same earrings, same color lip gloss. One clone is white, the other is deep brown, and somehow they manage to look just like Lissa, who is somewhere in the middle. Weird. Kind of like the way people start to look like their dogs after a while.

They all have a look that says, *Who let them in*? They probably think I'm like every other girl they imagine from the hood. A roughneck. A hoodrat. And whatever other words they know from watching MTV because I know none of them have actually been to the hood. So I stare back at them, using the crazy look that had Smythe more than a little concerned.

"I hate being the new girl," Bethanie says. "It seems like I'm always the new girl."

"You change schools a lot?"

"Enough to know what this feels like. The scrutiny, people trying to figure out where you belong."

I ask the cafeteria lady for extra potatoes, and she obliges.

That never happened at my old school, where the cafeteria ladies fussed at me like we were related and told me to move my greedy behind down the line.

"Sounds a lot like an *Animal Planet* documentary on pack order," I say.

"That's exactly what it's like, which is why we have to stick together."

Marco has already picked a table for us, and I hope I don't look too eager as I make my way over to him.

"Lissa's over there staring at us. I think she wants us to come join them." Apparently Bethanie is reading them a whole different way.

"I'm not getting that at all," I say. "Besides, I thought we were supposed to stick together."

"We are, but it doesn't hurt to get in good with the alpha dogs. Marco, don't you want to go over there?"

"I'm fine where I am. They're just like all the other people staring at us. They don't want us here."

I think Marco is reading the situation wrong, too. I don't know what the boys are thinking, but I'm pretty sure all the girls are staring at him out of lust. Which makes me dislike all of them because even if I'm the only one who knows it, Marco is *my* fantasy guy. Already claimed. Already more real than any of my previous lust objects by virtue of that handshake. Even though he seems to do that with just any ol' body.

I decide to buy dessert, which is off the menu plan, which means I have to pay for it myself. That's when I realize my wallet is missing from my bag. There are only three dollars and a bus pass in it, but still.

"Hey guys, I'll be back in a second. Don't let anyone take my tray—I'm still working on that."

"I know it's like restaurant food, but I think you still have to empty your own tray," Marco says. "But I'll guard it with my life."

God, he must think I'm some kind of glutton. At first I think he's serious, but then he smiles and I just about lose the ability to stand. And talk.

"No, it's just that . . . wait, what was I about to do? Oh, right . . . I think I left my wallet in the classroom. At least I hope so. I left it somewhere. . . . I'll be right back."

I get out of there as fast as I can before I make matters worse. What is my problem? I've won debate-team awards, can talk my way out of anything, but bring a cute boy into the picture and I turn into an idiot every time. When I get to the classroom, Smythe is just leaving.

"You still have twenty minutes before the end-of-lunch bell. I'm about to go get something myself," she says.

"I think I left my wallet in here."

She leaves the room, but not before she warns me to be back from lunch promptly. Everything is right where we all left it, including my wallet on the floor under my desk. I guess it fell out of my bag. Again. I grab it and walk back to the cafeteria thinking of something clever to say to Marco so I can redeem myself. I'm looking through my wallet to make sure my three dollars are still in there and not looking where I'm going, and I run into a girl in the hall. I mumble my apologies, but don't waste time returning to the cafeteria. I don't want Marco to finish his lunch and leave before I get back.

When I return, they're both still at the table. I'd half expected Bethanie to defect, but when I look over at Lissa's table, I don't see her or her clones.

"Where are your friends?"

"They left right before you came back in," Bethanie reports, sounding disappointed. "Maybe I can catch up with them. I'll see you later."

Part of my notice-everything superpower is that I'm usually a good judge of people, but I can't get a good read on Bethanie. I'm guessing she's more like me than Lissa since she's here on scholarship, and yet I think she'd commit a crime to become the third clone.

"I have to run too. I need to see the coach so I can get on the tryout roster," Marco says. "I'll see you back in the immersion class, okay?"

Was it something I said? I try to make myself feel better about being deserted with a nice banana split, which I start eating the minute I give the cashier my money. Chocolate ice cream's medicinal properties can't fix everything, however. Before I can get back to the table, Smythe is on my tail. She can't even give me a break at lunch.

"Miss Evans, do you have my Montblanc? I just returned to the classroom and it isn't on the desk where I left it."

"I gave it back to you."

"No, I mean just now. While you were there looking for your wallet. Maybe you had a reason to *borrow* it again."

"I told you—I *don't* have it," I say, trying to keep my voice steady and not reveal that I'm a little freaked out by what she's suggesting.

"Well, I don't see how it could just disappear." She gives me a look that says she knows I took it and walks off.

What a way to start a new school, having the principal accuse me of being a thief. Thanks, Lana. This is *sooo* much better than North High.

Chapter 4

At the end of school, I'm sitting on the steps at Langdon's main entrance waiting for a ride from Lana. The campus is mostly deserted. The last of the moms who don't have to work pulled around the circular drive half an hour ago. The last teacher just gunned it out of the teacher's lot, taking the turn so fast I was afraid the little orange car would flip over. That teacher must *really* be looking forward to getting home and making work assignments.

When my phone rings and I see Lana's number appear, I know I'll probably be waiting a little while longer.

"How did the first day go?" she asks.

"It was hell."

"Is it possible you're exaggerating? You always blow things out of proportion."

"I suppose it's possible, but I don't think so."

"Just give it some time. Look, my stakeout is running longer than I expected. This perp just won't come out of the massage parlor. You can wait a couple of hours until I'm relieved or you can take the bus."

"Well, I can't lug all these books on the bus so I guess I'll have to wait. Can't you just go in there and bust them already?"

"Two hours, Chanti," she says, and hangs up.

I'm trying to decide whether to wait for Lana or put all the books in my locker and not do my first homework assignments when Bethanie appears.

"You're still here?"

"My mom's late picking me up."

"Where do you live?"

"Aurora Avenue, off Center Street."

"Where is that?" Bethanie says, sounding like she expects it to be on Saturn.

"On the East Side, in Denver Heights."

"That isn't too bad. I was afraid you'd say somewhere in West Hell. I don't do outback. Text your mom you have a ride."

"Thanks," I say, not sure I mean it. I think I detected an insult. And who is she to talk? I can't imagine she lives near Langdon, either. I'm not sure why she's offering me the ride, but I know I don't want to carry all these books on the bus. Maybe she's trying to bond, part of that whole sticking-together thing she suggested we do.

"Where are your books?" I ask.

"I already put them in my car. I left something in my locker and had to come back. Which reminds me." She takes a card out of her backpack and hands it to me, along with a pen that looks really familiar. "I bought a card at the bookstore. I thought we could sign it and give it to Headmistress Smythe. Sort of a thank-you for her warm welcome to Langdon. I'll get Marco to sign tomorrow before school."

I don't take them from her. For all I know, it could be some elaborate ruse to get my fingerprints on her stolen merchandise.

"What? It's too much, right? I thought it was the proper thing to do, but I don't want to come off as a suck-up."

"That pen looks just like the one Smythe had today."

"Really? I didn't notice."

How could she not notice when she was clinging to Lissa's every word, which included a compliment about that pen. I don't like associating with people I suspect are thieves, especially when someone else thinks I committed the theft, but I also don't want to wait two hours for Lana, so I gather up all my books and head for the student parking lot. But Bethanie starts walking down the long driveway toward the main entrance.

"Not the student lot?"

"I prefer to park on the street."

And not just on the street. Down the hill, around the corner, and into a subdivision. I'm thinking maybe her car is imaginary.

"Here we are," Bethanie announces.

I still don't know where the car is because I'm looking around for a hooptie, which is what I'd be driving if I had a car, given I'm broke and needed a scholarship to get into Langdon. But Bethanie opens the trunk of a BMW, and not some ancient BMW that a relative had been kind enough to donate, but a current-year model.

Okaaay. If it were me, I'd feel compelled to explain why I was driving a brand-new, fifty-thousand-dollar car. Especially when I'm at Langdon on a scholarship for the economically disadvantaged. But all Bethanie says is, "You mind a quick stop first? I could use an iced chai."

Before she puts the key in the ignition, she checks herself out in the visor mirror.

"A little lip gloss first. Never know who you might meet."

I can't stand it anymore, and I don't even care if I'm being rude. "So what's with the car? Did you borrow this from your rich uncle or something?"

She doesn't answer, just smiles at me and puts on the largest pair of sunglasses I've ever seen, like she's an Olsen twin trying to hide out from the paparazzi.

The coffeehouse is on the same block as my bus stop so we're there in just a couple of minutes, which makes me wonder why she'd get all glamorous for such a short trip—until we walk into the coffeehouse and there's Lissa. So Bethanie knew exactly who she was going to run into. That's why she offered me the ride. With me along, it could look like she just casually ran into her. Or it could all just be a coincidence.

"Lissa, wow, that's so funny running into you here," Bethanie says the minute we walk in the door and see Lissa sitting alone at a window table. A coincidence not so much.

Lissa looks up from her texting for a millisecond. "Hey."

Bethanie stands there waiting for an invitation that isn't coming.

"What about that chai?" I ask. She finally takes the hint, and looks crushed until Lissa comes up to the counter.

"Did you guys drive here?" Lissa asks, flipping her hair behind her back. She can't seem to keep her hands away from her head. I guess if I paid as much for my hair as she did, I'd be obsessed with it, too. "A friend dropped me off and my idiot brother was supposed to drive me home, but I think he's forgotten about me."

"He drives the Escalade, right?" Bethanie asks.

"We both do. My father thinks sharing the car will teach us the value of money and hard work. It's lame."

Yeah, a 50 percent time share on a new Escalade provides a classic lesson in sacrifice. I wish Lana could afford to teach me that lesson.

"I'm lucky—I get a bus pass all to myself," I say, but Bethanie's expression makes it clear she doesn't find me as amusing as I find myself.

"Anyway, I was just taking Chanti home and thought I'd grab a drink for the ride. She lives way across town—Aurora Avenue or something. It's a hike, so I thought a coffee would be a good idea. Your brother's Justin, right? The quarterback? I hear he's very good. It must be so fun to have a twin. You

live in Cherry Creek right? I don't live too far from there. I'd
love to give you a ride after we drop Chanti."

Bethanie is the opposite of me. I get around a boy I'm
jonesing for and can't string together three coherent words.
She gets around a girl she's jonesing to be, and she can't shut
up. We get to the car and somehow I get the backseat. So
much for the new girls sticking together.

"What's the story on the car?" Lissa asks. She looks relieved she won't be riding in the wreck that a scholarship girl
ought to be driving, if she's lucky enough to be driving at all.
"Aren't you supposed to be socioeconomically disadvantaged?"

"I have a rich uncle. He let me borrow it."

"Did he let you borrow that Coach bag, too?" Lissa says.

Not that I'd ever want to have anything in common with
Lissa, but I'd like to know the same thing. She probably borrowed the bag the same way she "borrowed" that pen from
Smythe. Maybe she really does have a rich uncle because she
couldn't have stolen the car. Or could she? For all I know she
might be part of a car-theft ring. At least that would explain
why she has to park over hill and dale.

"You're too funny. It was a gift from him."

"Too bad he couldn't get you a gift of tuition money,
huh?"

"Right!" Bethanie says, laughing way too hard.

I tell Bethanie the fastest way to get me home and then
shut up while they discuss the joys of attending Langdon
Prep. When we finally take my exit off the interstate, my first
thought is that I'm so glad to be home. My next thought is
how much home is a helluva lot different from Langdon, and
I begin to see it through Lissa's eyes. Between the graffitied
walls and the *rejas* on all the windows, Bethanie probably
thinks she's arrived in West Hell, after all.

"Chanti, now what?" Bethanie says when the red light
stops us at Center and Lexington, where Crazy Moses is

about to push his shopping cart/living room into the park. They probably don't have a Crazy Moses in their neighborhood.

"Just go two more lights to Aurora Avenue. It's about a quarter mile on your right," Lissa says.

Well, that's correct, but I didn't say it. How does Lissa know this neighborhood? Maybe she's got a little less Cherry Creek in her than we thought. As if she's read my mind, Lissa offers, "Our maid lives off Lexington. I was with Daddy once when he gave her a ride home."

Right. The maid. I can't get out of that car fast enough when we finally get to my street. The minute I step on the sidewalk, smell the year-old grease frying wings up at the Tastee Treets, and hear Jay-Z blaring from someone's window, I feel like a fish let off the hook and thrown back into the water.

My relief at being home lasts just two seconds. That's when I notice that I arrived at the very time it seems everyone on the street is outside—washing cars, unloading groceries, throwing a football. I know I'm going to get a million questions about rolling up in a brand-new BMW wearing this fugly uniform. And they'll all come from Tasha and Michelle, who are sitting on Tasha's front steps. I asked Bethanie to drop me there because I don't want her or Lissa to know exactly where I live, at least until I know what else Bethanie is hiding and why she's so desperate to become Lissa's BFF. A little healthy paranoia comes with being a cop, or the kid of one.

"Oooh, look at Miss Thing stepping out of that car,"

"Now she's on the red carpet. Michelle, what's she wearing?"

"Well, Tasha, I believe that's the latest couture from the House of Burberry Knockoffs."

"Who is she? Is it Beyoncé? Could it be . . . no, wait, it's our very own Chantal Evans, fresh from the other side of Denver."

They break out laughing.

"See, I was going to tell you about my new school," I say, trying not to laugh myself. "And I wanted to hear what it was like at North, but you people make somebody want to go inside and do homework."

"Sorry, Chanti, we'll be good. We want to hear all about your new school." Tasha makes room for me on the step.

"But first," Michelle says, sticking an imaginary microphone in my face, "tell us if they're letting you keep your ensemble, and whose car you and your friends jacked to bring you home following the show."

Then I do laugh, because it feels good to be back home and I have a whole fifteen hours until I have to deal with Langdon Prep again.

Chapter 5

Fifteen hours goes by fast, 'cause now I'm starting my second day of hell. I still can't believe this is where I go to school, a place that looks like something from a Hollywood film lot. I can totally see an ad for a Lamborghini or Ferrari being shot here—red car, green grass, gray stone, and a woman leaning against the car sipping champagne. Or maybe one of those rich-prep-school shows on the CW. That's what I'm thinking as I make the walk from the bus stop, until I see Marco sitting on the bench under the tree where we first met yesterday. How could I forget my silver lining?

"Hi, Marco."

"Seems like only yesterday."

"Yeah."

My goal for today is to talk to this boy in sentences with more than two words. I swear.

"I thought I'd hang out here in case you and Bethanie, you know," Marco says.

"I know. The first day, right? We should compare schedules. Maybe we have some of the same classes."

There. I knew I could do it. But I cannot be smooth no matter how I try. The minute I take my schedule out of my backpack, the wind snatches it out of my hand.

"I'll get it," Marco offers.

"No, I have it," I say, but I don't. But what kind of second impression would I be making to have the guy run all over campus chasing down my schedule?

I try to step on it, but it gets away again. Now I'm running after it, wondering which is worse—looking like an idiot chasing a piece of paper across the windy quad, or missing out on the chance to sit way too close to Marco while we look over our schedules. I decide it's too early in our relationship to make him think I'm a complete moron and let the wind have my schedule.

"Do you think this planet is your trash can?"

I turn around to find someone who I can only guess is a teacher walking toward me, holding what looks like my schedule.

"Excuse me?"

"Mother Earth is not here to accept your refuse," she says and shoves the schedule against my chest. "Treat her like the goddess she is."

All righty then.

"Hey, that lady caught your schedule. Cool," Marco says when I get back to the bench.

"You mean the psychotic hippie?" I feel some attitude coming on, but I let it pass because I'd rather get all worked up over Marco than some crazy teacher. "So what do you have first period?"

"Maybe we should wait for Bethanie. She might have some of our classes, too."

"I don't think Bethanie will be showing up."

"She already dropped out?"

"Hardly. She'd kill to stay here. I don't think she'll be showing up to meet *us*. I think she's already ditched us for new and improved friends."

I'm about to tell Marco about yesterday's adventure when

Bethanie appears, proving yet again that when it comes to her, my superpowers of observation are no good.

"I didn't expect to see you here. I thought you'd be part of Lissa's crew by now. How'd the ride home go?"

"It was great. She was telling me about a back-to-school party one of her friends is having next weekend."

I give Marco a look that says *I told you so.* "So she invited you to a party?"

"Not in so many words, but why else would she tell someone about a party unless she wanted them to come?"

"Because she's Lissa. From what I know of her, sounds exactly like something she'd do."

I'm about to explain to her how the haves treat the have-nots when we notice Mildred from yesterday's vacuuming incident dragging a bookshelf across the quad, and having a hard time with it. She drops the bookshelf, falls to the ground, and grabs her foot. We run over to her since it appears we're the only people to witness this out of the hundred kids walking around and across the quad.

"Are you okay?" Bethanie asks. "Should we call someone?"

"Why are you trying to drag this heavy bookshelf by yourself?" Marco asks.

"Because it's my job, even if I don't get paid nearly enough for it. Oh, my foot is killing me."

"Seems like a two-person job, at least. You think you can grab the other end, Chanti? Or should I grab one of these guys?"

"You mean one of the guys who don't even seem to notice we need help over here?" I say the last five words loudly, in the hope someone might care, but no luck. "Sure, we can carry it together. Where were you taking it?"

"Over to the administration building. Headmistress Smythe's office."

Of course.

"Do you think you can put pressure on your foot if I help you?" Bethanie asks. She'll never fit into Lissa's crowd, lucky for her. I noticed Lissa and her entourage had walked right past us.

Once we get the bookshelf into Smythe's office, Mildred tells us where to place it. Marco is about to go find the nurse's office when Smythe arrives.

"What are you doing in my office? Who let you in here?"

"I did," says Mildred. She's lying on the sofa, out of Smythe's view from the door. "They helped me get the bookshelf you wanted moved from the library."

"Mildred, we do not ask our students to help our custodial staff with their duties."

"She didn't ask," Marco offers. "She was trying to drag that heavy thing across the quad by herself, and dropped it on her foot."

"If she needed help, she should have asked one of the other custodians, not our students."

"But you just called me on the Nextel and told me to get it over here ASAP," Mildred is saying. "I tried to tell you I needed to wait for . . ."

"That's neither here nor there. You children should get to class. First bell will ring any second."

"We were going to help Mildred get to the nurse," Bethanie says.

"I'll see to Mildred."

I doubt it. I imagine poor Mildred still here on this sofa at the end of the day, thirsting to death and Smythe laughing at her while she sips a glass of cold lemonade.

Just as we're leaving the office, Smythe stops us.

"Since you're all here, I can ask you about my Montblanc. It went missing yesterday." She's looking directly at me when she says this. "You remember, Chantal, the one you almost walked off with. I've had it for years and have never misplaced it."

I look over at Bethanie, waiting for her to confess so I don't have to narc on her, but she gives me a blank look. I guess she's going to let me take the fall.

"As I told you yesterday Mrs. Smythe, *I* didn't take it," I say, and walk out.

If my life had a soundtrack, the shower-scene music from *Psycho* would be playing right now. When I walk into my next class, I see the psychotic hippie at the whiteboard writing her name. Ms. Reeves. My biology teacher. I grab a seat at the back of the class. As soon as she turns around, Ms. Reeves's eyes lock on mine, and I can no longer hope she doesn't remember me. She comes straight back to my desk, her long tie-dyed skirt billowing behind her, bracelets tinkling. I can't believe Smythe lets her dress like that. It's so un-Langdon.

"And you are . . . ?"

"Chantal Evans. New girl."

"Since we last spoke, have you reconsidered your treatment of Mother Earth?"

Last spoke? We didn't speak. She made an accusation, shoved my schedule at me, and went off in a huff, as I remember it.

"I wasn't polluting. My schedule blew out of my hands. I was chasing it in the wind, but it got away."

"What I saw was you giving up the chase."

She walks back to the front of the room, tinkling and swooshing. That's going to be really annoying on test days.

"Welcome, class. I'm Ms. Reeves, a new teacher here at Langdon. This is an environmental science class, but it will be taught from the perspective of Earth and your place on this planet, rather than from your perspective and what the Earth can do for you."

From the sighs and groans around the class, I know I'm not alone in thinking the woman is a little off. Now I get why she's at Langdon. They've gone green. Langdon is trying to be environmentally aware because everyone knows green is the new black. I think I know who convinced the board to replace the Smythe Botanical Garden with sagebrush and limestone.

"Take a look around this room at all your . . . *stuff*."

I know what she really wants to say.

"Your *stuff* is your carbon footprint, and I can look around this room and see that the twenty of you will likely leave a footprint the size of a landfill. Just look at the number of plastic water bottles I see on the desks. It breaks my heart."

It's true. I think she's tearing up. Some girls sitting two seats over from me don't seem to notice our teacher's pain, though. They're too busy oohing and aahing over something one of them has taken from her bag. When I stretch to get a better look, I find it's Lissa and a clone. I must have missed them when they walked in, since I was busy licking my wounds after Smythe accused me of being a thief.

"What's going on back there?"

Uh-oh. Busted. Here she comes, swooshing and tinkling down the aisle.

"What is this?" she asks, snatching a small pink box from Lissa's hands. Then she starts opening it, and I'm hoping it's something embarrassing like a sex toy or a colonic kit.

"Face cream," Ms. Reeves announces, which is a little anticlimactic. "And look at the packaging. An excellent example of carbon footprint. We have the cardboard box. Inside that, we have the plastic platform the bottle rests in. *Plastic!* Now the bottle itself. A bottle within a bottle, just to make it pretty. Do you know how long it will take the earth to break down this bottle? *Never!*"

Ms. Reeves reassembles the cream in its packaging, but instead of giving it back to Lissa, she takes it to her desk.

"Hey, what are you doing with my cream?"

"I'm confiscating it. Langdon policy. A teacher can confiscate anything a student brings into class that is not germane to the class or is causing a disruption. This abomination fits both categories."

"But that's a brand-new, unopened bottle of *Il Mare*."

"How ironic that it's named for the sea, because that's exactly where the packaging will probably wind up."

"But that cost me twelve hundred dollars."

Ms. Reeves almost passes out after this news. Seriously. She has to brace herself against the whiteboard.

"Twelve hundred dollars? *Twelve hundred dollars!* Are you kidding? Do you realize how many acres of rain forest that could save? Do you know how many trees could be planted in the Northwest forests to stop soil erosion? I can't believe you people. I just can't!"

She throws the cream in her bag and walks out of the classroom, but before we can all start talking about what just happened, she's back. She calmly goes to the lectern at the front of the class, opens her teacher-copy textbook, and says, "Please turn to page three."

Seriously. Cue the music from *Psycho*.

Chapter 6

After spending an hour with crazy Ms. Reeves, my mood can't even be improved by the cheery French café music playing in the background or the delicious scent of galettes Madame Renault is cooking on a waffle iron while she teaches verb conjugation. French class is my favorite, though even when I'm here, I still hate Langdon. When I should be listening to Madame Renault running through verb tenses, I'm mentally cursing everything that is Langdon—the long bus ride to get here, the crazy teachers, and the clueless kids who wouldn't know real life if it smacked them upside the head. At least I do my mental cursing in French, though that puts some limits on me because I only know two French swear words. It isn't the kind of thing they cover in class.

Right now, it's just two minutes before the bell and I'm focused on trying to finish the short story I should have written last night instead of hanging out on Tasha's porch, listening to the latest gossip that I miss by not going to North High. Another reason to hate Langdon.

I smell the faintest hint of familiar cologne mixed with something else that makes me weak every time, and I don't have to look up to know Marco is standing within a few feet, and suddenly every part of me is warm.

"Has anyone claimed this seat yet?"

"What are you doing here?"

"Way to make a guy feel wanted," he says, pretending to be crushed but smiling in that way that gets me all hot and bothered.

Oh, you're wanted all right. That's what the Chanti in my head wants to say, but all that comes out of my mouth is, "No one ever sits there. It's your seat now."

The first lie of our relationship. A girl who chose *Fifi* as her French name has been sitting there. That's what she gets for giving herself a name reserved for poodles and strippers from old black-and-white movies.

"Good. It's mine now. I just did a drop/add into this class."

"Wasn't it hard to get a schedule change?"

I imagine Marco in the registrar's office begging the man to change his schedule so he could be in a class with me. When the registrar says it's against the rules, Marco finally admits that he's crazy about this girl but doesn't know how to tell her, and if he could only take French class with her, he'd figure out how to tell her his true feelings. French being the language of love and all.

"I was in Spanish because I thought it would be an easy A, but the teacher caught on to me. My advisor told me to find another language, one I wasn't already fluent in."

Or that could have been what was said in the registrar's office. But he had Russian or Mandarin (Chinese) as options. He chose French, and he chose the seat next to me.

"*Étudiants d'attention. Nous avons un nouvel ami joignant notre classe—Marco.*"

His name sounds even better with a French accent. *Marco.* It sounds all powdery soft and sexy. From now on that's how I'll say his name, which I can get away with since we're both taking French. Otherwise it would just sound stupid.

"*Merci, Madame Renault. C'est mon plaisir.*"

He speaks French! The way he just said *It's my pleasure* kills me.

"You speak French, too?"

"I took a year of French already. Why do you think they let me into French II?"

I don't know—to make it impossible for me to ever focus on verb conjugation again? Maybe because God is making up for all those times I asked him to send me winning lottery numbers in a dream, or a new bike on my tenth birthday, and He ignored me both times. But it's okay now. Having Marco sitting next to me in French class, speaking in that accent, makes up for everything.

Fifi arrives two minutes after the bell and heads toward us like she's about to tell Marco he's in her seat. I work up the most evil eye I have ever given anyone, and shoot her a look that says, "Unless you want a beat down, you'll take that seat in the back corner." Lucky for her, old Fifi gets the message and changes course. That's one benefit to the scholarship-girl stereotype Langdon kids have of me. They assume I'm dangerous.

When Madame Renault asks if anyone would like to work with Marco to help him catch up with where we are in the French book, I knock my notebook onto the floor trying to raise my hand before anyone else can. Smooth. Can I look any more eager? But when Marco reaches down to pick up the notebook, gives me that smile, and says, *"Merci,"* being smooth isn't all that important anymore. I just got myself a reason to talk to Marco about more than the lunch menu.

After school, I'm standing on the edge of Langdon's football field wondering why I never got into the sport before. It's a gorgeous afternoon and buff guys are running around in uniforms that only accentuate their buffness. What's not to like about this? Maybe it's just more interesting when I'm watching my future boyfriend wrap up practice. Marco suggested I meet him after practice so I could give him a copy of my French notes, but I'm hoping to turn this opportunity into a full-blown study session at the coffeehouse, if I can come up with an invitation that sounds casual and not at all desperate.

A man who I assume is one of the coaches starts talking to me.

"That kid is pretty good. Never seen him before. Do you know who that is, number seventeen?"

"Marco Ruiz," I say, because the only player I've been watching is number seventeen. I don't know if he's any good in terms of football, but I know he's good to look at.

"Is he new? He can't be a freshman. Not with that game."

"He's a junior. He and I both just started Langdon Prep this year."

"Are you two part of that scholarship program?"

Uh-oh. Here it comes. The pity/fear/disgust that Langdonites have for anyone whose parents make less than a combined income of a quarter million a year.

"Well, thank you, scholarship program. That kid is good."

He's the first person I've met around here who is happy to have us. Well, he's happy to have Marco, and I'm going to take that to include me since Marco and I are practically a couple.

"He is good," I say, hoping he won't ask me to explain why I think this since I don't know a thing about football.

"Friend of yours?"

"Yes. I'm just waiting for him to finish practice."

"Name's Mitchell," he says. "That's my son there, the quarterback who acts like he's never seen the playbook."

"Justin Mitchell?" Mr. Mitchell seems like a nice enough guy. Too nice to have spawned Lissa.

"That's the one, though the way he's been playing, I'm not sure I want to claim him."

The coach whistles to end practice, and Marco runs over to me. *Runs*, as in eager to see me. Justin is dragging behind him, as though he knows his father has been discussing his suckage on the field.

"Son, that was excellent scrimmaging," Mr. Mitchell says to Marco, not his actual son. "You've got hustle, something Justin here has been lacking lately."

Well, I wouldn't have much hustle either if I'd smoked a joint before practice. One look at Justin and I can tell that was his problem, or at least one of them. He's stoned. Surely his father sees it, or the coach.

"Lay off, Dad. Why are you even here?"

"I'm here to check out my investment. I'm the biggest booster this team has. I'd like to see where my money is going, and I'm glad to say that some of it went to that new scholarship program. You don't step up, Justin, and this young man might be our next quarterback."

"Him? He's a junior."

"A junior with an arm. Precision, too. Marco, is it?"

"Yes, sir."

Between calling Mr. Mitchell "sir," shaking his hand, and having a lot of hustle on the field, I think Justin's father is more crazy for Marco than I am.

"I like your style, Marco. I could use someone like you at my company. Are you looking for a job, by any chance?"

Oh, I am. Pick me. I'm so broke I'm willing to take a job without even knowing what it is. But then I remember it's Marco's style he likes, not mine.

"Yes, sir, I am. What's the job?"

"I own a moving company," he says, producing a business card out of thin air, as far as I can tell. "Mitchell Moving and Storage, the . . ."

". . . the largest minority-owned moving company in the state, started from the ground up when he was just eighteen years old with a beat-up old van and fifty dollars in his pocket," Justin says, completing his father's sentence. "Yeah, we've all heard it before."

Actually, no, *we* haven't all heard it before. I'm beginning to think Justin is Lissa with a Y chromosome.

"My son has no appreciation for hard work. Can't get him to work a week at the business he'll one day take over."

"What kind of work do you have available?" I say, trying to move the conversation away from awkward dysfunctional family moment to something more important, like me and my bank account.

"I need movers. Are you Marco's agent?" He smiles at this, and I realize Mr. Mitchell takes Marco and me for a couple. I like this guy even more.

"No, but I could also use a job."

"There's some heavy lifting involved so I like two guys on the team. But my teams work in threes. Two men and a project manager."

"I can do that, the project managing part," I say. "What is it, exactly?"

"I think you might have a little hustle in you, too. Call that number on the card, talk to Paulette to set up an interview. She'll want to meet both of you so she can figure out the second guy to team you with. She'll explain everything, including the project-managing part."

"So we have jobs?" I say, excited a job has just fallen into my lap.

"Paulette will put you on this weekend. No weekday work for students, but she'll keep you busy on Saturdays and Sundays."

"Thanks, Mr. Mitchell. You won't be disappointed." Marco and Mr. Mitchell shake on the deal.

"You two will be my first employees from Langdon Prep. Seems like this school has been trying to build leaders of the future out of people who don't see fit to do any hard work today." He's looking straight at Justin's bloodshot eyes when he says this. "I'll see you at dinner. Don't be late."

"Whatever," Justin says, giving a dirty look to his father's back and to Marco's face. "My old man's crazy. I'm sure you'll be great at moving mattresses, but don't think you're ever playing quarterback as long as I'm at Langdon."

When he walks past us, he rams his shoulder into Marco's arm.

"Excellent. We have jobs," Marco says, as though he didn't notice any of that family drama or Justin's threat. "I totally needed one. My pops had his hours cut last week. Now I can help out a little."

"What about him hitting you just now?"

"That's just football stuff. Nothing to worry about. Coach won't put a junior in to start."

If Marco isn't worried, I suppose I shouldn't be, but I don't think Justin's threat was empty. He and his father have some serious issues. Even if you're Justin and it can't be helped, it must be tough to have a father so disappointed in you. Maybe I'm the only one who sees it, but Justin's eyes were filled with something more than dilated blood vessels. There's some rage in that rich boy.

Chapter 7

"I seriously need a trip to the mall after school," Bethanie says, slamming her lunch tray onto the table. Honey-balsamic glaze from today's chicken entrée goes flying, just missing my shirt.

"Tough day?"

"That's an understatement. Come with?"

"I'll pass. Retail therapy doesn't do it for me, not that I could afford it. I prefer a Baskin Robbins fix. You could definitely talk me into getting ice cream."

"We can get ice cream. My treat."

She gets distracted when Ms. Hemphill walks by our table, as do half the people in the cafeteria. Every school has that one teacher who makes you wonder why she's a teacher: they're too hot, too cool, too stylish. At Langdon, that teacher is Ms. Hemphill and she's too everything. She even drives a brand-new Mercedes, which means she also has too much money to be a teacher. The boys lust after her, I'm pretty sure the other teachers hate her, and girls like Bethanie want to grow up and be her.

"She always wears the cutest stuff—trendy but classic at the same time. You know what I mean?" Bethanie says.

"No, I really don't. Wouldn't you rather go shopping with one of your friends, someone who actually likes shopping?"

She gets quiet for a second, then says, "I don't know that many people. Besides, I thought *we* were friends."

Wow, she must not have a whole lot of friend-making experience if she thought that's what we are. At this point, what we have is more like an alliance—two countries surrounded by a bunch of other countries that don't want us as neighbors. But it does give me a little more insight into who she might really be.

"So when you said you hate being the new girl, you meant totally new, like new to Denver?"

"I never said that," she says, sounding more defensive than my comment called for. "I never said we just moved here. Where'd you get that idea?"

"Whoa, I was just trying to get to know you better. That's what new friends do. I just figured if you didn't know that many people, it was because you haven't had a chance to meet any."

"Sorry. I guess I'm just peeved that I have to buy a new phone."

"I saw you on your phone just this morning. And you sent me a text about some cute guy in first period." Bethanie has a brand new BlackBerry that makes my free-with-contract-renewal phone look like two paper cups and a string. Did she steal that, too? "What happened between first bell and lunch?"

"Ms. Reeves is what happened. She confiscated it and refuses to give it back."

"She did the same thing yesterday with Lissa's face cream."

"She's doing it to everyone. Only a few days into the school year and she must have a serious stash already."

"Were you using the phone in class? She told Lissa she

had the right to take her cream because she was showing it off and being disruptive to class."

"Not even. I was standing outside her classroom door and only pulled it out to check the time. She walks by and just snags it right out of my hand."

"You were in the hall when she took it?"

"Yeah, and class hadn't even started. She called it a pre-emptive move because she knew I'd try to use it in class."

"I wonder what she's doing with all that loot."

"She says I can get it back at the end of the quarter. Can you imagine—no phone for three months?"

"You should fight it. Maybe take a look at the Langdon handbook and see if she violated the confiscation rule."

"It isn't worth the hassle. It's easier to get another phone."

I guess that's true if you've got money to blow. Or you're not averse to "borrowing" a phone from the AT&T store.

"Well, I can't go with you anyway. I have a job interview after school."

"Where?"

"Mitchell Moving and Storage. Lissa's dad owns the company and he offered Marco and I a job yesterday."

"Why do you have to work for Justin and Lissa's father? They're like the king and queen of Langdon. Surely there's some less conspicuous kids' parents you could work for."

"I have cash-flow issues. Doesn't matter to me if I'm slinging burgers or working for madame president."

"I never thought of it like that. You *are* kind of working for her, aren't you? That's just weird."

Right then I'm thinking that Bethanie and I are probably never destined for friendship. I have friends at home. I don't need her, although it's nice to have an ally in enemy territory. But how great is an ally who's all the time trying to figure out how to defect to the other side? And who thinks the world is coming to an end because you'd stoop so low as to work for the king and queen of the other side.

"I don't see why you have a problem with me working when you're in the same situation I am. Isn't that why you're here on a scholarship—because you don't have Lissa and Justin's money?"

"Work where you want to work. None of my business," she says, poking at her chicken with her fork.

"Are you going to eat that?" I ask because there's no sense wasting good food.

"You know what? Let's go off-campus for lunch."

"Only seniors can do that."

"I'll buy, you pick the place," she says, which, of course, are the magic words. Why should seniors get all the perks? Isn't it enough that they only have a year left of high school?

While we walk the quarter mile to Bethanie's favorite parking spot, I can't decide if I'm terrified or thrilled to be breaking the rules. I always hear that cops' kids are like preachers' kids—always looking to rebel—but that's never been me. Until last summer anyway, and even then I wasn't looking for trouble. Leaving campus for lunch feels like I'm inviting it.

"You still have your uncle's car? You must be his favorite niece."

"Want to drive it?"

I tell her no, but I absolutely want to drive this car.

"You know you want to."

"I probably shouldn't," I say, but she's already thrown me the keys and gone around to the passenger side.

It doesn't take a lot of coaxing before I'm in the driver's seat and cruising down the street like I own it *and* the car. I even glance up into the rearview mirror to see if I look any different from behind the wheel of a car that could cover a year's room, board, and tuition at my Ivy League school of choice. That's when I go up the curb, into someone's yard and come to a stop in the middle of a flower bed, after I take out a birdbath. I always wondered about those news reports of people driving into houses and buildings and wondered how that could possibly happen. Now I know.

"Are you okay?" I ask Bethanie.

"Yeah, how about you?"

"No, I think I'm dead."

"I'm pretty sure you aren't dead."

"I will be if my mother finds out about this. I only have a learner's permit and I don't even have it on me. Plus I'm off-campus. I'm so very dead."

Just then we see the owner of the birdbath coming out of his house.

"Quick, jump over me," Bethanie says.

"What?"

"You jump over, I'll slide under. Then it'll look like I was driving."

I do what she says and not too soon because the man is already halfway down his driveway.

"Are you kids okay?"

"Yes, sir," Bethanie answers for both of us.

"Good, because I'm calling the cops. You kids took this curve entirely too fast."

I get out of the car and look at the damage. The birdbath is in a couple of pieces and the car has flattened all the flowers. Plus there are two very long tire marks where grass used to be. I am in so much trouble, especially after the summer I just had. Lana's going to kill me, then ask God to raise me from the dead just so she can kill me again.

"Sir, I am so sorry for this damage. Calling the police and having them make a report would just be such a hassle—" Bethanie says before the man interrupts her.

"A hassle for you, especially when your parents find out you've damaged their car."

"It's her uncle's car," I offer because I feel like I should contribute something.

Bethanie cuts her eyes at me like she'd prefer I'd shut up.

"Tell you what. Let's just not involve the police or exchange names or anything like that." She points to the birdbath and says, "It's a thing. Things can be replaced."

"That *thing* was custom designed and cost me five hundred dollars. Plus you've ruined about a thousand dollars worth of prize rosebushes."

"So two thousand dollars would more than take care of it, right?"

"You have two thousand dollars lying around?" the man says, looking at Bethanie like she's crazy, same way I am.

"Let me just check," she says, reaching into the car to open the glove compartment. I don't know what she's going to pull out of there—a gun, Monopoly money, a tire pressure gauge—but not two thousand dollars. Except she does.

"Hold out your hand."

"What the . . ." the man says as he obeys her command and lets her count twenty hundred-dollar bills into his palm.

"Let's make it double your cost—three thousand dollars and zero questions," Bethanie says handing over ten more bills. To me she says, "In the car."

Like the stunned homeowner, I obey. She gets in, backs up to the street, and drives off, tires screeching.

"Let's hope he didn't get a chance to get my tag," she says.

"What just happened?" I ask.

"I saved your butt."

"And I'm grateful for it, but what's up with the ATM inside your glove compartment?"

"You know what the best thing is about secrets? Well, the only good thing really," she says, but doesn't wait for me to answer. "When someone knows your secrets and you know theirs. It brings you closer together."

It's true. Anyone who keeps me from getting arrested, expelled, or getting killed by Lana is going to have my loyalty. That's how MJ and I became friends. I mean, before we stopped being friends. But the stopping part was MJ's doing, not mine.

"Now your mom won't ever know about you driving without a license, and now you know I'm not really broke."

"So why pretend to be?"

"Langdon doesn't let anyone in after ninth grade and I really wanted to go there so I applied for the scholarship."

"So are you not broke, or are you rich? There's a big difference."

What I really want to ask is why all the cash in the glove compartment. The only people I know who keep a stash like that are thieves, dealers, and people on the run from the cops. But the only people I know with real money got it illegally since I only know them from Lana's cases, so my experience is limited.

"One secret at a time," is all she says.

Chapter 8

To show her solidarity, or to prove we really are bonded after what happened at lunch, Bethanie gives Marco and me a ride to Mitchell Moving and Storage when Marco's car refuses to start. We have to leave his ancient Pontiac Grand Prix in the student parking lot. During the long walk to her secret parking place, she explains the car to Marco using the rich-uncle storyline I'd inadvertently given her. The fact that I'm the only one she trusts with her secret life of bling may be something we can build a friendship on, unless it turns out she stole it all. She even wishes us luck before she drives away, leaving us to get home on our own. Good thing I have a bus pass.

From the outside, the place seems to be a big nondescript warehouse, but once we're inside, the main lobby looks like it belongs in some office building downtown—cool and modern with lots of steel and glass. Marco and I are ten minutes early for our interview, so the receptionist hands us both a job application on a clipboard and asks us to have a seat, then disappears down a hall, leaving me completely alone with Marco for the first time since we met. I've had plenty of daydreams of what I'd do in this moment, but now that I have it, I can't think of a word to say. So I study him like I do everyone else, and try to learn things about him I'm too nervous to ask. Like I noticed at lunch today he used his left hand to carry his tray to the table, but used his right hand to open his soda. Now he's filling out the application with his left hand, but he took notes in French class with his right. He's ambidextrous. This doesn't reveal the secrets of his heart, but now I know something about him that I didn't this morning.

I notice a faint tan line around his wrist, from something he wore recently when the summer sun made him darker, but not since school started because his wrists have always been bare. Believe me, I would have noticed. Times like this I wish my conversational skills were as subtle as my ability to watch people, but they aren't, so I'm just out with it.

"You usually wear a bracelet. One too small for your wrist, probably."

He looks up as though he's already forgotten I was there. I guess he was really focused on that application.

"Not a bracelet, but one of those friendship things, you know—the kind someone makes you from yarn or something."

Someone like *who*, I want to ask.

"How did you know that? I lost it right before I started Langdon."

"I noticed you have a faint tan line there."

"How do you know it wasn't a watch?"

"See?" I just realize I've reached out and touched him where the bracelet used to be. My face grows hot and I pull my hand back. "The size of the band is uniform all around your wrist. No watch face. And the line is too thin to be a man's watchband, anyway."

"That's crazy. You're pretty observant."

Now he thinks I'm a freak, one who stares at his wrists.

"I just pick up on things around me, that's all."

"Well, I don't pick up on things like that. Most people don't. But that's cool, like ESP or something. Kind of special."

I am the least special person I know, so I don't know whether he's trying to make me feel better about being a freak, or if he really believes what he's saying. But the way he's looking straight into me makes me know he believes it. He thinks I'm special.

"The clues are there for everyone to see, I just notice them when others don't. More like being a detective than having ESP."

"Well, however you do it, maybe you can help me solve the case of the missing friendship bracelet." His phone beeps and he pulls it from his pocket, quickly reads a text, and puts it away again. "I need to find it soon because I've run out of excuses to give my girlfriend. That's the umpteenth time she's asked if I found it yet."

Of course there's a girlfriend. There always is. I don't want him to see my disappointment, so I just go back to my application and hope he doesn't notice I hadn't even filled in my name yet because I was too busy checking him out.

After we finished the applications, Paulette, the office manager, shows us around the warehouse. I'm wondering how she can work around a bunch of guys all day wearing a low-cut slinky dress and still get respect, but somehow she does. Every guy we pass calls her *Miss* Paulette and shows great restraint by looking at her face and not her cleavage. There isn't much to see on the tour—the storage area, the loading dock—all of it kind of dark and gloomy. The ceiling in the warehouse is so high that the lights up there don't seem to make it down to ground level. It smells of wood palettes and diesel fuel. It's hard to imagine Lissa or her brother anywhere near this place. I can see why Mr. Mitchell is so disappointed. He knows it ain't ever gonna happen.

The interview turns out not to be one, really. Back at the administrative area, Paulette tells us we have the jobs and she wants to team us with an experienced mover. She makes a call and a minute later, a guy shows up at the door.

"Malcolm, I'd like you to meet Marco and Chantal, your new team. They'll be starting with us this weekend."

It's an understatement to say Malcolm does not look thrilled to meet us. When Marco extends his hand, Malcolm just looks at it until Marco gives up. I guess Malcolm isn't as impressed by formality as Mr. Mitchell. He greets my "Nice to meet you, call me Chanti" with silence. The only movement from him is his left hand. He has it down at his side, but he's holding what looks like a ball of modeling clay or Play-Doh. He presses his thumb into it until it begins to squeeze through his fist, then shapes it into a ball again, all with one hand. He does this over and over. It reminds me of Lenny and his mouse in *Of Mice and Men*. Eeek.

"Malcolm's a little quiet," Paulette explains.

Malcolm's also a little weird.

"He's been with Mitchell's for years, but just came back after a short break, right, Malcolm?"

"I liked my old team," Malcolm says.

"We discussed that Malcolm. When you went . . . on your break, we had to team them with someone else. The world keeps spinning, you know."

"Make *that* guy work with these two. They're just kids."

"That's why I'm putting them with you. With your experience, you can teach them to be quality Mitchell employees."

I can see how Paulette got her job. Her customer-service skills are excellent. She probably never had to, but I'm sure she could talk down a meth-head who thinks his Tastee Treets value meal is out to get him. Of course, that may be what she's doing right now. I'm beginning to think Malcolm's break was at a rehab clinic or maybe one of those rest homes for people who just lose it one day while standing in line at the bank. At least I'll always be in the van with Marco. If I had to ride around with this guy by myself, I'd just decide to stay broke.

Paulette's still talking as though Malcolm is as enthusiastic as she is, instead of nuts.

"You'll start with smaller jobs, like clearing out a kid's bedroom for empty nesters or partial moves to a winter home. Since Marco is seventeen, he can only drive the small van, anyway—employment laws, you know. At sixteen, Chantal can't drive at all."

That works out great since I won't actually be sixteen for a couple of months. One benefit of being the smartest kid in elementary school is being skipped a grade, which happened to me when I went from first to third. I'm a year younger than your average high school junior, but Paulette doesn't need to know that yet. I fudged my age on my application, but I figure by the time Paulette learns my true age, I really will be sixteen and by then they'll be so convinced I'm a model employee that it won't matter I didn't tell the whole truth. Or any of it.

"If you do a good job on those, we'll put you on full-house moves with Malcolm as the team driver and supervisor. We get lots of those in the summer—you kids could make good money if you work full-time."

She sends poor Marco away with rehab Malcolm so he can learn proper packing technique and get a uniform. A uniform! First Tastee Treets, then Langdon. If I have to wear another uniform I will scream. It turns out I get a reprieve. I'm supposed to dress business casual, which I hope is nothing like Paulette's outfit—a little too trendy and a whole lotta clingy for someone her age.

"You two might be our youngest employees yet," Paulette says, looking over my application. "You must have really impressed Mr. Mitchell."

Younger than you think, in my case.

"So what is the job exactly?" I ask, hoping I sound mature and businesslike.

"You'll be the face of Mitchell Moving and Storage to

our customers. First you'll meet with them to assess the job—what they want moved, how they want it stored, what they want us to pack—that sort of thing. Do you have customer-service skills?"

"Definitely. I have worked in a retail environment where I assessed our customers' needs and delivered the appropriate product in a timely fashion."

See, that's what you call embellishing. I was a cashier at the Tastee Treets, but I just made it sound better without really lying. As long as it doesn't involve a cute boy, I can talk my way into, around, or out of anything. Like the time Crazy Moses came in ranting he was going to sue Tastee Treets, scaring the customers. He said whenever he walked in, he heard voices and they were driving him insane. Instead of telling him the boat had sailed on that one, or that the voices he heard were just the Muzak system, I told him if he heard the voices whenever I was at the counter, it was a code that I'd give him a free coffee. With my discount, it only cost me a buck or two a week. Since I quit, I wonder if Moses is now threatening to sue because he stopped getting free coffee.

"Wonderful," Paulette is saying. "On moving day, you manage the move—make sure items are packed to our standards, keep the guys on schedule, and deal with any issues that may arise."

Uh-oh. I detect some BS. "Issues?"

"Well, our clients are all high-end. They're paying more for our services and they have . . . let's just say they have high expectations. That's where your customer-service skills, and a dose of maturity, will really help."

Translation: rich people going off on me when we scuff their credenza. But I got this. At my old job, I had people going off all the time. Like I said before, I bet Paulette never had to deal with a meth-head coming off his high.

"Don't worry. I'm used to working with challenging personalities."

"I think you'll do just fine, Chanti. I'll go with you this weekend on your first project assessment. I'll just need to get a copy of your driver's license to file with your employment paperwork."

"But I thought because of the law I was too young to drive at work."

"You won't be driving, but we need something on file for identification. Don't you drive?"

"Yes, ma'am. I'm an excellent driver, first in my driver's education class."

That doesn't mean I have a license, though. In all my excitement about the new job, and slight fear of working with weird Malcolm, I'd forgotten I'd have to show proof of my age. I don't even have my learner's permit with me since Lana is holding it temporarily. I borrowed her car without permission a few weeks ago and she got a little ticked off about that. So I make a big show of looking in my wallet and being surprised not to find my license, but promise I'll bring it with me Saturday. I just hope Lana will be so happy I found a job nowhere near our neighborhood that she'll give me back my permit, and that I impress Paulette so much on Saturday that she won't mind I tweaked my birth date.

Chapter 9

I'm hanging out with Tasha and Michelle after my interview, telling them about my new job. We're in Michelle's kitchen, which looks like the set of one of those cooking shows on cable and nothing like my kitchen. It's the only room in the house that doesn't have some kind of cross or Bible in it so it must be the only room Pastor Owens didn't get a say about how to decorate.

Thanks to her mother working overtime all the time, every appliance is stainless steel—not the hodgepodge of mismatched appliances at my house, where Lana buys what's cheap, not what coordinates well. There's a block of knives on the counter that must be crazy expensive because no one in the house can touch them except Mrs. Owens. They even have a cappuccino maker. As you can imagine, Mrs. Owens is a great cook. She always leaves something good in the oven or refrigerator before she goes to her nurse job on the second shift. Michelle and I are fighting over who will get the last pork chop, and eventually I have to concede since it's kind of her food. Okay, it *is* her food.

"But I'm a guest. A good hostess always lets the guest come first."

"Since when are you a guest? Nobody invited you, or

Tasha, for that matter. And Tasha had the nerve to bring her sister."

"She'll be in there glued to Nickelodeon for the next hour, like she's not even here," Tasha says. "I'm watching her tonight so I couldn't leave her at home."

"Y'all could have *both* stayed home instead of coming over here eating my food," Michelle says. I notice her voice goes up an extra octave when she's miffed. "Why don't we ever go to your house, Chanti?"

"Her mother doesn't like people visiting when she's not home," Tasha says.

"I'm starting to wonder if you even have a mother. Tasha, have you ever seen her?"

"Yeah, I've seen her. We *have* known each other since third grade."

Yeah, and don't you forget it, Squeak. She was my friend first, though I do appreciate your mother's baked apples. Maybe I could get to like you after all.

"Well, she's never home, to hear Chanti tell it. Even when her car is parked right there in front of the house."

"She's like Chanti. Not very social. And we don't go over there because her mother can't cook," Tasha adds, helping herself to more macaroni and cheese.

That's true, Lana is the worst cook, which is why I do most of the cooking, although my skills are limited to anything that comes from the store in a box, bag, or a frozen food container. Which is kind of sad since I love to eat. But the other problem with going to my house is Lana's job. She keeps odd hours, but she's at home as much as any working parent. I just can't risk taking friends over there and walking in to find a gun on the dining-room table, or Lana coming out of her bedroom dressed for work, i.e. like a prostitute, because she didn't know I had friends over. That would be pretty hard to explain. So I shut up about the pork chop and being a guest, and make do with more mac and cheese.

"Guess who got out of jail?" Tasha says, and like she always does when she asks you to guess something, she immediately follows with the answer. "Donnell Down-the-Street. He was out this morning. He came by to see Michelle just as we were leaving for school."

"How'd he get out?" I ask, wondering if he broke out because I'm sure he was guilty of whatever they took him in for.

"Because he didn't do it," Michelle says, sounding convinced.

"He also claims he didn't cheat on Michelle, and that you lied about seeing him and Rhonda Hodges making out at the movies," Tasha says, adding, "He had some four-letter words for you Chanti."

"Now why would I lie about that? Michelle, think about it. What would I gain from telling you your ex is a lying cheat?" I mean, other than a beat down for my trouble.

"Like Donnell said, you're probably just mad because me and Tasha are girls now."

"Chanti's still my girl," Tasha says, "but I'm beginning to think it may not be safe hanging around her with all these criminals on her case."

"Donnell is not a criminal," Michelle protests.

"Yeah, right," Tasha says. "All I'm saying is Donnell and MJ are two people I don't want to be on the bad side of."

When I get home from eating all Michelle's food, Lana surprises me with dinner.

"I made my famous tuna-artichoke-raisin casserole."

Believe me, its only claim to fame is the vast number of people it has sent running for a bottle of Pepto. But I hate to tell her I already ate at Michelle's since she looks so proud doing the mom thing, so I confirm her delusion that her casserole tastes good.

"But you took so little. How about another big spoonful?"

"Watching my calories," I say, and change the subject before she can make another offer. "I heard Donnell Down-the-Street was out. Did he make bail?"

"No, they had to turn him loose. Kind of hard to hold someone on suspicion of theft when the evidence you thought you'd find in his car, at his house, or on his person, can't be found. It also doesn't help when you can't place him at the scene of the crime."

"Theft? I thought he'd been picked up for dealing again. I guess he's been expanding his business."

"Something like that," Lana says, and then looks up at me, almost catching me spitting her casserole into my napkin. "Why are you so interested in Donnell? You haven't been hanging around that hoodlum girl again, have you? Those two probably run together."

"MJ wouldn't have a thing to do with Donnell. She's gone straight."

"Yeah, and every perp who swears on his mother that he's innocent really is."

I figure Lana's anger is still too fresh for me to defend MJ, so I take another approach.

"Michelle told me. She and Donnell used to go together, and he came by to see her today."

"If that's the kind of boy she attracts, I want you to stay away from her, too."

Luckily she doesn't know how tight Michelle and Tasha are now, or I wouldn't have a friend left on The Ave. She leaves the table, saying she needs a shower after a long day trying to convince her confidential informants it would be in their best interests not to hold out on her.

Donnell being back on the street is not what I wanted to hear. But it's only a matter of time before he's arrested for something else, at least this is what I tell myself so I can stop worrying. Because if Donnell really cares about Michelle (how could he when he had his tongue all down Rhonda Hodges's throat?) and he thinks I'm the one who ruined it for him, I admit that Tasha might be worried about me for a reason. Just because you played kickball with someone back in the day doesn't mean they grow up to be right in the head. And Donnell DTS wasn't right in the head even back then.

But Lana and Tasha are all wrong about MJ. In fact, I could use her friendship right about now. I mean, she saved my life. Or at least, saved me from a beat down. When it happened, I didn't know how to thank MJ for keeping me from getting my butt kicked, because words didn't seem to be enough and, if I'm being honest, she scared me, too. The two guys posted at the front door didn't even try to stop her when she crashed the party, said she'd heard it was the place to be, and asked if they had a problem with her being there. Apparently her reputation had already spread to the south end of Denver Heights. I figured if she was living on The Ave, she'd be a good person to make friends with, and I'm nothing if not a diplomat. When she told me she had walked to the party (she was wearing Doc Martens boots, and wouldn't know a stiletto from a wedge heel), I gave her a ride home from the party. Now that I look at it, this wasn't such a grand gesture since she lived half a block from my house, but I can tell you that not a single other person at that party would have given her a ride.

Michelle and Tasha were just plain rude about the whole thing. Since Lana was on stakeout—and the party was less than a mile away and she'd never spot that on the odometer— I took her car, the backseat of which doubles as a landfill because my mother is a little messy. The three of us fit just fine on the front seat on the way to the party, and as tiny as Tasha is, she could have easily sat on Michelle's lap on the way back. But those two refused to share the front seat with a Blood/Crip girl, as if she could do a drive-by on them from *inside* the car. So we spent about ten minutes moving food wrappers, several pairs of shoes (including a pair of mine I thought I'd lost a year ago), old newspapers, a couple of blankets, a locked suitcase with half a blond wig hanging out of it, and a set of binoculars (I had a hard time explaining those last two items) into the trunk so they could sit in the backseat.

But MJ must have thought me giving her a ride was a big deal, because after that, she wanted to hang with me. This meant I had two different sets of friends because Tasha and Michelle didn't want anything to do with her. I didn't know what the big deal was. Aurora Ave has enough madness going on that a Blood/Crip girl is hardly noticeable. But Michelle and Tasha have their standards. Drug-dealing Donnell DTS is one thing, but MJ apparently crossed a line. She was the first girl ex-con on The Ave.

I liked having a double life, sort of like Lana. I had to hide my friendship with MJ from Lana, who would never approve, which made the friendship all the more solid. Everything I did before MJ met Lana's approval. I was about to be a junior in high school and I was way overdue for breaking out. Suddenly my life was not so lame. People who'd been picking on me since grade school stayed out of my way. And that girl who threatened me over Robert Tice? She even came by to tell me I could have him. Which would have been nice if I knew what to do with him because Robert is fine, but unfortunately he lost all interest in me once he heard I was friends with MJ. Even *boys* were afraid of her.

A few weeks into hanging out with MJ, I felt as close to her as I ever did to Tasha. Having someone save you from a serious ass-kicking will bring you together quick because you get to bypass all the usual girlfriend, frenemy drama. And because MJ knew I was forever indebted, she felt completely safe in telling me the real story, which she decided to do one day when we were watching TV at her grandmother's house.

People thought it was wrong that her grandmother, whom everybody had called Big Mama long before MJ showed up, had to take in a juvenile delinquent in her golden years. Part of MJ's probation agreement was that she not associate with the people she ran with when she was arrested. Her mother thought it best she just get out of town altogether, which was how she ended up with Big Mama, who is not exactly frail and helpless. When she's not attending her church meetings, she's running her numbers game—an illegal lottery for people who like the halfway decent odds of winning five hundred dollars from the numbers more than the impossible odds of winning 10 million in the state lotto.

That was another thing I liked about MJ—there really was no wild and crazy side to her, even though that was what I originally wanted from our friendship. She liked some of the same things I did, like books and detective shows (except I silently rooted for the detectives while she cursed them out loud). Tasha and Michelle imagined we were out knocking over liquor stores or something, but mostly we just hung out at MJ's place watching game shows and reruns of *Law & Order*, which is kind of interesting when you watch it with an ex-con after years of watching it with a cop.

One day a few weeks into our friendship, we were watching *Jeopardy*. Neither of us had spoken except to answer Alex Trebek in the form of a question, so it surprised me when she offered a confession that I hadn't even asked for.

"Okay, I'm going to tell you what really happened in L.A. I've heard all the BS that's out there and I want to set the record straight."

I muted the TV because even though I hadn't asked for her confession, I'd been dying to hear it.

"First, stop calling me Blood/Crip girl. I know you thin' it's funny, but it's kind of annoying. I was never a Blood c Crip."

I didn't say anything, but was surprised how disappointed I was in hearing this. Blood/Crip girl was part of MJ's mystique.

"If you get all your information from TV, you'd think those are the only gangs out there. I was part of the Down Homes. Never heard of them right?"

"I don't think so."

"Down Homes don't get any respect outside of SoCal. I think it's because it's two words. A single word like Blood or Crip just sounds *harder*, you know?"

I didn't know, but nodded in agreement, pleased to learn that (a) MJ really was a gang girl after all, and (b) she agreed with me about the oversaturation the Bloods and Crips have gotten in the media.

"I did spend some time in jail, but I was fifteen, so it wasn't so-called hard time. That's what people say who haven't been in juvenile detention. Let me tell you, it's hard in JD, especially in L.A. County."

"So what did you go in for? That's what no one seems to know. Not that I've been gossiping about you or anything . . ."

"It's a'ight. I know people are talking. I know you have my back when they do, which is why I'll tell you. Wrong place, wrong time, that's all."

"That's all?" I was really hoping that wasn't all.

"My boyfriend was in the Down Homes. I knew that when I met him. Where I lived, just about everybody wore colors, so I either had to be a nun or go out with a G. I also took my books seriously. I wanted to go to college, the whole nine. But I was in love with that boy for real. So I stayed with him even though I knew what he was about."

She stopped to ask if I wanted a Coke.

Uh, no. I wanted to hear about the boy she loved enough to do time for, which was obviously where the story was headed.

"One day he says he needs to go to the bank, and could I

drive him because his license was suspended. I should have known something was wrong right there because of two things. One, he kept all his money at home where he could keep a better eye on it. He always said there was no better vault than a shoebox and a Smith and Wesson. He was funny as hell, way better than Chris Rock."

MJ stopped to laugh at the memory of this bit of comedy. I prompted her back on track by asking her about the other thing that should have clued her in about her hilarious boyfriend.

"Oh yeah. He never cared before about driving on a suspended license. All of a sudden, he was law-abiding. He was almost twenty, and hadn't had a license in two years. That's just another way for the man to keep track of you."

"So he was really going to the bank to rob it?" I asked, in case she got sidetracked by stories of keeping ahead of the man. I know all about staying ahead of the man, since I live with him. Her.

"You guessed it. I'm sitting in the car, and he comes out and says, 'Let's go.' So I do. I don't even know what's happened until there's a blue light on us. Then two more sets of blue lights. My first thought is whether we have any pot in the car. It didn't even dawn on me that he'd just robbed the bank until the Five-Os jumped out of the car screaming 'Put your hands up!' They wouldn't do all that over some weed. Not in L.A."

"So they got you as an 'accessory after the fact.' "

"Man, Chanti you watch too much *Law & Order*. Sound just like a cop. I'd probably been better off with you as my public defender. That dude was clueless, just out of law school. Got me close to two years in JD."

"So wait, how old are you? You said this happened when you were fifteen."

"I lied. I'm not sixteen. I'll be a legal adult my next birthday, but I feel like I've been grown for a long time."

MJ was done with her confession. She took the TV off mute just in time for the Final Jeopardy round, which I got wrong and she got right. During the closing credits, a cruiser went down Aurora Ave running hot. MJ stopped smiling over her victory in Final Jeopardy and with a voice like ice said, "Man, do I hate the cops."

Chapter 10

It's one of those late-summer days that make me think I'll never leave Colorado, even when I'm grown—mid-eighties, sky bluer than you could ever make up in a dream, the highest mountain peaks dusted with early snow. The sporting-goods stores have started running ski sales, but winter and snow seem so far away that you forget how cold November will be. It's a day made for a convertible.

I guess Bethanie isn't certain she has my friendship yet because she insists on taking me shopping after school—her treat. When I told her I needed to dress business casual for my new job but I didn't know exactly what that meant, she suggested I get a subscription to *In Style* magazine and said we were going to the mall. She doesn't need to buy my loyalty, but I'm not doing much to stop her. If nothing else, I figure it will be a chance for me to see if she'll be "borrowing" clothes from the mall or if she'll be dipping into the glove box for some spending money. She still hasn't let me in on the source of her funds.

I text Tasha and Michelle that I won't be joining them for our usual Friday happy hour—the buy-one-get-one deal on tamales at the Center Street bodega, then kick back and enjoy the ride to the mall. Call me shallow, but I like riding around in a brand-new BMW with the top down, people looking at us and assuming we're rich girls. If I was with Tasha and Michelle and two girls went by in a car like this, we'd immediately start hating on them, angry it was them and not us.

The wind blows a receipt from somewhere in the car into my lap. Bethanie doesn't notice so I take a look. It's from the campus bookstore, dated the first day of school, for a greeting card and a Montblanc pen. I see why Smythe got all agitated—it cost three hundred dollars! So the only thing Bethanie lied about that day is not noticing Lissa's compliment about Smythe's pen. Not only did she notice, she ran out and bought one just like it. I'd be embarrassed to admit that, too. But I'm glad to know the only thing she's guilty of is having low self-esteem. Except now I'm wondering how she can afford to buy something that expensive. Bethanie says she isn't broke, but it's a big leap from not being broke to being able to buy overpriced stuff you don't even need.

Finding the receipt also leaves the question of who actually stole the pen. I know it wasn't Marco, and the only other person in the room, the one who thought it was such a great pen, was Lissa. She was in the cafeteria when it went missing, but I still want to get the story on her because if anyone could make my life at Langdon miserable—other than Smythe—it would probably be her. It's smart to have information on people who might one day cause problems.

"You never gave me all the details of your ride with Lissa after y'all dropped me off. So what's she like?"

Lissa knew all about a neighborhood she'd never be caught dead in (mine). She says her maid lives around there, but I'm sorry, I just don't see Lissa riding with her father to take the maid home. She's the type who probably doesn't even know her maid's name.

"At first she was kind of standoffish, but after we started talking fashion, we found some common ground."

"Enough to build a friendship on?"

"It's not about friendship, Chanti. This is business."

Now here's something new. "Business?"

"I want all the best. If she's the person I need to run with to get it, then that's what I'll do. Friendship would be good, but that's secondary."

I thought she already had all the best, but I keep quiet about that. And I make a mental note whether I can trust Bethanie with anything real, even though we now share secrets. She makes friendship sound a little disposable.

"That's why I'm going shopping today, too. For her party next weekend. She mentioned I might want to rethink my style, because your sense of style says more about you than words or actions."

"Wow, that's deep."

"Well, I happen to agree with her."

"So she gave you style tips based on what? How you iron your uniform skirt? No one has any style wearing a uniform—thus the name. *Uniform*."

"Sure you can. She pointed out that my old manicure was inconsistent with my Coach bag. See?" she says, waving her right hand in my face. "I've changed it to a French manicure. More understated."

When I first met her, Bethanie had what I thought was a cubic zirconia glued onto her manicured pinkie fingernail. Now I wonder if it was a real diamond, but that's still a little ghetto fabulous for a girl trying to feign Langdon style. I have to agree with Lissa on one point. Bethanie is a walking inconsistency. She might be trying to cop Lissa's style, but sometimes I get the feeling Bethanie is from around the way just like me.

When we pull into a parking lot full of shiny new cars made everywhere but in America, Bethanie announces, "This is Cherry Creek Mall," as if we've just arrived at the end of the yellow brick road. We're walking toward the mall when a woman running away from it nearly knocks us down as she passes by.

"Watch where you're going!" Bethanie yells at the fleeing woman. "What was her problem? She's running like she stole something."

It's true. I've seen plenty of people running out of the Denver Heights Mall and usually someone was after them. In most cases, it was the off-duty cop the mall hired as security. I didn't get a good look at the woman, but being Lana's daughter, I watch to see where she goes. She stuffs two huge bags into the trunk of a tiny orange car, gets behind the wheel and guns it out of the lot. License-plate number 431ZTF2. The way she's moving, I expect to see a couple of security guards run out the door after her, so I'm ready to give them a description of her car. But no one follows her.

"Maybe she was just in a serious hurry to get home."

"Forget about her. We've got shopping to do," Bethanie says.

I have never seen so many designer bags and jeans on the arms and butts of girls my age, or younger in some cases. How is it possible to be thirteen and afford the kind of clothes these girls are rocking? Where I come from, you'd have to be a baller, rapper, or dealer to afford this stuff. Michelle had a Louis Vuitton wallet after she spent a few paychecks on it, but there was no way she could afford a whole bag. I thought it kind of defeated the purpose when she had to pull her LV wallet out of her Payless purse. But at least Michelle earned the right to spend stupid money; I doubt the girls in this mall earned theirs.

"You ever been here before?" Bethanie asks, leading me

into a store so shiny and bright that it almost makes sense some shoppers are wearing sunglasses inside. Even the sales racks appear to be made of gold. Ms. Reeves would pass out if she just walked past this place.

I say, "A few times," which is a lie because I've never even been in the mall before. Most of the stores there are so far out of my price range that I never saw the point. I'm not sure why I lied about it—hopefully I'm not turning into Bethanie, pretending to be something I'm not. It's scary that Langdon might have that effect on me.

Right away, I see I was accurate about the place. Besides the fact that I can't even afford to pay attention in a store like this, much less a pair of shoes, the minute we get three feet inside, all employee eyes are on us, and not because we look that good. There's another girl in the store, about our age, who someone ought to be following around instead of me, because that huge Louis Vuitton dog carrier she's sporting is a lot more full than it was when I noticed her out in the mall a few minutes ago.

While Bethanie is ooh-aahing over something ridiculously overpriced, I watch the girl with the growing bag. She's so confident she doesn't even watch the store, doesn't notice me checking out that bag. This is the perfect place to steal—they won't risk ruining a four hundred-dollar blouse with a hole from a security sensor. I bet she didn't pay for a thing she's wearing, including the dog carrier. Hello? Is no one wondering where the dog is or why it's so quiet?

I guess not, because here comes a saleslady running up to us right now.

"Hi, ladies. How can I help you today?"

"We're just looking," I say. "Maybe that girl over there needs your help."

The saleslady ignores me and again asks what kind of help we need. My conscience is clear—I tried to do the right thing. Now I hope the shoplifter robs the place blind. Bethanie acts like she didn't just hear me say we don't need any help. "I'm looking for some jeans."

"I can help you find your size."

"We can find them ourselves. Thanks though." Apparently my tone isn't dismissive enough, because the saleslady doesn't leave us alone until she's helped Bethanie find several pairs of jeans and tops, counted them all, and placed them in the fitting room. But she's still keeping an eye on us from her cash wrap. Louis Vuitton girl is heading for the entrance unnoticed, dog carrier bulging.

"What is your problem?" Bethanie whispers from inside a dressing room.

"I can't stand when they follow us around like that. Even in these uniforms with the Langdon crest all over them, they figure we're stealing."

"Shhh. You're embarrassing me."

"No one's out here but me. That saleslady can't hear us, but I wish she could."

"She wasn't following us. It's called good customer service. Maybe you aren't used to it."

"Good service? Are you serious?"

"Look, Chanti, maybe where you shop, service isn't part of the experience the way it is here. No one needs to steal around here."

"I'm guessing that girl with the dog carrier just ripped off a few thousand's worth in under three minutes, and not because she needed to. Number-one lesson in solving a crime is understanding the motive. Need is not always the motive."

"Who are you? Nancy Drew, girl detective?"

Soon as she opens the dressing room door, here comes the saleslady to see what all we've stolen so far. Bethanie comes out wearing jeans worth two Tastee Treets paychecks—a size too small and a couple of inches too low—almost requiring a bikini wax. The silk and lace tank she's wearing looks more like underwear. I don't think this is the style change Queen of the Preps was suggesting.

"What do you think?"

"It's a little skanky," I say, at the same time the saleslady says, "It's a little expensive."

Bethanie yanks off the tags, hands them to the saleslady, and says, "Excellent. Ring it up, then."

But I can tell she's really saying to both of us, *Screw you.*

Chapter 11

Bethanie was ticked off with me after I called her outfit skanky, but she still hooked me up with business casual, a khaki pencil skirt and a black blouse, both in cotton. Both from Target. Asking Lana for money after being used to making my own is starting to get old, and every time Bethanie treats me to something, I feel this twinge of guilt because I keep wondering how she can afford it. I've been waiting for her to tell me she's got a trust fund, or her parents are in the import-export business, but so far she has told me as little about herself as possible. Not that I don't keep asking. But soon I won't need to mooch off Bethanie and/or plead my case to Lana because here I am at my first day on the job, which means I'll soon have a paycheck again.

It's a warm morning so the air-conditioned lobby of Mitchell's is a relief after the walk from the bus stop. I check out my reflection in the mirrored wall behind the receptionist's desk and see that my new outfit still looks crisp, and I hang around in the lobby a couple of minutes trying to cool off so I don't look a sweaty mess when Marco sees me. That makes me a couple of minutes late because he and Malcolm are already in Paulette's office when I get there.

"Our team is complete," Paulette says brightly. I think she's hoping her enthusiasm will rub off on Malcolm.

"I'm still with them?" he asks Paulette.

She gives him an exasperated look and ignores his question.

"Before we separate, I want to go over your schedule. If all goes well today and tomorrow with your training, I have a few small jobs to assign you for next weekend."

"How are things going with that new guy?" Malcolm asks, fiddling with the drawstring on the mini-blinds. The Play-Doh is gone. I guess he needs something to keep his hands busy.

"Things are going great. He's not so new anymore. You were gone six months, you know."

Gone where? The state asylum? A drug-induced coma? I really do need to figure out the deal with this guy because there's no way I'm getting into a truck with him behind the wheel, even with Marco there. I mean, it might be slightly romantic to die beside your beloved as you plunge to a fiery death into a canyon off Highway 40 because your driver snapped, but I'd kind of like to enjoy the being-alive part first. At least a first date. Which won't happen until he dumps his bracelet-weaving girlfriend for me. So I'm not quite ready for the death scene yet.

"Chanti, did you remember to bring your license?" Paulette asks as she looks through a folder.

"Oh no, I completely forgot about it," I say, which is true. I also forgot to make up some story of why I won't have it tomorrow either, but fortunately for me, Paulette gets distracted.

"This is odd," Paulette says. "Marco, there's a note in your file that says we need to speak to HR before we start the training. Something about your I-9 form."

"Really? What's the problem?" Marco looks scared, and I

try to remember which of the many forms I had to fill out was the I-9.

"Oh, I'm sure there's no problem. It says on your application that you were born in the United States."

"Yes, I was." Marco says this a little too defiantly.

"I'm sure it's nothing to worry about. Let's just go take care of it now."

Paulette and Marco leave me alone with Malcolm, which is both scary and fortuitous.

"So, you really liked your old team, huh?"

"I don't know. It's my job. I don't come here to like people."

"Marco and I will work really hard, I promise. We aren't like the other kids at Langdon; we've had other jobs," I say, thinking this might be the reason for his reluctance to work with us. Maybe he's met Justin and Lissa and thinks all Langdonites are like them. That would frighten me, too.

"I *knew* my old team. They knew me. It was okay. None of this figuring each other out."

"I don't much like meeting new people either."

"Hey, I don't need some kid trying to analyze me, okay?"

Uh-oh. Hot button. I'm thinking the asylum was a good guess.

"My bad. Just trying to make conversation."

"Well, your conversation sounds a lot like interrogation to me."

Jail. Hadn't thought of that.

I keep quiet for a full minute (I know because I was staring at the wall clock the whole time), hoping Paulette and Marco return soon. They aren't back when the minute hand strikes twelve, and I can't help myself.

"So you went on a break, huh? That's cool. I could use a break myself."

"From what—homework? Didn't school just start?"

"Yeah, but summer break is just a couple of months. But six months—that's a *real* break. What was it—a sabbatical or something?"

"A what?"

"Like a long vacation from work."

"You need to stay out of other people's business, kid." His tone says *shut the hell up*, and I do.

I'm more than relieved when Paulette and Marco return. Marco looks relaxed again when he offers an explanation. "I just forgot to sign the form, that's all."

I'm trying not to think about Marco alone in a truck with a madman when Paulette and I arrive at the house of our first client of the day, which is in Cherry Creek and not far from Langdon Prep. I'm guessing this is where a lot of Mitchell Moving and Storage's customers live, since it's his neighborhood and he specializes in moving and storing the stuff of people who have more money than they know what to do with. If that describes your financial situation and you live in Denver, odds are good you live in Cherry Creek.

As we walk up the steps of a house that could easily fit three of my houses inside of it, Paulette warns me, "Now let me do all the talking and you just observe."

That's like telling the sun to shine. This I can do.

The front door is huge, big enough that Shaquille O'Neal could walk through the doorway and still have a foot of headroom to spare. On either side of the door is a tall potted bush that someone has shaped into three uniform balls stacked on top of each other. Rich people must have nothing but time. Well, time and money.

"This is Chantal, my assistant," Paulette says, making introductions. "She'll be your service representative on the day of the move."

"Nice to meet you, Chantal. That's such a lovely name."

I almost tell her to call me Chanti, but I get the impression Paulette used my full name for a reason. Chantal fits this scene.

"So what will we be moving for you?"

"My daughter's away at college and needs some furniture. We bought her a condo rather than paying for a dorm. Better investment than dorm fees, you know."

"Very smart," Paulette says, agreeing as if she knows from experience, which seems unlikely on an office manager's salary. I'm really hoping my job won't include pretending I have some idea what it's like to be rich. Paulette may be able to pull it off, but I would fail miserably.

We spend the next hour walking through the house, Mrs. Stone pointing out what will be moved, Paulette laughing at more rich-people inside jokes, and me writing it all down on an inventory form. It should have only taken twenty minutes tops, but Mrs. Stone has to tell us where she got everything, even the stuff that isn't being moved, like the mother-of-pearl backgammon board she got on a little junket to Madagascar. Who says *junket*? And I have no idea where Madagascar is.

I'm starting to dislike her daughter. Not only will she get a free condo, she'll have an almost-new plasma TV and a leather sectional that feels like butter (Paulette gave me an evil look that said *Get off that sofa now*! when I tried it out). And that's only from the first floor of Mrs. Stone's house.

After we left Mrs. Stone, there were four more houses and I swear each one was bigger than the last one, with more expensive stuff than the one before it. When we pull into the parking lot of Mitchell Moving and Storage and I see Marco leaning against his ancient Grand Prix with at least three different colors of paint, I have a moment of culture shock, like someone has blasted me back into the real world and now I have to figure out how to make do with hand-me-down cars and weekly bus passes.

"Hey, you're still here," I say to Marco after telling

Paulette I'd see her tomorrow. "I thought you guys only had a couple of small moves."

"We did, but I thought I'd wait for you, see if you wanted a ride home."

He waited, probably hours, just to give me a ride home. Someone call an ambulance because I am about to die from happy. I try to stay calm, sound nonchalant.

"A ride would be great."

"I was thinking if you want, we could get something to eat and discuss our French project."

Did I say I love my French class? I love my teacher even more. She had the brilliant idea of doing skits, and had us pair up into teams. Marco and I are a team, and the best part about it is *he* asked me. The minute the teacher said pairs, I started thinking up how I'd ask Marco but still play it cool like I didn't really care if he's my partner or not, but while I was busy coming up with a scheme, he just asked. One day I'll learn the direct route is sometimes best, and stop analyzing everything to death. But not today, because I spend the whole ride to the restaurant thinking of what I should do next and end up not saying a word. Not a single word.

When we pull into the Sonic parking lot, I try to decipher his choice of restaurant. Did he pick Sonic because we could have the food brought out to the car and have more privacy? That would mean he wants private time with me, which is great. But if I eat in the car I know I'll make a mess, and then he'll think . . .

"I hope you like Sonic—they have good slushes," Marco says as he gets out of the car, resolving all my questions. I *really* do need to stop overanalyzing everything. "You're pretty quiet. Did training go okay?"

"Oh, it went fine, but I can't believe how *rich* rich people are."

"I know. We moved a room that I'm sure if you totaled up the contents, it cost more than everything in my house."

"How was it working with Malcolm?"

"He's a little strange, but not serial-killer strange, if that's what you're thinking."

"Was I that obvious?"

"Well, you seem a little freaked out by him. And he told me you were grilling him about his time off the job."

I wouldn't call that grilling. Believe me, Malcolm would know if I was grilling him. I've had a great teacher, and if he didn't weird me out so much, I'd know everything I want to know about his extended vacation. But he did weird me out, so I ask Marco what he knows.

"He didn't tell me, exactly. My take on it is he doesn't have anything against us, it's just that he's not good with people, and he'd been working with his old team for a while and had gotten used to them. Now he has to get used to us."

"So it's not like he came at them with a hatchet and they refused to work with him ever again."

He smiles at this. "I'm pretty sure not."

The place is empty because it's that limbo time between lunch and dinner when everyone uses the drive-through, something I learned working at Tastee Treets. It's almost as private as if we'd stayed in the car. After we order and take our food to the table, I get my French notebook from my bag. Now that we don't have Weird Malcolm to talk about, I'm once again at a loss for words. So I focus on squeezing mustard on my hotdog while I steal quick looks at Marco. God. He's *so* cute. I try to fake like I'm completely at ease, but it's all I can do to keep down my hotdog while my stomach turns flips.

"Do you not like hotdogs? You've only had one bite, and I'm almost done with mine."

I should have ordered something else. How do you eat a hotdog and not make a mess? I can't pull it off, though I'm dying to finish it before it gets cold. But it isn't worth risking mustard all over my shirt on our first not-a-date-but-could-be-a-date.

"I guess I'm not as hungry as I thought," I say as I inhale our basket of fries. If you leave off the ketchup, fries aren't at all dangerous.

Awkward silence ensues. We could always work on the French skit, but I'd rather find out more about him, beyond what I can get from just watching him. I remember that moment in Paulette's office when she asked about his I-9 form, and his reaction when she asked if he was born in the States. Maybe I can start from there. He can tell me about his family, where they're from.

"That was strange, Paulette asking if you were born here."

"Why was it strange?"

Immediately I sense him going on guard, and wish I had never brought it up, but now I had to come up with an answer.

"She didn't ask me if I was born here. I don't know, it seemed kind of like she was suggesting something."

"Like what? Like I'm an illegal?"

"No, not like that. Well, maybe like that. Kind of like she was judging. I mean, you aren't, right? Not that it matters." And it doesn't. I'm just trying to make conversation and as usual, when it comes to boys, I'm only making a mess.

"I'm Mexican-American. I was born here. But I could be from anywhere—Puerto Rico, Spain—every brown person in this state isn't Mexican, and every Mexican in this state isn't illegal. Maybe you're the one judging. You should know better."

This is going wrong on so many levels.

"You know what? Let's forget about Paulette and work," I say, trying to sound light and airy, as though the last minute didn't happen. "We're supposed to be working on the French skit, right?"

"We should just go. I have to meet Malcolm early tomorrow."

Before I can try to make things right, he's already taking our trays to the trash can and heading for the door. I'd try to fix it, but I know I'll probably make it worse. Other than giving him directions, I don't say a word as he drives me home. And when I get out of the car in front of my house and tell him I'll see him tomorrow, he says, "I guess."

Without understanding how it even happened, I have completely ruined our first not-a-date-but-could-be-a-date.

Chapter 12

Marco managed to avoid me all day Sunday. He and Malcolm had already left the warehouse by the time I got to work, and when Paulette and I returned from the last client assessment, his car was gone. By Monday morning, I still haven't thought of how I'll apologize, mostly because I'm not sure what I'm apologizing for. A lot of what was said, and insinuated, came from him. But I started it and whatever I said wrong really ticked him off, and I couldn't sleep all last night thinking about it. I've been trying to distract myself with my classes, hoping the right words will come to me by French class.

PE should keep my mind off Marco since I can spend the next fifty minutes hating it. It isn't that I'm lazy, I just hate to sweat. And I get tired. That means I tend to be a slacker when it comes to PE. It's the only class I've ever gotten a C in since first grade. My sophomore year I would have had a perfect grade point average if not for PE, which makes me hate the class even more. Even worse luck is the fact that Lissa is in my PE class. When I walk into the locker room, she's talking to one of her clones, whose back is to me. Lissa breaks into a smile, but not because she's happy to see me. It's the kind of smile that only the evil can make, a smile that says something is about to go down. But before I can prepare for whatever she's about to do or say, I'm thrown off by the clone when she turns to face me, because it's a new one. And somewhere at home, she's got a Louis Vuitton dog carrier.

"Chanti, this is Annette, a friend of mine."

Lissa's entourage is like a Benetton ad—it includes just about one of everybody. I'm guessing Annette is Korean based on the charm dangling from her necklace, a single letter of the alphabet. I don't actually speak Korean so I could be wrong, but Aurora Ave isn't far from Little Seoul and I know what the letters look like from all the business signs. I also spend a lot of time going over the menu at the Korean barbecue on Center Street. She has probably never driven a single street in Little Seoul. Whatever her nationality, Annette somehow manages to look a lot like Lissa. How *do* they do that?

She also looks bothered, like it's some great effort to be introduced to me. Like I even care who she is. I already know more about her than I need to.

"Annette just started today. She got mono at the beginning of summer, so she's just now back. Chanti's one of the scholarship kids."

I don't say a word to either of them, and just walk to my locker. This doesn't stop Lissa from talking to me, of course.

"So Chanti, Headmistress Smythe's pen still hasn't turned up. Any developments on that?"

"Not unless you have it, seeing as you had as much opportunity to take it as any of us."

"Like I need to steal a pen."

I nod at the still-silent Annette. "Like she needs to carry a dogless dog carrier around the mall."

Yeah, I thought that would shut her up.

I figured I was done with Lissa and Annette until they come up behind me while I'm running my laps on the track. Well, fast-walking my laps. Seeing as how they'd already lapped me twice, I knew their slowed pace had everything to do with me.

"What did you mean about the dog carrier at the mall?" Lissa asked.

"She knows what I mean. Ask her."

They flank me so I get to hear them in stereo.

"Look, I'm not sure what you *think* you saw, but that's not why we wanted to talk to you," Annette says. "Lissa was just giving you crap before. That's just how she is."

How she is what? Evil?

"All we really wanted to do was ask if you'd heard about the party Annette's throwing Friday. It's to celebrate her having a life again after that whole mono thing."

"My parents will be out of town," Annette says. "It should be fun."

"I'm busy this weekend."

"The party will be at 218 Prado, nine o'clock—in case you reconsider. I hope you do," Lissa says before she runs off.

Bethanie will probably hate me because I got an actual invitation to the party, even if it is just a bribe, instead of a casual mention in conversation just to let you know there's a party, but you aren't invited, which is all Bethanie got. That's why I won't tell her about it, because it would be mean, like something Lissa would do. And she might try to talk me into going so she can come with me. That'll happen when Bethanie starts shopping discount. Meaning never.

"Where's my bracelet?"

This question follows a shriek, which comes from a girl on the other side of the locker room. I look over to see it's Zoë, the girl who, if it's possible, is even less athletic than I am. At least I was fast-walking my laps. If she'd gone any slower around the track, she'd have fallen over. She's definitely a Langdon misfit. I wonder how she survived this place for two years without either dropping out or going crazy on somebody. But now the poor girl is just about in tears and probably not worried about eating alone at lunch. Worse, every girl in the locker room pretends not to notice her. So I'm right, she *is* the social misfit. Well, the other one.

"What's wrong?" I ask, since no one else cares.

"My bracelet, it's gone. My dad's going to kill me. He didn't think I was ready for serious jewelry. I haven't had it a week and now it's gone."

"Are you sure you had it on today?"

"Of course I'm sure," the girl says, looking at me like *Who are you, and do you think I'm an idiot?*

"Maybe it's on the track," I suggest. "I'll help you look for it."

"No, no, no! I didn't wear it out there. I put it in my locker when I dressed out, and now it's gone."

"You mean this locker, with no lock on it?" I say, and I admit it probably wasn't the most sensitive thing I could have said, but it was certainly the most obvious. These people at Langdon are supposed to be so smart, but they don't have a lick of common sense.

"You're one of those scholarship girls, aren't you?" she says and the tears stop instantly. "How do I know you didn't do it?"

Can you believe this?

"Hey, wait a minute. Chanti's a friend of mine. I don't know what you're suggesting, but you're all wrong."

This comes from Lissa, which is even more unbelievable, unless you consider her friend's an apparent klepto who I have the goods on, and who they no doubt guess I suspect as the bracelet thief.

For effect, Lissa puts her arm around my shoulders and adds, "I think you'd better keep looking for that bracelet and stop making accusations."

"Come on, Chanti, let's go," Annette says, looking a little guilty if you ask me.

The minute we're out of the locker room, they dump me like I'm the one with mono, without even so much as a good-bye.

My world history classroom is too warm and the subject matter too boring. Add that to the tryptophan in the turkey sandwich I had at lunch and I'm trying hard to suppress a yawn when the headmistress comes on the PA system and interrupts a riveting lecture on the Peloponnesian War.

"I'd like the following students to come to my office immediately: Marco Ruiz, Bethanie Larsen, and Chantal Evans."

As soon as she says Marco's name, I know the rest of the names she'll call. I know the rest of the school is wondering what The Scholarship Kids did, hoping that after a couple of weeks trying to pretend we were absolutely no different, Langdon Prep had finally come to its senses and decided saving the poor wasn't worth the effort.

We all arrive at the office at the same time. Mildred is there and smiles at us but looks worried. She's standing behind Smythe, dusting ancient, first-edition books that have likely never been read by our fearless leader. She doesn't strike me as the type to read Aristophanes.

"Good morning, students," Smythe says, all business. "What I have to say is of a very delicate nature, but it must be said. It has been brought to our attention that there has been a rash of small but not inconsequential thefts around the school. Now, I'm not suggesting that any of you have had anything to do with the thefts . . ."

Yeah, but she brought us all in here anyway.

Mildred, who has given up any pretense of dusting (and why bother since Smythe doesn't seem to know she's there, anyway?), stands behind the headmistress's chair and shakes her head.

"Then why'd you call us in here?" Marco asks.

"Well, Langdon Preparatory has never had a problem like

this, and suddenly we have these thefts that coincide with your arrival."

"But the whole freshman class started when we did," I say.

"All the thefts have occurred in Percy Hall, an upperclassman building. Freshmen would have been very noticeable wandering around Percy Hall. You three are the only new upperclassmen in school," Smythe says, sounding victorious.

I've mentioned that I try to avoid conflict, and that's true, especially when it involves people who see no problem in pressing their thumb against my larynx before we've been formally introduced. But now I'm being falsely accused. Been there, done that. I have to say something in my defense.

"What about Annette Park? She's kind of new. She started school late."

And I know she's a thief because I caught her in the act.

"That's precisely why she cannot be blamed for the disappearance of my pen. She started school after it went missing. Besides, Miss Park hardly needs to steal."

I guess she's never heard of the thrill of the steal. Not everyone *needs* to steal.

"You mean this pen?" Bethanie says, holding up the pen that I now know she didn't steal.

"Where did you get that?" Smythe says, taking it from Bethanie and appraising it like it's a rare jewel.

"I found it in the library. I figured someone must have left it there."

Smythe looks at her skeptically and while I'm grateful Bethanie is taking the heat off me, she's opened herself up to Smythe's suspicion. Bethanie and I are the only ones who know that isn't Smythe's pen.

"From now on, don't assume because you find something you are now the new owner of it. We have a lost and found in the main office."

So not the response I expected from Smythe. I figured

she'd be on the phone to the police by now. It throws me for a second, but I get back on track.

"I just can't believe Langdon has never had thefts before we showed up," I say.

"Oh, we've had a few thefts and other discipline problems, but we deal with them before they get out of hand."

"And sometimes you get things wrong," says Mildred, startling Smythe and confirming what I thought—that Smythe had forgotten she was there. "Sometimes you make false accusations and hurt people."

"This is none of your business."

"This is every bit my business," Mildred says.

"Leave my office. Now."

Mildred looks like she's considering whether she'll leave or not, but then she heads for the door. I get the feeling it's only because she chose to, and not because her boss told her to.

"We'll discuss this later," Smythe says as Mildred leaves the room.

"I look forward to it," Mildred says, slamming the door behind her.

Smythe smoothes her hair as though she and Mildred had a real fight and not just a verbal skirmish. Given the hostility between them, I wouldn't be surprised if they'd thrown down before. It's clear Mildred shook her up a little, but now Smythe's back to business.

"As I was saying, we've had thefts before, but it's a rarity, and never of this magnitude. Not on the order of a two-thousand-dollar tennis bracelet."

I almost choke on that bit of information.

"Miss Evans, are you still here with us?"

"I was just thinking."

"Well, it seems you should have done some thinking last summer. Maybe if you'd given your actions some thought, you would have made better, wiser choices."

"Last summer? I don't get it," says Bethanie.

"So now you're suspecting us of something that happened before we started Langdon?" Marco asks.

"I'm not referring to all of you—just Chanti. Let's just say I always know more about our students than they think I do."

I know I'm pushing it, but I can't let this go without saying something.

"I sure hope you're looking at other suspects, and not singling us out just because we're the scholarship kids."

"Dismissed," is all the headmistress says.

Chapter 13

I'm home on the sofa trying to write a sonnet for my English lit class, but I can't stay focused. It's kinda hard to concentrate on homework when your principal has accused you of stealing a two-thousand-dollar bracelet. That's felony theft. Two to six years. If I tell Lana, all she'll do is ask how I get myself into these situations, and then answer her own question: bad judgment, wrong friends.

When the doorbell rings, I'm happy for the diversion. I see MJ through the peephole and I wonder two things. First, am I clairvoyant 'cause it's like I conjured her up thinking about bad judgment and wrong friends. Second, has hell frozen over?

"MJ, what's up?" I say all casual, as though she hasn't sworn never to speak to me again.

"I found this at my house," she says, holding up my iPod. "Thought you might want it."

I'd been wondering where it was. It must have fallen out of my bag while we were still friends and I was hanging out at her house. Why it took her so long to return it I don't know, but I sure don't plan to ask.

"Thanks. I've been looking for that." An awkward moment of silence passes, and then, "I was about to nuke a frozen burrito. Want one?"

"I'm just returning what belongs to you. That don't make us friends again."

She starts to leave, but turns around.

"Did you hear Donnell Down-the-Street got arrested?"

"Yeah, but he's back out. They couldn't hold him."

Her face turns hard and she says, "Yeah, I guess you'd know all the details."

"That's common knowledge on The Ave," I say.

"Is it common knowledge he's pissed with you?"

"How'd you hear?"

"People talk. That girl Michelle has a big mouth."

I can't imagine Squeak saying boo to MJ, but she's already stolen one friend from me. Not that MJ is still a friend.

"I'm not worried about Donnell, but thanks for caring." I say, hoping the sarcasm is obvious.

"Look, I don't really care what happens to you; but maybe you ought to be worried."

"I've got homework," I say, because this is beyond awkward and I don't see her point in trying to scare me about Donnell other than to just be mean. I get the point. We're no longer friends. "I'll be seeing you, MJ."

"I doubt it. Just wanted to return the iPod. Can't have you thinking I'm a thief or something. You might have your mother arrest me."

Lana is sort of the reason MJ hates me now. I'm mostly the reason, but Lana didn't help. The only thing MJ hates more than me are the cops. I can see her point, but that's because she was falsely accused and should never have gone to jail. I believe her story about her boyfriend's botched bank robbery, even though I don't understand how she missed those clues. Tasha's kid sister would have seen that disaster coming, and she's like seven or something. That's why I don't have a boyfriend (Michelle would give you other reasons). Boys mess up your head, make you want to go to jail for them. Even when they're so stupid they leave the money bag in the car, put what they can in their pockets, and go out to the car for the bag so they can get the rest, during which time the teller trips the alarm and the manager locks the doors so they can't get back in. When MJ later told me that bit of information, I started thinking there was a legit reason why the Down Homes got no respect outside of SoCal. I questioned how much respect they got *inside* SoCal.

Anyway, I knew MJ was an innocent. An innocent who could probably break your neck with her bare hands if you got on her bad side, but it would take a lot to get on her bad side. Unless, like I said before, you wear a badge.

I was thinking about this while I sat outside the Tastee Treets a few weeks after MJ and I had met. The girl who had reluctantly offered me Robert Tice had just walked up. At first she looked like she was about to snatch me bald, and the next minute she was smiling at me like I was about to give her my lunch money. That's because MJ had just walked out of the restaurant with our food. That's how my summer was going. I got respect from everyone, all because MJ was my new best friend. Which is why I thought nothing of doing the favor she asked that day.

"My grandmother took her car on a church trip down to Colorado Springs. You think you could give me a ride across town tonight, over on Colfax, around ten or eleven? There's a hotel down there my cousin is staying at. He wants to know if I could visit him while he's in town."

I didn't want to tell her I only had a learner's permit. MJ was almost eighteen and worldly compared to me. If she knew I was just fifteen, I figured she wouldn't want to hang out. Instead of telling her I couldn't legally drive, I began asking questions that might help me get out of doing her the favor.

"Why so late? Why not tomorrow when your grand-mother's back in town?"

"He's passing through on his way to Chicago, leaving to-morrow. We're like brother and sister, and I haven't seen him in a long time. It would be nice to see him, just for a few minutes at least."

"Passing through from where?" The Lana angel over my right shoulder was whispering *No good can come of anything, especially a hotel on West Colfax, late on a Saturday night.*

"I know what you're thinking, Chanti. Yeah, he's from L.A., but he wasn't a Down Home. He wouldn't have a thing to do with the Down Homes."

So I thought, *Why not?* It was already mid-July and my association with MJ had brought very little excitement to my summer, and I was tired of evading Tasha and Michelle's questions about what MJ and I did when we hung out. Okay, so I didn't evade their questions; I answered them. I was get-ting tired of embellishing. It didn't seem like lying if I made the stories we watched on *Law & Order* sound sort of like they had happened to MJ. Lana was on a stakeout, the car was free, and I knew where she kept the extra set of keys. I'd be in my bed long before she got home. I'd already taken the car a couple of times without her ever noticing the odometer had moved—part of my ill-fated summer of rebellion. But this drive would be ten miles roundtrip, not two. Since I didn't want to risk Tasha or her parents seeing us and maybe telling Lana, we agreed to meet back at the Tastee Treets at ten o'clock.

Maybe MJ didn't know the difference between a hotel and a motel, but that place was definitely not a hotel. It was barely a motel in my opinion, but the huge red flashing sign out front disagreed. When MJ got out of the car, she said she'd just be fifteen minutes, but now it was twice that and still no sign of her. I remembered the instructions from the card in the seat pocket on the one plane ride I ever took—you're supposed to walk around every so often so you won't get a blood clot in your legs and die. I imagined there were worse ways to die around there, but I had a moment of bravery and got out of the car to stretch my legs.

Forty-five minutes and still no MJ. I'd never been mad at her before, but I was starting to get angry. To keep my mind off how long she was taking, and how the red flashing motel sign made the oil spots in the parking lot resemble blood-stains, I played the game I always play when I'm somewhere new. It's something Lana taught me when I was a kid, the way other mothers teach their kids to lay on the grass and detect bunnies and kittens in the clouds passing overhead. It's called *Observe Your Surroundings.*

The motel had two floors in the shape of a square, with a courtyard in the middle, two passageways into the courtyard on each side, one on each end. The loud hum of a soda or ice machine came from the passageway nearest me. I could hear it over the televisions blaring through open motel windows (no AC in this place) and cars going down Colfax. Very close, a car backfired. At least that's what I hoped it was.

There was only one access point from motel to street. One way in or out. The glass lobby doors directly faced the entrance from the frontage road, so the front desk clerk would be able to see anything coming in or out of the parking lot, as long as he didn't fall asleep. I'd definitely want a room near the lobby given my choice, which I'd have in a mostly vacant motel the city should have condemned and bulldozed about twenty years ago. But MJ's cousin had chosen a room in the back. Since I'd been waiting, several cars had entered the lot and gone straight to the back, and then exited the lot five minutes later. I got back in the car because

I had a bad feeling all of a sudden. That's why I nearly peed myself when there was a knock on my window. When I saw who it was, I went from fear to relief to fear all over again.

"I thought this was my car. What are you doing out here?"

"Mom."

"Don't *Mom* me. If I wasn't on the job, I swear . . ." Lana stopped talking, and I knew she was listening to someone in her ear. It was then I noticed a row of cars parked in the next motel's lot. It was dark, but there was enough light from the motel to make them out if you knew what you were looking for. They were all Crown Vics, cop car of choice. Why hadn't I noticed them before?

"Chanti, don't leave this car. Stay low. It's about to go down." That's the last thing Lana said before she went walking off into the dark, her platinum-blond wig made orange by the red, flashing sign.

Chapter 14

So I know all about being in the wrong place at the wrong time, and that's how I'd describe my whole Langdon experience. But up to now, having to attend Langdon was an annoyance. Smythe suggesting I've committed a felony goes way past annoyance.

The next day at lunch, Marco, Bethanie, and I find a table in the back of the cafeteria so we can discuss what went down in Smythe's office yesterday.

"Did you say anything about it to your parents yet?" I ask.

"No," Bethanie says. "I'm just hoping this thing goes away."

"I haven't said anything," says Marco.

"Good. I'd appreciate it if you gave me a couple of days to figure this out first," I tell them. "I'd love to bust this case and set Smythe straight. If parents get into it, it'll turn into a whole big thing and I won't get a chance to find out who really did it."

"Only if you tell us what you did last summer," Bethanie says. "What was all that about?"

"I have no idea what Smythe is talking about," I say, which is mostly true.

"I can wait," Marco says. "My parents are already stressed about my dad's hours being cut at work and they're dealing with some serious family stuff. They've got enough to worry about. I can lay low unless she gets real crazy and calls the cops on us."

"It won't get that far. I'll figure it out before it does," I say, hoping I sound more confident than I really am.

"I know you play girl detective on TV, but what makes you think you can actually find the thief?" Bethanie asks.

"She's pretty good at observing people, and isn't that mostly what being a detective is about? Maybe we should give her a chance."

We haven't talked about what went wrong over the weekend, but I'm hoping this means Marco is willing to give me another chance on that front, too. It helps that he smiles at me after he says this, just barely, but I notice.

"I guess I can give you a couple of days. If my parents get dragged into it, then it might come out that I'm . . ."

Bethanie stops midsentence, and I know what she was about to say—that she's afraid her cover will be blown, the school board and her parents will find out she lied her way into Langdon, and she'll be expelled faster than Smythe can conjure up crazy accusations.

"I mean, you know, the farther you can keep the parents from school, the better, right? They stay in my business enough at home."

"Thanks, guys," I say, letting Bethanie's weak story slide. "I think I picked up a clue or two before I walked out of Smythe's office."

"So give it up," Bethanie says.

"Number-one lesson in solving a crime—don't let on what you know until you have your suspect in custody, and even then, don't tell much."

"That's number one?" Bethanie asks. "I thought you said it was 'understand the motive'."

When Lana first became a cop and I wanted to know everything there was to know about her work, she'd teach me lessons in crime-solving. I'm pretty certain both lessons were high on the list of importance, but that was a while ago, when I was still young enough to think my friends would agree being a cop was the coolest job on the planet. I still believe it is, but no one else on Aurora Ave would.

"Well, it's somewhere in the top ten. On that note, I have someplace I need to be," I say, leaving them to wonder what I'm up to.

I go looking for Mildred. I already knew she disliked her boss as much as I do, but while we were all in Smythe's office, she seemed to have a definite opinion on Smythe falsely accusing people. I'm betting Mildred is sympathetic to our getting railroaded, and has some history on Smythe that might help my case. I find her in the janitor's supply room/office in Main Hall.

"I won't take too much of your time, Mildred. It's related to that whole thing in Smythe's office earlier."

"You're still here, so I guess she hasn't expelled you yet."

"She's not expelling us. We haven't done anything wrong."

"That won't stop her."

"So you've seen it happen before?"

"Up close and personal. She expelled one of my kids."

"Your kids go to Langdon?"

"They did. One of the employee benefits used to be free tuition for children of staff after ten years of service. I put three kids through Langdon. They all graduated and got full scholarships into some good universities. The fourth, my youngest, would have been starting his senior year, but she expelled him just before winter break. Some Christmas that was."

"For what?"

"Graffiti and theft. She claims he stole some paint from the art department—that was the theft part—and then 'defaced' Langdon property."

"And you don't believe it?"

"Of course not. I know my Reginald isn't an angel, but he didn't do that." She points to a photo tacked to the wall above a shelf full of cleaning products. "He's the one in the middle. Got an honest face if ever I saw one."

I look closely at the photo and see the middle boy is cute, kind of familiar-looking, but I don't know why, considering he was kicked out before I started Langdon.

"You said free tuition used to be a benefit. Not anymore?"

"Not since *she* arrived a few years ago. She talked the board into offering it to faculty only. Said it should be a perk for attracting the best teachers, but staff like me come a dime a dozen. Reginald had just been accepted to ninth grade, so he was what you call grandfathered in."

"I suppose Smythe didn't like that."

"Not one bit. I was the only staff member who had a child attending, and it just ate at her that he was still here. I think she just made up that charge to get rid of him."

"Why was Smythe so set on expelling Reginald? Does she dislike you that much?"

"Not *me*. Anyone like me. Anyone like you. People who don't have money or a fancy upbringing. Sort of the way you don't want flies hanging around your picnic."

"So where is Reginald now?"

"Neighborhood school. But not for long, I hope. I brought a complaint to the board and I'm getting myself a lawyer. That's the only reason I'm still working here—if her decision gets overturned, Reginald's coming back. He'll graduate from Langdon like my other kids."

"That reminds me why I'm here," I say, really motivated to prove Smythe wrong after hearing Mildred's story. "I have a favor to ask. I need your help proving my friends and I aren't guilty."

"If you can do that, it would surely help Reginald's case. It would show the board she just goes around willy-nilly accusing people. Just let me know what you need me to do."

"I need information about what was stolen and when. If you could get me into her office, keep watch for me while I'm in there, that's all I need."

"I can do that. How about today after school? She leaves every day at four o'clock. I can let you in then."

"That'll work. Maybe you can keep an ear out, too. If you're in the office next time something's reported stolen, let me know what's going on."

"Wouldn't it be fun if it was Smythe doing the stealing?"

"You think?"

"Nah, I'm just talking. I hate that woman and *wish* it was her so she could be fired. But she'd never do her own dirty work. That doesn't mean she wouldn't get someone else to do it for her. Now *that* I wouldn't put past her."

My old school had security cameras everywhere, but lucky for me, Langdon only has them on the grounds, not inside. Or maybe that isn't so lucky in this case—if there were cameras, we might know who was stealing and I wouldn't be in Smythe's office trying to clear my name. Mildred is standing in the main office pretending to mop the floor, but she's really keeping an eye out for me. She made sure the floor was good and slick with wax, and put out one of those yellow plastic signs that warn people not to enter or they'll slip.

Once I get the information I need, I'll go out the back entrance.

It doesn't take me long to find what I'm looking for. Smythe is as transparent as the wax Mildred's using on the floor. There's a folder in her file cabinet marked SCHOLARSHIP STUDENTS and that's where I find the report of the stolen items. The witch. I make a quick scan of the list and return it to the folder. That's when I hear Mildred's voice in the outer office.

"You'll have to wait until the floor is dry, or I'll have to start all over again."

"That's your job, isn't it? Another pass with the mop won't take more than a minute or two. I need to get into my office."

Oh, snap.

"Those are some pretty expensive-looking pumps you're wearing. Leather soles, right?"

"So?"

"So I'd hate to see them get all gummed up with this wax. And once they dry, every time you wear those shoes, you'll be slip-sliding all over the place."

"Well, what do you suggest I do? I can't very well leave without my car keys."

"I'll get them for you. Won't matter if these old work shoes get a little wax on them."

Thank you, Mildred.

"Well, that makes more sense than ruining a perfectly good pair of Ferragamos. They're on the desk. No, wait, in the pencil drawer. I remember—I threw them on the valet where I hang my jacket."

I look around the room and find them in none of those places, but I do notice the sweater draped on the back of her chair is hanging lower on one side. I quietly fish out the keys so they don't jangle and hand them over to Mildred when she walks into the office. She gives me a reassuring smile, as if to say *It'll be okay, I won't let you get caught,* and goes back out to Smythe.

"That was quick," Smythe says, sounding suspicious. Or maybe I'm just paranoid.

"They were right where you said they were, on the valet by the door."

"Of course they were. I knew where I left my keys."

I cannot wait to set this woman straight.

Chapter 15

Langdon is just ten miles from Denver Heights, but it takes two buses to get home. It's not bad because the route takes me close to Downtown—just ten more minutes and one extra bus connection—and there's all kinds of benefits to that. So far I've only discovered the food benefits, but I hear there are others. I need sweets when I'm stressed so today I made a detour to one of those candy stores that sell stuff from back in the day. I bought Lana's favorite candy from when she was a kid so that ought to score me some points with her— and I might need her help. Since I got the information from Smythe's office yesterday, it's all I can think about, but I still haven't narrowed the list of suspects.

I'm working on some banana Laffy Taffy when Tasha boards the bus but doesn't notice me. I call her over.

"What are you doing on this bus? Shouldn't you be on the tin can from North High?" I ask.

"I had a job interview at the movie theater. If I get it, there's an employee discount."

"How did it go?" I ask

"I feel good about it, but we'll see," she says, taking my candy bag from me and digging through it. Something about how easily she did that makes me think we're still as close as we ever were, we just got a little off track.

"Don't eat all the chocolate."

"Uh-oh. What's going on?"

"What do you mean?"

"You only get territorial over chocolate when you're seriously stressed. So what's up?"

I'm glad Tasha knows me so well because I really do need to talk to someone.

"You can't tell anyone about this, especially loudmouth Squeak. Or my mother."

"You know I won't. Tell me."

The bus has stopped to pick up a bunch of people and I wait until it moves again so no one can hear us whisper over the loud engine.

"My principal suspects I'm stealing stuff at school."

"Seriously? Why you?"

"She's had it in for me since the beginning. She never wanted to offer scholarships and is profiling on the kids who got one—we're not rich so we must be thieves."

"She can suspect all she wants, but what proof does she have?" Tasha asks, unwrapping a Squirrel Nut Zipper.

"I broke into her office to find out that very thing."

"See, that right there won't help your case that you aren't a criminal."

"I didn't have a choice."

"This is like the time in fifth grade when you had to prove you weren't stealing food out of people's lunches in Miss King's class. You got profiled because everyone knew how much you liked to eat."

"A stolen Snickers bar wouldn't have gotten me arrested. This time the loot is expensive enough to make it a felony charge." I'm so upset I barely notice when a kid walking by knocks me in the head with his backpack. Barely.

"Dang, Chanti, that's serious. Have you figured out anything yet?"

"Until today, five thefts had been reported, all from girls, so I figure it's a girl doing the stealing, or maybe a boy who has a thing for the girls he's stealing from."

"Yeah, but even the biggest player won't be mad crazy about five different girls."

"I thought the same thing. So I ruled out boys. Next thing is the stolen property: an iPod, a BlackBerry, a netbook."

"Stuff that's easy to sell in a pawn shop," Tasha says. Every third business on Center Street is a pawn shop, so she knows the deal.

"Exactly, but I doubt anyone at Langdon even knows how a pawn shop works, or where to find one, so I ruled out anyone stealing because they *have* to."

"That's the only reason someone at North would steal. It must be a whole different world at your school." Tasha points to my candy. "Can I have another one?"

"But the other two stolen items have nothing to do with electronics," I say, handing her the bag. "One was a tiny bottle of perfume. I had to go online to find out why anyone would steal it. Turns out it goes for tall dollars—it's produced in France for two hundred an ounce and impossible to find in the States. The last item on the list is a Kate Spade bag."

"How much money was in the bag?" Tasha asks because in Denver Heights, thieves steal bags to get what's inside.

"That's the crazy thing. The thief dumped the contents in the victim's locker, and took the bag. That didn't make any sense until I checked the Net. From what I can tell, the bag is produced in limited quantities to create a false inflated market for it."

"English, please."

"Sorry—I'm taking Econ 101. They only make a few

bags so everyone wants one, no one can find it except a priv-
ileged few, and once they find it, they have to spend a ton to
buy it."

"Like this overpriced candy you just bought," Tasha says,
fishing out another piece.

"Right, so maybe you should stop eating it," I say. "Then
I was trying to figure out what the stolen goods have in common besides all being top of the line and stupid expensive."

"And?"

"They were all taken during study-hall periods. But there
are two study-hall rooms in Percy Hall."

"That school has so many buildings they have to name
them?" Tasha asks. "North only has one building, unless you
count the overflow trailers, and no one's naming those. One
day you need to take me over there to see it."

"Assuming I'll still be there and not in jail."

"Oh yeah. You were saying?"

"Since we only get one study-hall period a semester, and
each item was stolen from a different study hall period, it
would be impossible for one kid to do all the stealing. They'd
have to have help."

"Maybe there's a ring of thieves, like a porn or drug ring."

Tasha's suggestion sounds a little Hollywood, but I don't
dismiss it. A theory, even a crazy one, is a possibility until you
can disprove it.

"Wouldn't it be kinda hard to steal in study hall? I mean
everyone would see the thief," Tasha says.

"Maybe at North, where it's just a regular classroom. At
Langdon, they also have study rooms like you see at the public library—little rooms with a small table, a chair, and a large
window looking out into the main room. Everybody tries to
get there early enough to claim one of those rooms so they
can nap or text or whatever they want because the teachers
can't see them unless they walk by. All the thefts happened
out of those rooms."

"So the kids must have been out of their study rooms when the items were stolen, but wouldn't someone have noticed the thief going into the rooms?"

"That's what I keep thinking. To complicate things, today something was stolen from a PE locker so now I can't even confine the thefts to study hall."

I've been so focused running the case by Tasha, I'm surprised to find we're already halfway home. Tasha has helped me lay out all the facts (and eaten half my candy). Now I just need to connect them into a story. That's always the fun part.

When I get home, I find Lana at the kitchen table reading blueprints. They're spread all over the table and floor with sticky notes stuck to them. She does this whenever she's on a new case, studying not only the building she's staking out, but buildings nearby. That's a big part of being a detective—knowing your surroundings. She says it's a gift we have, the ability to look at a thing once and understand it better than other people, to see how it fits into everything else. Even though she sometimes treats me like I'm already one, she claims to hate the idea of me becoming a cop. Too dangerous, she says.

"Lana, now I don't want you to get all crazy when I tell you this."

"Oh no, don't tell me you're pregnant. . . ."

One thing Lana fears more than chasing down an armed suspect is me getting pregnant. I guess because she knows how hard it was to have me when she was in high school. I'm sure I could tell her anything else—I'm on drugs, I'm a compulsive shoplifter, maybe that I gamble on the weekends when she's working a late surveillance—and she'd be fine with that, just as long as I don't tell her I'm pregnant.

"I'm not preggers, Lana. You'll be the first to know when it happens."

"Don't even joke about that." She knocks three times on

our wooden table in case I've jinxed myself. But unless you can get pregnant from just dreaming about sex, I'm safe. "So what is it you don't want me to get 'all crazy' over?"

"Look what I got for you," I say, handing her what's left of the candy. "There's some Mary Janes in there, and some Sugar Babies."

"Bribes, Chanti? It must be bad."

"The headmistress is trying to set me up for some thefts at school."

"Oh, thank goodness. I thought it was something serious," Lana says. Not quite the response I was hoping for, but pretty much what I expected.

"I consider a theft charge pretty serious, especially when I'm the accused."

"Sure you aren't overreacting a little? You tend to do that, you know. Remember the time you called the fire department because you smelled smoke, certain our house was burning down, and it was the neighbors' barbecue? Had an ambulance and three fire trucks over here."

"That was being cautious, not overreacting. And in this case, I've got proof."

"What kind of proof?"

"Monday Smythe called us all down to her office. . . ."

"Who is *us?* Don't give me half the facts."

"All the scholarship kids . . ."

"Is that what they call you?"

It's hard to get a story out when Lana goes into interrogation mode.

"Never mind that, Lana. She called us all down to say someone had been stealing and, not that she wanted to make any accusations, but it must have been one of us."

"Because . . ."

"She claims they had no thefts until we started at the school."

"That woman better watch herself," Lana says, and I

know from the inflection in her voice that it isn't an idle threat.

"Or what?"

"Just a mama bear looking out for her cub."

Now I know something is up. Lana would never reference a mama bear and her cub. When I was a kid, her bedtime stories were G-rated versions of her day at work. Sort of like an Officer Friendly version of *Snow White and the Seven Dwarfs*, except that the dwarfs were juvenile delinquents, and Cinderella was more worried about her probation officer than her evil stepmother.

"You have something on her, don't you? Is *Smythe* the favor you used to get me into Langdon?"

"Chanti, you're getting off track."

"Let's see. She must have committed some crime for you to have any dirt on her."

Lana says nothing, just stares at her blueprints, and I know I'm right.

"Nooo! Did you catch her in a sting? Is Smythe a drug dealer after school?"

"You're talking crazy."

"Was she stealing something? Maybe she's my suspect. She really wants us scholarship kids gone—maybe she'd set us up just to get us out of Langdon."

"Don't be ridiculous, Chanti."

"You know I'm going to figure out how you met her, so you might as well tell me."

"I'm not telling you anything."

"So there *is* something to tell. I knew it. Does she know your cover?"

"No, I stayed under."

"A-ha! Vice Bureau *has* arrested her for something."

Silence from Lana.

"I guess I don't need to know what she did, but it explains why she treats me the way she does. She thinks I'm the daughter of one of your alter egos. Hooker, crackhead, con artist, drug dealer—doesn't matter which one. No wonder she's convinced it's me."

"You know what happens when you can't verify a theory. No evidence, no case."

"You're just peeved because I outsmarted you."

This new revelation about Smythe doesn't give me much in the way of solving the school thefts, but at least I know who I'm working with. For the first time since all of this began, I feel like I'm one step ahead.

"Can we get back to the school thefts, please?" Lana asks. "Why are you just telling me about this?"

"I thought I could handle it on my own, but I need help. I was able to get a look at the list of what was stolen."

"I probably don't want to know how you were able to get a look at that, right?"

"Right."

No doubt I'm the only kid at Langdon whose mother would beam with pride over the fact I may have done a little B and E for the sake of solving a case. I lay out the facts as I know them. We don't need to write them down because we're both looking at the same list in our heads. We're quiet for a minute while Lana processes what I've told her.

"I agree, it isn't a boy, for all the reasons you said. Given the way the study rooms are set up, someone would notice a student going in and out of another student's study room, certainly the study-hall teacher would. It has to be someone who could go into a study room while the student is out and be above suspicion."

"So that leaves the study-hall teacher?"

"Or some other staff, like facilities people."

Oh no, I couldn't imagine Mildred doing that. But she isn't the only facilities person at Langdon. There are lots of them because the campus is so big.

"Not just facilities staff," Lana continued, as if reading my mind. "Was someone in there changing out lightbulbs on the days the thefts occurred? Could they have had contractors in to paint or fix a stuck window, anything like that?"

"I'm not sure. But it has to be someone who is in the school every day because the thefts haven't been clustered in sequential days, they've been spread out since our first day at the school. They wouldn't allow the facilities people to disrupt class time. I can't rule out friends of the victims, who no one would suspect if they went into a friend's study room. So that leaves staff or students who have access to study hall during that time."

"You said the bracelet was stolen from the PE locker room, so you can't limit your search to just the study halls."

"Yeah, but I think that theft might be unrelated," I say, still believing Annette was behind that. Now that I think of it, I should find out if she has study hall this semester. Maybe mall shoplifting has lost its thrill.

"What's going on in that school? I sent you there to stay out of trouble. . . ."

"See what I'm saying? Okay, if I ignore the bracelet for a minute and just focus on study hall, I can narrow it down to a couple hundred people, including the alleged victims. They could be trying to set someone up, or one of them could be a thief. Two hundred suspects—not very narrow."

"Well, let's look at it again. Use the advantage of being new to this world and examine the anomalies. What jumps out at you about the girls who had their property stolen?"

"They're all rich, but that doesn't set them apart at Langdon. Everybody is rich."

"Instead of looking at wealth as a common denominator, look at it as the backdrop for the anomaly."

"So someone who isn't rich? But you always tell me shoplifters are usually females who don't need the loot, they just want the thrill."

"That's true of shoplifters. But I think we're dealing with

something different at Langdon. I don't think this is a thrill seeker, or they wouldn't limit their hunting grounds to the study-hall rooms. They'd branch out, get bolder. As an outsider, tell me what you think about the items stolen."

"Well, first off, I can't believe kids are walking around with five hundred dollar BlackBerrys and messenger bags. Even if we could afford it, there's no way you'd let me spend that kind of money on a phone. Sometimes I want to introduce those Langdon kids to the real world, like closeout sales and after-school jobs and praying all winter that the furnace won't die. They don't know how good they got it."

By the time I was done, my observations had turned into a rant. Lana looks at me like I've just cracked the case.

"Find someone as angry as you are about some people having too much and others not having enough, and you'll have narrowed that list considerably."

Maybe Lana's right, but I don't know anyone remotely as angry as I am about overindulged Langdonites. Well, except for one really ticked-off bio teacher. I'm about to go back to my room and make some notes when Lana stops me.

"Chanti, on second thought, I want to look into this. If she's really suggesting you're a thief, that's a serious accusation."

"But if you go down there and talk to her, won't that blow your cover? She thinks you're what—a drug dealer? Or a pro?"

"I never told you what she thinks I am."

"Whatever it is, she must not be too worried about you exposing her if she's willing to pick on me like this."

"I'm not going to tell you, Chanti, so give it up. But you do raise a good point about blowing my cover, since she thinks I'm doing time right now. Maybe she thinks I can't expose her from a prison cell."

"Prison?"

"It was part of my story to get you into Langdon. You

know, 'I want to save my child from a similar fate, let her into that school,' blah blah."

This is why I'm such a good liar when I need to be. It's inherited.

"And you asked her to let me into the school in exchange for . . . ?"

"My silence about that which shall not be named. She probably figures she held up her end by letting you into the school and now that I've been locked up in a land far, far away, she can renege. Who will people believe, anyway? The principal or the con? By the way, she thinks you live with a foster family."

"Oh my God, Mom. Did you have to make the fake me into such a mess?"

Between Smythe's accusations and having two ex-cons mad at me, the real me has enough problems. Lana ignores my anguish.

"I'll just have to send someone from the office to have a chat with her, let her know she has no case against you."

"Unless one of your cop friends has a student at Langdon who knows I've been accused, that won't make any sense, some detective just showing up out of the blue when Smythe herself hasn't involved the cops yet."

"You don't know all my cop friends."

"I know if you have one with kids at Langdon, he's probably got Internal Affairs all over him 'cause a cop's salary could never swing the tuition."

Lana tries to think of a comeback, but accepts defeat.

"So I'm supposed to just let this woman call my kid a thief?"

"After talking to you, I have some ideas I want to check out. If I don't find the real thief soon, or if she escalates and goes to the police, then you can go after her. But at this point, setting Smythe straight is not worth blowing your cover."

"How'd you get so smart?"

"Good genes."

She smiles, but only for a second before she turns into Officer Mom.

"I don't want flattery. I want to know everything you find out. Don't hold out on me, Chanti."

"Deal," I say, hoping her mom/cop radar won't pick up on the mental finger-crossing I'm doing as I say it.

Chapter 16

I was actually looking forward to school when I woke up this morning. Not only do I have a lead on catching the real thief, I also have a lunch date. Some would call it a study session at the library, but I like to think bigger. Langdon's library is nicer than most city branch libraries, with two floors, a ton of books, and a multimedia center. It gets more use than the library at my old school, but Marco and I manage to find a secluded table in the humanities section. We're sitting side by side, so we can collaborate on our skit for French class.

"I want to apologize for last weekend," he says, and I'm so relieved we're finally going to talk about it.

"I'm sorry if I said something stupid."

"No, it was all me. I'm just a little sensitive about that subject."

I hope he tells me why because that would mean he trusts me, but he doesn't say any more about it and opens his French book. But that's okay. He isn't angry with me and we can get back to turning our friendship into something more. The table we picked is the perfect spot for a little extracurricular activity, but unless he makes the first move, I know it'll never happen. I can't think of anything to restart the conversation, so I focus on unwrapping my sandwich, part of the contraband lunch we've sneaked into the library.

"So what do you think we should do?" Marco asks.

I think we should kiss, but that's not what I say. What I say is, "About what?" because I'm an idiot.

"What should our skit be about?"

"I don't know. Maybe this, what we're doing now. *Petit-déjeuner au bibliothèque.*"

"Except that's breakfast. Lunch would be *dejéuner au bibliothèque.* And we're breaking Langdon law by having lunch in here. Maybe we should move lunch to the café for our skit."

I'm feeling the whole French thing, so I tell him it's a great idea: *"C'est une grandes idée, Marco."* I hope the way I say his name sounds seductive instead of ridiculous.

"Let's come up with the dialogue, or should we do the setting first?"

"Let's do the setting. But after we eat. I'm starving."

Oops, yet again I've broken the first rule of dating—don't let on to the guy that you are ever hungry. Oh well. That's a stupid rule, especially when he's already seen me go through a basket of fries like there might be gold hidden at the bottom of it. So I bite into the sandwich and try to think of something else I can do to let him know I'm a delicate flower, because I know my hips and butt will never convince him that all I ever eat are salads.

He opens a bag of chips and I notice that the tan line on his wrist is nearly faded away.

"Any luck on finding the missing bracelet?"

"It doesn't matter anymore. She broke up with me."

"Over that? No way." I try to look sympathetic instead of incredibly happy.

"It was more than the bracelet. I saw it coming. She says I'm different now, and Angelique does not like different."

Angelique. Sounds like a beautiful girl's name, the kind of girl who could make him forget she ever left him, forget my name, and take him back, all before breakfast. I pretend I didn't hear it.

"What's changed?"

"From the minute I applied for the scholarship to go here, she started in on me. Why do I want to go to some snob school? Did I think our public school wasn't good enough? It's good enough for her. Maybe I thought she wasn't good enough, either. Crazy noise like that, you know?"

"Yeah, I do know. A couple of my friends said the same thing when I told them I wasn't going to North."

"North? That's my old school. You weren't there last year. There's no way I'd have missed you."

I'm hoping he means because it would have been love at first sight.

"My old school is the one that closed down and merged into North. My mom saw it as an excuse to get me into Langdon."

"I'm glad it worked out the way it did. We may not have been friends at North. Angelique could get pretty jealous."

Hate her. But I can do that later. Right now I need to move the conversation back to us, not his emotionally unstable ex-girlfriend.

"I still hang out with my old friends, but not as often," I say. "It hasn't been two weeks at Langdon, but it seems like we're already in different places. We don't have the same things to talk about. . . ."

"It's like they think wanting something better is a bad thing," Marco says, peeling an orange. Without asking if I want some, which I do, he just hands me half. Is that not the sweetest thing? "And I'm not saying Langdon is better, but it might get me better opportunities—I can't deny that."

"It's the only reason I'm here." Well, that, and Lana forced me.

"Friends say I have to keep it real. I'm trying not to hear

that. I just want to get into a good college, help my parents out. To me, that's keeping it real."

"And I can still be an around-the-way girl just because I'm wearing this uniform. I'm still Chanti, just Chanti with more prospects."

"See, Angelique didn't get that." Marco turns to me and smiles. "I'm glad you get it."

Kiss me. I try to suggest this to him subliminally since this would be the perfect opportunity, but all he does is unwrap his sandwich and tell me how amazing it is that I'm so aware of things. Yeah, but I'm not aware of how to make boys think of me as something more than a friend.

"Well, I'm hoping all this awareness will help me solve the school thefts."

"Have any ideas yet?"

"No, but I'm working on it."

Later in the day, I'm sitting in study hall and instead of doing homework, I'm watching Ms. Reeves. The study rooms are set up in a squared-off U-shape, the open end of the U being the front of the room where Ms. Reeves sits. I made sure I got to class early enough to get a study room, otherwise I'd have to share one of the tables inside the U and I don't want any distractions. In fact, I got here so early—after pretending I was sick at the end of my last class—that I was able to watch the study hall class before mine empty the room. I didn't see Annette, so I guess I can eliminate her as a suspect for the study-hall thefts.

I don't know how I'll get a chance to watch the other study-hall teacher, but I don't think I need to. I'm pretty sure Ms. Reeves is the one. The other teacher, Ms. Hemphill, fits the Langdon scene perfectly—she's got that whole *I'm a person of culture* thing going that all these teachers try to pull off, like they're better than teachers at other schools just because they teach at Langdon. You get the feeling she can afford to be a teacher because she came from money. That's the only explanation for her car, a Mercedes so new the temporary tag in the back window still has a month before it expires. Even at Langdon with its trust-fund teachers, that big shiny car stands out in the parking lot. She's not a woman struggling to understand how these kids have the money they do.

Ms. Reeves, enviro-psycho, is the total opposite. She's already decorated the study hall with posters of decimated rain forests and endangered seal pups. A jar sits on her desk with a sign next to it that reads: THE CHANGE LEFTOVER FROM YOUR SUPER VALUE COMBO COULD FEED A THIRD WORLD VILLAGE FOR A WEEK. It's always empty. She drives a tiny hybrid that looks more like a Matchbox car than something made for grown people. It also looks brand new, so I figure Ms. Reeves is another trust-fund teacher, just one with a guilt complex.

Wait a minute. Her car. The tiny hybrid with a tiny trunk. I grab a dollar from my wallet, go up to her desk, and drop it into the jar.

"May I have a hall pass?"

"Thank you for your donation," she says sweetly, handing me the pass.

I head outside toward the teachers' parking lot, looking for a brand-new orange Honda, the little car I saw speeding away while I waited for Lana on the first day of school. I find it at the end of the lot, sporting a license plate that reads 431ZTF2. So that was Ms. Reeves at the mall. And I'd bet my Langdon meal plan ticket that she *really* was running because she stole something. I don't have a motive yet, but I think I might have my suspect.

Back in study hall, I grab my books and move to one of the shared tables inside the U so I can have a better view of the study rooms. I'm hoping the boy I sit next to doesn't think I moved because I'm weird or I like him or anything. But he just looks up at me for a second, then goes right back to texting, holding his cell under the table so Ms. Reeves can't see it.

I watch Ms. Reeves like I'm Lana on a stakeout. She has her back turned to the room while she hangs a poster of endangered snow owls on the wall behind her desk. If the perp was a student, this would be the perfect time for the thief to make her move, but no one even shifts in their chairs. I see Angela from world history pretending to study while she reads the manga mag placed strategically inside her textbook; a few students trying to get next period's homework done since they didn't do it last night; one with her study door closed and talking on her phone, violating school policy; a boy named Brad I recognize from English playing a game on his PlayStation Portable; another asleep with his head on the desk.

Brad puts the game into his backpack, leaves the backpack in the room, and goes up to Ms. Reeves's desk. She hands him a hall pass, and the minute he's out of the room, she picks up the cardboard box she keeps beside her desk and heads toward the study rooms. It's one of those boxes with lids that printer paper comes in. She has cut a slot in the top of the box lid and marked on it in big letters SINCE YOU DIDN'T SAVE A TREE, AT LEAST RECYCLE ONE. Ms. Reeves walks slowly, deliberately, as if she's trying not to look deliberate. She stops in Angela's room and asks her something. Then the girl hands her a few sheets of paper that Ms. Reeves slips into the slot on the box lid and continues her pass of the study rooms.

Now she smiles at a student as she walks by his room, but he doesn't smile back because he's the one asleep and drooling onto one of his textbooks. She keeps smiling, and even nods her head at the boy who doesn't know she's there. What study-hall teacher would let a kid get away with sleeping? I think that's their favorite thing to catch us doing. Teachers live to scare kids out of a good midday nap in study hall. But

Ms. Reeves just keeps smiling and moves along, stopping in front of the room where PSP-playing Brad was.

She moves into the room and a few seconds later, exits and heads back to her desk. I notice that she never gets to the bottom of the U, never finishes her search for a tree that might be recycled. Now she carries the box differently, like it's a little heavier even though she only put a few sheets of paper in it. The clincher is when she puts the box under her desk in the space where her legs should go, where no environmentally conscious student could reach it to recycle a tree.

The second that box goes under Miss Reeves's desk, I ask for another hall pass. Since I add another dollar to the jar, she doesn't question the second request. I go straight to the headmistress's office.

Chapter 17

When I walk into Smythe's office, she looks as though she's been expecting me.

"I'm glad you've decided to come and see me, Chantal. This will be kept in confidence; the others need not know it was you who confessed."

"I'm not here to confess. I could have proven yesterday I had nothing to do with it, but I wanted to find out who the real thief is."

"And you know who the real thief is, then?"

"First I want to make sure you know why it couldn't possibly be me. The first day of school, from the moment we arrived, someone was with us. First you took us on the tour of the school, followed by the immersion workshop. At lunch, every kid in the place was watching us. Then we went to the registrar's office to build our schedules. The only time we were anywhere near Percy Hall was when we stood in front of it during your tour. There was never a moment for us to have stolen anything from Percy Hall that day."

"But the thefts have been occurring for nearly two weeks now, and I know for a fact that all of you have at least one class in Percy Hall."

"Yeah, along with two hundred other kids. The important

clue here is that you told us the thefts began on the first day of school."

"Well, that may well be an isolated incident. Perhaps that first student *thinks* her property was stolen and it was really lost, but the rest of the missing items are truly stolen."

Even Smythe must know that explanation is weak, because she adds, "What about my pen? That was stolen the first day, when I left it in the classroom during lunch. You'd been in there just minutes before. Alone."

"Bethanie found it in the library, remember?"

"She found someone's pen, but it wasn't mine."

So that's why Smythe was giving the pen such a hard look the day Bethanie said she found it. She knew then that it wasn't hers, but let us go on thinking we were off the hook for it.

"In fact, I don't even think it was found. It appeared brand new to me, as though someone bought one just like mine."

"Why would Bethanie do that?"

"To end my suspicions that it was stolen, perhaps to protect a friend."

"I'm telling you it wasn't me. Just like the Percy Hall thefts weren't me, and now I have proof."

In spite of herself, Mrs. Smythe moves forward in her chair and lays her palms flat on her mahogany desk.

"It's a teacher."

"A teacher committing the thefts? That's ridiculous."

Little does she know that until a few minutes ago, Smythe herself was on my suspect list, even if Lana thought the idea of Smythe setting us up to get us out of Langdon was farfetched.

"No, that's a fact," I say. "But you won't know if you don't check it out before sixth period ends and she has a chance to get rid of the evidence."

"You've got some imagination, and you know all the police lingo, don't you?"

This isn't a question. She says it as though she's insinuating something.

"I'm well-acquainted with all of our teachers, and there is no way one of them is the thief. Why should I believe you over any of our faculty?"

"Because I have proof. And you probably don't know this teacher very well at all. She's new to Langdon."

I'm about to remind her she's also the teacher who wants to replace her precious garden with gravel and ragweed, but I don't need to. Smythe's eyes grow wide.

"Mrs. Smythe, I promise if you go down to Ms. Reeves's room right this minute, you'll find a box under her desk with a PlayStation game in it that belongs to a boy in study hall who probably doesn't even know it's missing yet."

"I'm going to look into this. I want you to stay right here, because we're going to have a discussion about this if you're wrong."

When Smythe turns to leave, I roll my eyes at the back of her dyed-auburn head and give her thirty seconds, then follow her down to Ms. Reeves's room. There's no way I'm going to trust her to do the right thing. Even when she finds the PSP, I wouldn't put it past her to deny it. As much as she wants to save her garden, she may want to kick me out of Langdon even more. Or she might figure out a way to do both.

I feel like I'm in a bad detective movie, dodging behind a bush as we cross the quad to Percy Hall, and once there, walking softly so Smythe doesn't hear my shoes against the floor, ready to duck into a bathroom if she should turn around. But I guess Smythe is so confident in her command for me to stay put that she doesn't notice I'm following her. She goes into Ms. Reeves's room and I wait outside the door to watch through the window. I want to crack the door a bit so I can hear, but I'm afraid Smythe will notice. She looks down at Ms. Reeves—which she does to everyone she talks to whether they're sitting or at eye level—and says something. Ms. Reeves suddenly looks terrified. Now Smythe moves to look under the desk. She takes the box and nods her head toward the door, motioning Ms. Reeves to follow.

I consider running, but why would I punk out when I've come this far?

"Chantal, I thought I asked you to stay in my office."

"Did you? I must have misunderstood."

"I bet you did. Well, both of you follow me."

We do, into an empty classroom next door. Ms. Reeves looks like a woman on her way to the gallows. She doesn't look at me, and I'm glad because I feel like a snitch, which everyone knows is the lowest kind of low. But I had no choice. Better her than me. Smythe puts the box on a desk.

"What's this box for, Ms. Reeves?"

"Recycling . . . I ask the students to recycle paper. We're ruining the rain forests."

Smythe opens the box and looks surprised and disappointed at the same time—disappointed in Ms. Reeves or because she can't expel me now, I don't know.

"So why is this video game in here?"

"They just have so much, these brats." Ms. Reeves caves like they have her on surveillance tape. "You wouldn't let me do the fundraiser for the orphans in Africa, and they're running out of time. I needed to find a way to make money. These Langdon kids—it's just disgusting how much they have that they don't appreciate. They don't even notice when they lose things. Mommy and Daddy will just go out and buy another, doesn't matter if a seven-year-old's fingers are bleeding in some Chinese sweatshop!"

"I thought the orphans were in Africa," I say, because I really am trying to follow along.

"Oh, shut up! You're just as bad as they are, polluting Mother Earth, and you of all people should know better."

I want to ask her why, because broke people pollute, too. But I don't because that might just send her over the edge.

"Chantal, who does this game belong too?" Smythe asks.

"Brad somebody . . ."

"You're in on this?" Ms. Reeves yells at me. "You should understand better than anyone in this school about the tyranny of oppression. I never thought you'd be the one to help the man."

"Uh, I never thought the man would accuse me of stealing the stuff you've been stealing, and threaten to have me arrested."

"I never threatened that," Smythe says.

"Whatever."

Now Ms. Reeves looks like she's about to cry. "Oh, Chanti, I never thought they'd blame this on you. I should have known. And now I'm as unjust as the rest. I'm an unjust! I'm one of the unjust!"

This chick has lost it.

"Chantal, get the owner of this game and bring him here."

Smythe didn't finish her sentence before I was out of there. Anything not to see Ms. Reeves reveal another personality. By the time I return with Brad, my teacher is in full-on tears, the kind that make you snot your nose.

"Hey, how'd that get in here?" the boy says. As if to prove Ms. Reeves's point, he hadn't noticed it missing.

This time, it's my turn to be smug when I look at the headmistress, but I can't pull it off with the sobbing Ms. Reeves standing between us. Turns out she's crazy for real.

Chapter 18

It's the second morning in a row since I started Langdon that I didn't dread what waited for me at the end of my long walk from the bus stop. Knowing Marco would be there always made it better, but until today, I felt like I was walking around with a scarlet letter on my blazer—a big red O for *Outsider*. I still feel like that, but at least now I'm a victorious outsider, and I won't have Smythe on my back.

It all makes sense now. When I was looking into Ms. Reeves as a suspect, I found out her planning period was the same period as my PE class. That means she had an opportunity to take the tennis bracelet from that girl's locker. Zoë wasn't in any of Ms. Reeves's classes, but she could have easily cruised the bracelet during lunch, or maybe during a day when she had hall duty. Those diamonds have a whole lot of sparkle; you can't miss 'em. She could have easily walked into the immersion workshop room during her lunch break, especially if she was scoping out stuff to steal. What she expected to steal from the scholarship kids I don't know. But then she *is* crazy.

Today is a good day. Not only am I free, but I proved to Lana that I've got detective skills of my own and can handle my business. I'm a minor hero at school because I got Ms. Reeves, confiscator of all things good, ousted from Langdon. I may have even scored points with Smythe—with Ms. Reeves gone, her botanical garden may live to see another season. So I'm feeling pretty sweet about the whole thing.

"We should celebrate," Bethanie says when I find her at her locker. "Let's do something after school."

"As happy as I am to be out of Smythe's grip, maybe I should just go home and get as far away from Langdon as I can for a couple of days."

"Come on. It's Friday. You solved the case and the good guys won. Isn't that reason to celebrate?"

"I suppose," I say, trying to think of a way out. "But I have to drop by my job and finish some paperwork. The boss says I have to do it today."

It isn't a complete lie—I really do owe Paulette a copy of my nonexistent driver's license, but I plan on delaying that conversation with Paulette for as long as possible, or until I actually turn sixteen, whichever comes first.

"We could ask Marco to come with," she says. I guess Bethanie has caught on to my secret Marco-lust. I don't even try to play it off.

"We *should* celebrate. What'll we do?"

"Leave that to me. I'll think of something. I probably won't see you at lunch—I've got cheerleading tryouts. But you and Marco meet me here at my locker after school."

Over lunch, Marco tells me he can't go out tonight, and I have to act all calm like he hasn't just ruined my entire weekend, and possibly my life because, you know, we're just friends.

"That's cool, it was kind of last minute, anyway," I say, grateful I'm such an excellent liar when I need to be.

"I'd really like to hang out with you. But I've got this thing."

Oh, no. I'm getting the generic, can't-even-think-up-a-halfway-decent-excuse *I've got this thing* excuse.

"Seriously Marco, it's no big deal. I might not even go myself."

"It's a very big deal. You just saved me from a lot of trouble without ever involving my parents and I owe you big time. It's just that I have this family thing. I wish I could get out of it, but I can't."

He looks at me that way he does and I believe him. I can tell he'd really rather hang out, but family comes first. Which makes me that much more crazy about him.

"But I want another chance. Maybe one day when Bethanie has something else to do."

Did he just sort of ask me out? I don't need food, water, or chocolate—I'm pretty sure I can live on just those words for the rest of the weekend.

I completely forgot the lie I told Bethanie this morning until we pull into the Mitchell Moving parking lot, the first stop she makes after school. Now I have to keep up the pretense since I made out like my job depended on filling out the paperwork.

"It won't take but a second," I tell her before I jump out of the car so she won't follow me. Bethanie will take any chance she can to get closer to the Mitchells or anything Mitchell-related.

My plan is to stand around just inside the lobby for a few minutes and then go back to the car, but then I hear a voice behind me. A scary voice.

"What are you doing hanging around here?" Malcolm asks. "Thought you don't work until tomorrow."

I'm wondering the same thing about him since he's sitting at the receptionist desk. Mr. Mitchell is going to lose a lot of business if the first person prospective clients meet is Malcolm.

"I thought I left something here last week," I say, looking around the lobby like the missing thing is going to magically appear—a week later. "I'm always losing stuff."

Malcolm clearly doesn't believe my story, just stares at me. I wouldn't believe me either. The lobby is sparsely decorated and it's obvious nothing is out of place. I feel committed to carrying this lie through, especially with Malcolm acting as though if he stares long enough, I'll crack. So I kneel down and look under the lobby sofa, even behind a potted plant. As if to bolster my lie, when I stand up, my cell phone falls out of my bag.

"See what I mean," I say, holding up the phone as proof.

Just then the receptionist arrives.

"Thanks for covering for me, Malcolm," she says, patting her round belly. "Junior doesn't always want to wait for my break."

"Glad I was passing through," Malcolm says, giving me a mean look.

I don't waste any time getting out of there because that dude just creeps me out.

"This time you can wait in the car. I won't be long," Bethanie says when we pull up in front of her house so she can change for the party and redo her makeup. After school, we grabbed something to eat and the whole time she obsessed over what to wear, even though I reminded her it was just us, and I sure didn't care what she was wearing. Then she decided she needed to go shopping so we had to spend two hours at the mall. I ignored her when she told me there was no way I could go out celebrating still wearing my uniform and that I needed to buy something, even when she offered to pay.

I'm disappointed about having to wait in the car because I really want to find out what she's hiding. Turns out she doesn't live near Cherry Creek like she told Lissa that day she gave her a ride. She lives smack in the middle of the neighborhood. It was a stretch to think she might have stolen the car, but I'm pretty sure you can't steal a house, so Bethanie really does have Langdon money. After fixing my run-in with the birdfeeder and giving up her pen to keep Smythe off my tail, I really do believe Bethanie is almost a friend. Everyone needs a few secrets, but I get the feeling she's hiding a big one. We can't be true-blue until I know what it is.

Whatever it is she doesn't want me to see inside her house—her parents, her family's bad taste in interior design, I don't know—must be bad. So far, all I know is the house matches the extravagance of her car. So I'm sitting in the car dreaming up a dark family secret for Bethanie when her mother comes out of the house before Bethanie is halfway up the drive. Bethanie stops in her tracks, like the fear of what her mother might do or say freezes her to the spot. I know the feeling of mother embarrassment, so I pretend to look away down the street, as if something interesting has caught my eye. But here comes her mother anyway, off the front porch and into the yard, her hand over her eyes so she can get a good look at me. Then she waves and motions me to come in. Bethanie looks terrified and I wonder what she's so afraid of. I give up trying to pretend I don't see her mother over there waving me in like she's the guy on the airport tarmac with the big orange sticks.

"You must be Chanti." Bethanie's mother gushes all southern accent, and then she grabs me in a bear hug, nearly knocking me over, which is hard to do because I am not what you'd call waifish. She's dressed head to toe in animal print, and sadly, not one animal but at least three different species are represented. And I'm serious about head to toe: from the kitten-heel mules in leopard to the long flowing (giraffe?) scarf around her hair, which I believe is paying homage to one of those eighties bands. Is this what Bethanie's trying to hide from me, that her mother is a fashion victim?

"Bethanie talks about you so, and I've been wanting to meet you. Y'all come on in here and sit a while so we can meet proper."

If I hadn't spent my early years and most summers in the South, I'd almost think she was faking that accent because she's laying it on so thick. No doubt it's the real thing, the twang of it right as peaches in August. But it seems too heavy for someone who's been here awhile, which I assume they have since Bethanie got agitated when I asked if she'd just moved to Denver. Maybe Mrs. Larsen is like Headmistress Smythe—a fake, hiding something just like Bethanie.

Soon as I walk in the house, I see money can't buy style. The décor is nothing like those houses I saw last weekend when I was working with Paulette. It's like a jungle in here with all the plants, not a single one of them real. Everything is either white or gilded gold. The water-spouting cherub in the fountain at the entryway is both. It reminds me of some of the houses on *MTV Cribs*. You can tell which celebrity has had money long enough to know they should hire a professional designer, and the ones who just got rich last week and let their mother or girlfriend do the decorating.

A woman in a maid uniform appears and Bethanie's mom sends her off for some tea. I'm beginning to see why Bethanie wants to hang out with Lissa. It seems they have more in common than we do, right down to the housekeeper.

"Why don't you get comfortable, Chantal, and we can have a nice visit."

"Mama, it's eighty-five degrees out. No one wants hot tea."

"That's what air-conditioning is for. We adore high tea around here, don't we, Bethanie? Some days it's the only time we can all get together."

"When you say *we*, are you including Daddy in that? He's almost never home for high tea."

Mrs. Larsen makes a face like Bethanie has said more than she should, but like any good hostess, hides it behind a quick and easy smile. Anyone else may not have noticed it, but I notice everything.

"Bethanie's father travels quite often."

"Yeah, right," Bethanie says.

"Bethanie never talks about what her father does," I say.

"He's in oil," Mrs. Larsen says, except she says it like there's no *I* in the word. "It's very lucrative. What do your parents do?"

"Well, it's just my mom, and she's a paralegal."

"There isn't much money in paralegal work, is there?"

No true Southern belle would talk about how much people make, but I'm pretty sure this woman's no Southern belle, no matter how much she's pretending to be.

"Not very much, but enough."

"Then how can you afford to go to Langdon?"

"I got in the same way Bethanie did," I say, looking at Bethanie. She's shaking her head, hoping I understand that she wants me to shut it. Now.

"We're rich, honey. That's how Bethanie got in."

"I meant to say, I got in on a scholarship."

"Well, that's just wonderful."

"Mom, Chanti and I have to get ready to go out, so . . ."

"We have plenty of time," I say, because there is no way I'm passing up this chance to get Bethanie's real story.

I already know they haven't had their money very long because no one who's used to money talks about it the way Mrs. Larsen does. And Bethanie is lying about how long she's been in Colorado because her mother's accent is fresh off the Bible Belt. Then there are the lotto scratch-off tickets I noticed on the foyer table. People who can't really afford the lottery are usually the ones who play. Obviously the Larsens don't need to play, but I'm sure they once did. It's a habit hard to break.

All of a sudden, I hear a man's voice coming from what I'm guessing is the kitchen, since that's the direction the housekeeper had gone for the tea. I can hear him easily because he's yelling.

"Who bought this new dinette set? Y'all been shopping again?"

Bethanie and her mother look terrified, and Mrs. Larsen goes racing into the kitchen to run interference. She comes out a second later with the oil man.

"This is Bethanie's father," she says to me. To her husband, she says, "We were just entertaining Bethanie's friend. You probably scared her with all that fussing."

"Nice to meet you, Mr. Larsen. Mrs. Larsen was just telling me how you own an oil company. That's very interesting."

"It *is* very interesting. Oil is my passion. Love me some oil."

"So does your company do horizontal or conventional drilling?"

"Say what? Oh, yes, right. We do the conventional-type drilling."

"That's probably the best way to go, certainly the least expensive. That way your wellbore is always parallel to your oil zone."

Bethanie is looking at me like I'm crazy, and her father just looks lost.

"That's it exactly," he says. "That's the very reason I go conventional."

Oops. Wrong answer.

"You're just a little Einstein, aren't you, hon?" Mrs. Larsen says. "I can see why they let you into school with that scholarship."

Bethanie grabs my arm and hauls me off to the kitchen.

"What's the deal interrogating my father like that? And what are you—some kind of oil geek?"

"I wasn't interrogating him. I was genuinely interested. Science is my favorite subject."

"I thought French was your favorite subject."

"French is my favorite *class*. Big difference. Anyway, I've been reading up on oil exploration, you know, because of the political climate and all. I'm no expert, but I do know the closest your father has ever gotten to oil is the unleaded fuel pump at Conoco. What's the deal?"

"There is no deal, so mind your own business. I'm going to run upstairs for just two minutes. Don't you dare move from this spot."

Once she's out of the room, I do move, of course. There's a stack of papers on the breakfast bar and I suspect I'll find something there. But before I can have a look, I hear the makings of an argument brewing between Bethanie's parents.

"If y'all don't stop spending all my money, we gonna be broke again," says Mr. Larsen.

Broke *again*. So I was right. They are newly rich.

"*Your* money?"

"That's right. I earned it."

"Earned it? Is that what you call it? Well, at least I got something to show for my spending. What you got to show besides losing tickets from the dog track? At least I got *things* for my money."

Scratch-off tickets and Dad bets on the horses, too. Seems to be a theme. They must remember I'm in the house because they quiet down and I pick up the stack of papers on the breakfast bar. I don't even have to rifle through them because the evidence is right there on top. A letter from the lottery commission. And not just any old lottery commission. Bethanie is Powerball rich.

I can see hiding that from people, but I don't get why her family is pretending to be from oil money. If I'd won the lottery, I'd keep it on the down low just to keep long-lost relatives from hitting me up for money, or to avoid being a mark for a ransom hit. I sure wouldn't be trying to perpetrate a whole different kind of rich life. I mean, rich is rich. If you're going to flaunt it, why not just go with the truth? Solving Bethanie's mystery will definitely be my next case.

Chapter 19

Bethanie parks in front of a house just a few blocks from her place and I already regret saying yes to celebrating. She's scammed me into hanging out with some of her stuck-up friends. Not exactly my idea of a good time.

"Whose house is this, anyway?" I ask as we walk up to the front door.

"I hope there'll be some cute guys at this party," Bethanie says, ignoring my question.

"Party? Wait a minute. That street sign back there said *Prado*, didn't it?"

"Okay, don't get mad."

That's when I notice the house number over the door. *218.*

"Where are we, Bethanie?"

Before she can answer, and before I can make my escape, the front door opens. There's Annette, and I want to kill Bethanie. When Lissa walks up behind her, I want to kill myself. But that's a little drastic, so I just turn to leave.

"I think Chanti left something in the car. Will you excuse us a sec?"

I'm already standing at the car when Bethanie reaches me and whispers, "Come on, just give it an hour, please?"

"You tricked me into going to Lissa's party."

"Because you wouldn't have come if I'd told you."

"Damn skippy."

"Lissa invited me at the last minute and I didn't want to come by myself. I'm not all that comfortable around these people."

"I thought these *were* your people."

"I mean, I don't know them that well, and I want to. Come on, just half an hour, then we'll go. Besides, how will you get home? I'm your ride."

She has a point there. I suck it up, hoping nothing could be that bad for half an hour. When we get inside, it doesn't look like much of a party. For one, it's really quiet, except for a TV playing somewhere in the house. And for another, no one else is there, except for the other two clones.

"Are we early? Did I get the time wrong?" Bethanie asks, realizing there is not a single cute guy to be found.

"When you told me you were bringing Chanti, I figured it might be a chance for us to get to know each other," Lissa says. I half expect her to add an evil villain laugh. "You know, a real Langdon welcome to the scholarship kids. I was kind of hoping you'd bring that hot friend of yours, but just as well. We planned a girls' night."

"*Night?* We won't be staying long. Right, Bethanie?" Because I can manage half an hour, an hour even, but there is no way I'm staying here any longer than that.

"You have to stay. We're having a fashion show and doing makeovers, complete with goodies to take home. That was my idea. Sort of my version of public service, help the needy and all that."

"Oh my God, that sounds like so much fun," Bethanie practically squeals. Why she wants to be one of these people is beyond me, but I suspect it has a lot to do with that whole upscale Langdon life she's creating for herself out of a dollar Powerball ticket.

The fun starts with a full tour of the house, and I don't mean one of those important room tours like *here's the bathroom, here's the kitchen.* Because really, do I need to see the parents' room and their priceless figurine collection or hear the story of how the silver in their special dining room (they have two dining rooms—special and everyday) was handed down by some deposed Korean emperor generations ago? Okay, I get it. You're mad rich.

"Fashion show time," Lissa announces after we've seen every last room in the house. "But before we start that, guess what Annette snagged from the wine cellar? Champagne. The good stuff, too. This goes for five hundred dollars a bottle."

"My parents are collectors," Annette says.

"Won't they notice it's gone then?"

"Who cares?" Lissa says, laughing as though I'd made a joke. "What a weird thing to worry about. Let's just enjoy it."

Annette fills our glasses while the clones go upstairs and change into their first ensemble.

"So Bethanie, I see your rich uncle let you borrow the car again," Lissa says after sipping from her glass like she drinks rare champagne all the time.

"Yes. He doesn't drive that often, anyway," Bethanie says weakly. She won't even look in my direction.

"He's very generous, your uncle," Lissa says before refilling her glass.

That's interesting. Maybe Bethanie will be busted twice today. But Lissa quickly bores of Bethanie and turns on me.

"So what's the deal with you and that scholarship boy? Are you two a thing?"

"His name is Marco and we're just friends."

"Yeah, but I bet you want to make it more than that. I can tell."

I ignore her, hoping she'll focus back on Bethanie, who looks relieved not to be the one in Lissa's interview chair.

"My brother hates him. Their coach benched Justin so—it's Marco, right?—so Marco can start the season opener."

"He's starting?"

"You didn't know? Some girlfriend you are. Maybe he's not as into you as I thought."

"He's into me?" Even when I'm talking to someone else *about* Marco, I have a hard time forming complex sentences.

"Well, he's way out of your league as far as looks, but you do have that whole poverty thing in common. It might be enough to build a beautiful relationship on."

"You must have started the champagne early, Lissa. You're already drunk," I say. "Not pretty."

"Don't be mad. I wish the best for you two. Really I do."

The clones return then. I'm pretty sure they're wearing clothes I saw during that shopping trip to Bethanie's mall, clothes that ended up in Annette's dog carrier. I manage to sit through thirty minutes of conversation about Prada, Gucci, and Juicy Couture before I have to get away.

"You mind if I use the bathroom?" I say to Annette, but Lissa answers as though it's her house.

"Of course not, but use the one upstairs, in the master bedroom. The one down here isn't working. Isn't that right, Annette?"

Annette looks confused, like she doesn't know what Lissa is talking about. A little too much champagne, I guess. Five hundred dollars or five dollars—it all makes you drunk. Bethanie gets up to follow me.

"What are you two, joined at the hip?" Lissa says.

"I just need to talk to Chanti for a second. I'll be right back."

"Whatever," Lissa says, polishing off her glass.

When Bethanie and I get upstairs and out of earshot, she says, "I wanted a chance to talk, you know, about what happened at my house. We didn't get a chance to in the car and . . ."

"I want out of here, now! Isn't this supposed to be *my* celebration, you know, to say thanks for me keeping us out of jail?"

"I know, we'll go soon. But about what happened at my house . . ."

"Bethanie, I know about the lottery win."

"How do you know?"

"It's what I do, remember? What I don't understand is why you're faking a whole different life, but that's your business. If you're worried about me telling them you're only pseudo-rich, don't. Your secret's safe with me."

"Look, don't be calling me no pseudo-rich," Bethanie says in a voice I've never heard. All of a sudden she's got her mother's accent, but without the magnolias and mint juleps. Wherever she's really from, I'm thinking it's the Dirty South version of Aurora Ave. "Rich is rich, okay? No one cares how you got there. What I'm worried about is getting busted out of Langdon. Once I'm in there a minute and people accept me as one of them, they won't care about my money or hold me to that scholarship."

"Bethanie," I start, then realize that name doesn't match the hood girl she's suddenly morphed into. "Wait, is that even your real name?"

"It is now."

"Okaaay, whoever you are. Do you really need Langdon and those twits down there to make you feel good about yourself?"

"Don't get all Dr. Phil on me. I don't need your analysis. I just need you to keep your mouth shut. You don't know nothing about me or where I come from. I can tell you now—I'm never going back."

She returns downstairs to Lissa and her clones. I'm so shocked by this whole new person I just met, I forgot I was supposed to be escaping torture. I'm dying to know what happens now, so I follow her.

"You weren't up there very long," Lissa says, looking disappointed. "I thought you had to go."

"I changed my mind. Is that a problem?"

This girl has serious control issues. She'd better recognize I'm not one of her minions.

"Should we do makeovers now?" Annette asks Lissa, as though this is not her house and not her party. I can't stand Lissa, but I'd love to know how she works this mind-control thing she has over these girls. Maybe I could use it on Marco.

"I'm tired of fashion and makeovers," Lissa says, picking up her phone to send a text. Apparently she's bored of discussing Gucci and criticizing me. Wait—I spoke too soon. "Let's have some real fun and play a little truth or dare. I'll start."

The she-devil looks into my soul when she suggests truth or dare, and I really want to leave this place. Nothing good can come out of Lissa's mouth, no matter what she's about to say.

"I know a little truth about Chanti that no one here knows. Not even her bestest friend Bethanie. I don't know why she's hiding it, because it really makes for an interesting story."

I'm thinking she knows how I broke into Smythe's office to get information about the thefts, but that isn't it at all.

"Our little Chanti has a record. She's been to jail."

Chapter 20

Lissa's information was not quite accurate. I was arrested and I went to jail, but I absolutely do not have a record. But I didn't stay around to explain all that.

"Take me home, Bethanie," I said after Lissa outed me.

"Come on, we're having fun," Bethanie said.

"Maybe *you* are, and at my expense. Take me home—now!"

Bethanie looked around the room at Lissa, Annette, and the clones and decided they were what she really wanted before she stabbed me in the back.

"I told you I don't like living in the past—it's my least favorite place. That includes your past, Chanti. It isn't my problem."

I grabbed my bag and got out of there. I didn't care if I had to walk all the way back to The Ave, I wasn't staying there another second. Even when Bethanie's car pulled alongside me two blocks later and Lissa opened her window to apologize (like I believed her), I didn't say a word. Even when Bethanie told me to get over myself and get in the car so we could all go get something to eat, I kept walking. The whole time I spent looking for the nearest bus stop, which took forever because I didn't know where I was and kept walking in circles, I was wishing I'd told them all about Bethanie's lottery money. That traitor.

Making friends with Bethanie—or whatever her name really was—was a bad decision. I knew it from the time I met her. Lana says I make too many bad decisions. I never plan to get into these jams; they just happen. It's like Ms. Reeves—she probably didn't start from crazy. I'm sure she had a noble idea that just went wrong at some point. Just like me taking MJ to see her cousin at that motel. I had the best intentions, but everything still went very wrong. Getting busted by the cops, put into a squad car, and booked into jail was effective in scaring me straight.

Not that I'd ever gone crooked. Yeah, I was looking for a little excitement in my summer, but nothing like that. That's the thing that really bothered me. If I was going to get arrested, I think I should have at least had some fun. Not me. I went straight to jail. I did not pass go and I did not collect my two hundred dollars. Or my excitement. All I did was wait forty-five minutes in a car in the parking lot of the sleaziest motel in Denver.

That's what I was doing when Lana disappeared and cops came out of nowhere and swarmed all over that motel. There were uniform cops, detectives—even the SWAT team was there. To my credit, I wasn't so off my game that I missed a fleet of Crown Vics *and* a SWAT truck. The SWAT guys came from somewhere around the corner about the same time Lana was telling me to stay low. Which I did most of the time, but the very moment I decided to have a good look was when MJ came running toward the car screaming, "Let's go," with a uniform about two feet behind her.

Let me tell you two things: First, I seriously flashed back on that story about her not-so-bright boyfriend, and second, I am a wuss, as I've mentioned before. So, of course, I froze, the uniform handcuffed MJ, and his partner did the same for me. He put us both in the back of a squad car and left us alone. I realized then he knew who I was because they'd never leave two perps alone in a squad car. That gives them time to get their story straight. Which is what MJ tried to do.

"Look, Chanti, they don't have a thing on us. Don't worry."

"Worry? I just had the crap scared out of me. Why did you bring me here knowing your cousin was into something illegal? What's he into, anyway?"

"A little this, a little that."

"Can you be more specific?"

"Drugs and weapons," she says casually, like anyone else might say "arts and crafts."

"What the hell, MJ? Aren't you on probation?"

"I swear I didn't know nothing about it until I got here. And then when I saw what was going down, I wanted out of there."

"It took you forty-five minutes to figure it out? I mean, I already had my suspicions just by watching the cars come in and out. I was just about to text you that we needed to go when you came running out of there."

"I figured since I was there, I might as well visit a minute."

See, that's MJ. The innocent part I was talking about. She's in the middle of something that could land her back in jail, and I mean hard time since she'll be an adult soon, and all she can think to do is have a family reunion.

"I thought you said your cousin would never have anything to do with the Down Homes."

"That was true, he'd never be caught dead with a Down Home, except for me. Blood first. 'Cause how would that look, him associating with Down Home when he's X-2."

"What's X-2?"

"Down Home's rival."

At that moment, I could totally see Lana's point about my bad decision making.

★　★　★

"What were you doing at that motel?" Lana asked for the second time.

"I was just giving my friend a ride to see her cousin."

"Your friend? How do you know each other? Or better yet, how *long* have you known each other?"

"Just since the end of school. She lives on The Ave . . . I mean, she lives where I do."

"So that means your mother has met her?"

"Not really."

"And do you think your mother would approve of this friendship?"

"What kind of stupid question is that? You sure you even a real cop?" MJ had been quiet the whole time we'd been in the interrogation room, so she surprised Lana as much as me when she finally said something.

"I can assure you I'm very real, and so is my size-nine shoe. You want me to demonstrate how real it is? Because I will put it so far up—"

"Uh, now wait. Let's just be calm about all of this," I said, trying to diffuse the tension. Lana had told me more than once that keeping people calm is critical in such a situation, and that situation had a lot of tension.

"Threaten me and I'll cry brutality," MJ said, making me wish she'd just kept going with her stony silence routine.

"Nice friend you got here."

"It's all just a misunderstanding," I said. "MJ told me everything that happened. She really did just go over there to see her cousin. Her cousin from out of town that she hadn't seen in a long time, just passing through."

"Chanti, you don't have to say a thing to her."

"How could she know they were up to no good?" I wasn't hearing anything MJ said at that point. I was just trying to get out of that mess.

"I said don't talk to her," MJ said. Or more like growled.

"And how could she know they were part of some kind of a drug and weapon ring?"

"Would you shut up, Chanti?" She banged her fist on the table to make sure I got the message. To Lana, she said, "I know my rights. We don't say another thing without a lawyer. Better get a PD in here if you want any more information out of either one of us."

Lana smiled at this request for a public defender and then motioned to her partner to take MJ out of the room.

"Chanti, don't talk," MJ warned me as the detective led her away. "This is how they do it, separate us so we turn over on each other. Don't be fooled. Remember that episode of *Law & Order* we saw last week." Even with the door closed, I could hear her yell, "I hate y'all! I hate all y'all cops!"

With MJ gone, Lana could give her full attention to me, which was worse than the fingerprinting, mug-shot taking, and the smell of that holding cell they put me in when we first arrived.

"Mom, I swear," I started pleading my case right away.

"Don't give me *Mom* now. I don't want to hear it. What I do want to hear is how long you've been running with that girl."

"See, this is how—"

"But later. I've got business to handle. You and your friend can think about all this back in that holding cell while I finish some reports."

"Holding cell? But Mom, I mean Lana, you can't believe I was involved in any drug ring."

"Of course I don't. And I know your little gangster wannabe friend wasn't either."

I wanted to point out that MJ was definitely the real thing and not a wannabe. Well, she was at least a real gangster's girlfriend, even if he was in some B-grade gang. And she'd done almost two years in JD. But I figured it was a bad idea to correct Lana on the finer points of MJ's life of crime.

"So why are you sending us back in there? It smells like vomit."

"I want you to have a good look at what can happen when you hang out with someone like her."

"Some girl in there was talking about scratching out my eyes if she ever saw me again."

Okay, that may have been due to the fact I called her a skank as I left the cell, when I thought I was going home because Lana had cleared up this little misunderstanding. Now she wanted me to go back in there?

"Your friend looks like she can handle herself. She'll have your back. Isn't that how it works?" Lana said, looking down at a case file like she had something more important to do than save her only child from imminent death. Or at least blindness.

"Are you serious?"

"The guard won't let anything happen. She knows you're mine."

Chapter 21

Too bad I couldn't take that guard with me once I got out of jail. I could use someone around me who won't let anything happen, and I mean 24-7. Seems like the first day I stepped onto Langdon property, things started happening, most of it bad. The only good to come out of that place is Marco and my job.

The morning after being outed as an ex-con, I'm grateful for both. If not for Marco and Mitchell Moving, I'd be giving Lissa and Bethanie hell right now. Well, if I actually had the nerve to get in somebody's face, I would be. You can be assured that I'm giving them hell in my head. MJ could handle them both at the same time without even thinking about it. But that's just wishful thinking since MJ doesn't want a thing to do with me. So I'm just going to focus on my job, and be glad I'll get Marco all to myself today. Mostly. Weird Malcolm will be there, but he hardly talks so it'll be like we're alone.

Now I'm running late for that new job because I couldn't find my wallet this morning, spent too much time looking around the house for it, and missed my bus. It's forever falling out of my bag, I just hope it fell out somewhere in the house. I guess that'll teach me to buy a bag that closes (not!) with a drawstring instead of a zipper, just because it's cute. When I round the corner to Paulette's office, I hear Marco's voice and I'm surprised to hear my name, so I stop to listen. It isn't eavesdropping when the conversation is about me.

"What *about* Chanti?" Marco is saying, sounding a little defensive.

"Nothing, man. I was just wondering if there was something between you two." That's a male voice I've heard before, but I can't put a name to. And given the context, I'm guessing Paulette isn't in her office with them.

"Why you want to know that?"

"The way you hang out all the time, I was wondering if she was your girl. You know, because I might . . ."

"You're not Chanti's type," Marco says, making me wonder how he knows what my type is. "She won't ever give you the digits, so you can just forget about it."

"Dude, chill. No need for hostility. Besides, I think I just got my answer."

"We're just friends, that's all."

"For now, right?" Then I know who it is, because he says this line in such a sinister way, full of innuendo and suggestions. Not that I don't hope he's right, but he still makes it sound so dirty. As only Justin Mitchell can. "No problem, man. Your secret's safe with me. And so is hers."

"What's that supposed to mean?" Marco asks, at the same time Paulette comes around the corner from the other end of the hall.

"Chanti, did you just get here?" Paulette says, unknowingly about to bust me for eavesdropping, but I stay cool enough to act like I just walked in.

"Yes. Sorry I'm late," I say, following her into the office.

Marco looks guilty, his face turning just a little red. Justin looks very much like his evil sister did when she announced we should play truth or dare. So he knows about my brief incarceration, too. OMG. Was that what he meant about keeping my secret? What if he was just about to tell Marco when Paulette appeared? I'm pretty sure with all his handshaking and exquisite manners, Marco would not find a jailbird the most suitable date for the homecoming dance. I bet Angelique, owner of the beautiful name and weaver of friendship bracelets, has never been to jail. I'm doomed before I even get started. And right after finding out that he likes me. I mean, if Justin's suspicions are accurate.

"What are you doing here?" Paulette asks Justin. You can tell from her tone she's none to happy to see him.

"It says Mitchell on the building. I'm a Mitchell, aren't I?"

"Yeah, but you're the Mitchell who thinks he's too good to work for a living."

I love how Paulette came right back with that. She obviously doesn't take Justin's crap even if she does work for his father.

"Whatever."

"Can I help you?" she says, full of attitude.

"No, you can't help me with nothing."

"Is that what they teach you at that school, how to speak in double negatives?" She directs this to Marco and me, but we have enough sense not to get in the middle of this.

"My father asked me to pick up his briefcase. He left it in his office."

"Well, you know where his office is. Next door over. Same place it's been for twelve years."

Justin gives Paulette a dirty look and leaves.

"I can't stand that kid," she says, not even trying to say it under her breath or anything. "Acts like someone owes him something. Never mind him. We've got work to do."

"Are we going on our first solo trip?" Marco asks, doing a great job of pretending we didn't just witness a little Mitchell-family dysfunction.

"Not quite. We have two pairs of snowbirds who need an assessment today."

"What's a snowbird?" I ask.

"Retired folks who go south for the winter." She looks at her clipboard and adds, "In this case, Boca Raton. Most snowbirds duplicate everything in their winter homes, but a few like to move items back and forth."

"That seems like a lot of work, and expensive, too."

"They don't move furniture, but they like to take electronics—televisions, stereos, computers—the kinds of things popular with burglars. You'd think living in a gated community with state-of-the-art security systems would ease their worries about leaving their homes empty for six months."

"I can see their point," I say. But then, I worry about everything.

"We'll do the assessment this one last time, but I'll stay in the background. It's an easy job. The two couples are neighbors here and at their winter homes. I guess that's an old-people affliction—doing everything with your friends, even taking extended vacations together."

"So we'll pack today?" Marco asks.

"No, they don't want us underfoot. We'll wait until next weekend after they're out of the house. They leave town on Monday for a ten-day cruise, so we have plenty of time to get things packed and moved before they arrive at their winter homes. You'll do the packing Saturday. You know how Mr. Mitchell feels about kids working during the week."

"If it's only an assessment, what will I be doing?" Marco asks. I'm crushed because this means another weekend of us working apart. After overhearing—not eavesdropping on— his conversation with Justin, I think he may be as disappointed as I am.

"You and Malcolm will go out on a job. But I promise next week will be the real thing."

When we leave Paulette's office to go our separate ways, Justin is closing up his father's office.

"You're still here?" Paulette asks. "I thought you were just getting a briefcase."

Justin doesn't say anything, only holds up the briefcase, smiles, and heads in the other direction.

"That boy is up to no good. Been a bad seed since birth. Did you see those bloodshot eyes? High as a kite at nine in the morning. I don't know how he can afford it since his father cut him off a few weeks ago."

"Cut off his money?"

"Him and his sister. Mr. Mitchell's trying to teach them some values, but it's probably too late for that."

Cutting off Lissa from her money supply is like cutting off her oxygen. She must have had some stashed away to be able to afford that face cream she was showing off in Ms. Reeves's class. I'd love to know what kind of allowance they got before Mr. Mitchell came to his senses. I'm sure Paulette knows, but I figure this is a new job and I'd better not get too deep in the gossip so I just keep my mouth shut as we walk to the van. Which is just fine because Paulette keeps talking as though I'm responding.

"It's all because those children had no mother. The girl is just as bad. I mean, Mr. Mitchell is a good man, but children need their mother," she said, getting into the car.

I was just about to ask what happened to Mrs. Mitchell, but she answers my question before I can open my mouth.

"She died when they were young. With the business just starting out, too. She was the original office manager. That's how I came to work for Mr. Mitchell. To take her place. Not take her place," Paulette says, slowing down just long enough to get a little flustered. "Well, you know what I mean."

I think I do. Paulette's been pining for Mr. Mitchell, and hating his kids, for years. I almost tell her I know how hard unrequited love is, until I remember that's not me anymore. Marco is just as hot for me as I am for him, if Justin's instincts are to be believed. While I wouldn't trust anything about Justin Mitchell, especially after what Paulette says about him, I'm going to believe him on this one. But on everything else? I definitely need to watch my back, and maybe Marco should, too.

Chapter 22

On Monday, everything at school is different. I've only been at Langdon a couple of weeks and never really got in the groove of it; still, nothing feels the same today. People are staring at me in the halls like they did when I first arrived. But they'd gotten used to the new scholarship girl pretty quickly, so the stares I'm getting today are different. I hope I can find Marco before first bell so I can ask him if he's getting the same treatment, and if he knows why. Maybe they've found something new to hate on the scholarship kids about.

Smythe is standing at the door of the main office and when she sees me heading for my locker, motions for me to come over. *Now what?*

"Chantal, I want you to know that I still have my eye on you until we resolve the issue of the Langdon thefts."

"But I caught the thief. She admitted her guilt and you fired her last Friday, right?"

"Thank you for alerting us to Ms. Reeves's actions. She gave us quite a lengthy confession, even confessing to taking things that hadn't been reported missing. She did not, however, mention a Montblanc pen or a tennis bracelet."

Pregnant pause, for effect.

"I asked her about these items and she knew nothing."

"And you believed her?"

"Why would she lie about those items and be so contrite about everything else?"

"Maybe because the value of the bracelet would be a class-one felony charge instead of a misdemeanor. More jail time."

"It's certainly to your advantage that you know the justice system so well. You're going to need it," she says, all cryptic, before walking into the office.

Bethanie is coming down the hall toward me, and the minute I see her face, I know the school isn't hating on all the scholarship kids—it's only about me. Lissa and Justin must have spread the story about me going to jail. I'm about to ask her what's going on when she just passes right by as though she didn't see me. Okay, we had a little falling-out at the party, but now I know we have more in common than I thought, even more than the secrets we share. We come from the same place. She really is a scholarship girl, even if she's working hard not to be one. So I follow her.

"Bethanie, what's going on? Did Lissa tell everyone about me going to jail?"

She looks at me as though she's Supergirl and I'm Kryptonite, and considers whether to even talk to me. "You mean the first time or the next time?"

"Next time?"

"Whatever you did over summer break is old news. What the hell were you thinking, Chanti?"

"About what? Speak English, would you?"

Bethanie takes my arm and pulls me into an empty classroom.

"They're saying you did it, Chanti, and you know, you used to be my girl and I trust you to keep my secret about the lottery money and I want to not believe them, but it looks bad."

"*What* looks bad?" I'm on the verge of a major freak-out now, and still don't know what for.

"The burglary at Annette's house Friday night."

"Somebody broke into Annette's house?"

"She's saying the somebody was you."

"What the hell? Y'all were there. Did you see me break into Annette's house and steal something? I mean, this doesn't even make sense."

"We weren't there the whole night, and neither were you."

"Right. I was home in bed, no thanks to you."

"Yeah, but what did you do before you got home? It happened while we were out getting food. You should've just gotten in the car with us, and then this wouldn't have happened."

"I didn't do it, Bethanie."

"Whether you did or didn't, if you'd been with us, no one could accuse you of it. Look, I have to go. I'm sorry to leave you hanging, but I'm not trying to get kicked out of Langdon." She looks around the hall nervously, as though she's afraid to be seen with me.

"Wait, at least tell me what happened. When you got back to Annette's house, what did you find? Any signs of a break-in?"

"Sorry, Chanti. I'm out of it."

First bell rings and I'm left wondering what just happened.

I tried to find Marco before I ditched school, just to explain to him what little I know, which is that I had nothing to do with a burglary, and give him the real story behind my brief incarceration. But I couldn't find him before the second bell, and I couldn't stand being there with all the staring, all the accusations flying across classrooms and hallways. I just have to hope that Marco knows enough about me to know I couldn't be any part of this. There are only two people in the world I can trust to help me, and one of them won't talk to me. So I call the one who will always help no matter what kind of trouble I get myself into. And I need some help, because I've got a feeling it's all about to go down.

This is where my embellishing skills prove useful.

"Lana, I'm sick. You have to come get me," I say when she answers her phone.

"You were fine this morning. What happened between then and now?"

It's times like this when I wish I had one of those mothers who hears the words *I'm sick* and just drops everything to come get their kid—no interrogations, no need to make up a lie.

"I guess I must have picked up something. This girl in PE just came back to school after having mono. Maybe I . . ."

"Mono?" she says, sounding worried. "Seems like the school should have told the parents there was a student there with mono."

Caller, you're a winner. But just in case she hasn't fully bought it, I add some insurance.

"I'm at the coffeehouse near my bus stop. While I was walking to the stop, I had to puke in someone's yard, so I was afraid to get on the bus and get sick on whoever sits next to me."

"All right, give me twenty minutes."

It's hard to fool a detective, and I only manage to half the time, but that still says something about my special talent for storytelling. But I have to tell Lana the rest of this story in person and away from Langdon Prep because she will absolutely lose it when she hears I'm about to become a B and E suspect.

As soon as I get in the car, Lana slaps her hand against my forehead.

"You don't have a fever. It must not be the flu. Does it feel like a cold?"

"Yeah, I think it's a cold." I have to keep the lie going until we get home because we're only a mile from campus and if I tell her everyone at Langdon is fingering me for the burglary, she'll go right back up there and turn Langdon inside out. That's the last thing I need right now. But by the time we reach home, she's onto me.

"So what's really going on, Chanti? I was in the middle of a stakeout."

"Soon you might be trying to solve a case a little closer to home," I say, trying to make light of it, but Lana's not smiling.

"Please tell me you haven't gotten yourself into some new mess. That's why I sent you to that school, to keep you out of trouble. But you always seem to find it."

"Trouble finds *me*."

"Tell me what's going on."

I relay what little I know, which is my impending arrest for a crime I didn't commit, since I don't have any details of Friday night past the point of seeing Bethanie's taillights fade in the distance. Lana listens intently, but doesn't look nearly as distressed as I'd expected.

"So you think you're going to jail because a girl's house you'd been to earlier that night was later burglarized, and because of the way kids were looking at you in the hall."

"Exactly."

"Chanti, there's nothing in that story that points to you. If the girls didn't lock the house before they left—like one girl I know who got our TV and stereo stolen last year—anyone could have gone in there."

"That's true."

"Or it could have been some other girl at the party, for that matter. Even that girl you went to the party with."

"Bethanie? No way. She's my friend."

"You claim she tricked you into going to a party she

knew you'd never want to attend. Doesn't sound like much of a friend to me."

I can't see any way Bethanie could be involved in this. She rescued me after I wrecked that birdfeeder and tried to cover for me by giving Smythe that pen she bought. I've only known her a short time and she did ditch me so no one would think she was involved with the burglary, but I know she wouldn't set me up like this. Then I remember what she said in hall this morning: "You *used* to be my girl. . . ." Not to mention I really have no idea who Bethanie is after she revealed her Dirty South persona.

"But how?" I ask, a little more open to the idea that I truly may have been betrayed.

"Unless they pulled in there with a moving van and took everything, an inside job would be easy. If there were only a couple of small things missing, it could be anyone who was there that night. What was taken? Were there signs of forced entry?"

"I never found out all that. I just got out of there. Those kids were persecuting me with their eyes."

"Oh, the drama," Lana says, sounding tired. "You're not going to jail, but you *are* going back to school. And I need to get back to my stakeout."

Suddenly I feel the need to defend myself, even with Lana, because when she lays it all out like she has, there really is no case against me. Well, at least not based solely on the alleged burglary at Annette's house.

"Something's going on, Mom, and I know when you break it down the way you just did it doesn't sound like it. But there's other stuff happening."

"What other stuff? That business with the thefts around school? The teacher did it, right?"

"That's another thing," I say, remembering Smythe's warning. Ms. Reeves confessed to the thefts, but not all of them.

"They can't tie those thefts to you," she said, sounding like a cop when I wish she'd sound more like a mother.

"Yeah, but I just have this feeling."

"So do I, a feeling you hate that school and you're looking for a way to get out of it so you can go to North High with your friends."

"At Annette's party, this bi-atch named Lissa—"

"Watch the language."

"I am. That's why I said bi-atch. Anyway, somehow Lissa found out about my little incident over summer break and she told everyone at the party. That ticked me off, so I left."

"How did she find out? That was all expunged, there's nothing on your record. You *have* no record."

"Exactly. The only way I figure it is Smythe told her."

"Who?"

"The headmistress—the one you arrested for something."

"Don't get sidetracked, Chanti."

"Well, when she called us into her office to falsely accuse us, she said she knows something about my past, and this morning she says she has her eye on me. And Smythe loves Lissa. I don't put it past her telling Lissa about me."

"But there's nothing to tell. If they were to do a background check on you, they'd find nothing. You never told your friends at school, did you?"

"I don't have any friends at school."

Bethanie has made it clear she wants nothing to do with me, and I figure Marco has heard the rumors by now and he'll be the next victim on my friendship list. Maybe hearing I have no friends causes Lana to have some pity for me (though not much) because she lets me stay home.

"I still think you're blowing this out of proportion and it's more about you not wanting to attend that school. You're going back tomorrow," she says, heading out the door. "Do the laundry since you're home."

I can't believe Lana thinks I'd go through all of this just to create a reason not to go to Langdon. Okay, maybe my history might lead her to believe that, but couldn't she see everything I'm telling her is on the real this time? So much for thinking my own mother would have my back.

Chapter 23

Until today, I thought only one other person knew about my arrest outside of Lana and the cops. I didn't even tell Tasha. I knew she'd have nothing to offer but "I told you so" because she never liked MJ from the get-go. I'd always trusted her to keep my secrets, but once she started hanging out with Michelle, I didn't know if the best-friend rule about keeping secrets was still in play, though I know differently now. So that leaves MJ, and how could she have told Smythe or Lissa when she doesn't know anything about them? Besides, she's the only person other than Lana who I'd trust with my life because after all, she's already saved me twice.

After Lana forced me back into the holding cell, claiming she had to do it to keep her cover, though I knew it was to teach me a lesson. Then I discovered she had put way too much confidence in the guard's knowledge that I was her kid. Either that or the guard knew and didn't care because when I returned to the cell and saw that MJ was gone and the girl I'd recently called a skank was waiting for me, the guard was not at all interested when I told her about my looming death. She left me there to figure out how to keep myself from getting shanked or skived or whatever they call it when a fellow inmate takes you out with a knife made from a Pop-sicle stick.

Okay, the skank didn't have a knife, homemade or other-wise, but she did have a serious uppercut, which she landed against my chin the minute the guard was out of sight. I hoped that was all I'd get, but then she sat on my chest—which was easy because her punch had landed me on the floor so quickly I didn't have time to try to defend myself, which in my case meant assuming the fetal position. There were four other girls in the room, and no one seemed to notice I was about to get my butt kicked, except for the one who was standing over me saying, "Hit her again! Hit her again!" Now that girl seemed really interested.

I think the skank was about to oblige her audience when someone else whispered, "Guards."

"Turn away from the door," she said as she got off of me. "Don't say a word or you'll get a helluva lot worse when the guard leaves."

I would have, too, if the guard hadn't come with MJ in tow. You can believe the minute that guard was out of sight, someone got a helluva lot worse, but it wasn't me. MJ just about lost it when she saw my bruised jaw, which had already begun to swell. Lucky for the skank, I pulled MJ off of her before she could do her any serious harm. After that, no one came near MJ or me, and we had one roomy corner of the holding cell to ourselves.

"Maybe we should call the guards about your face. You probably need some ice on that."

"I hope it looks bad. Maybe now I can teach my mother a lesson."

"What are you talking about?"

That uppercut must have rattled my brain because I never slip up when it comes to Lana's cover, especially around MJ, who I'd figured would probably not have much interest in me as a friend if she found out that it was my mom who had just interrogated us.

"I mean, you know, when I get out of here, she'll probably be mad about me taking the car without her permission. Seeing my face like this might soften her up."

"Oh yeah. Big Mama is gonna give me hell, too. When I called to ask her to pick me up, she went from pissed to crying in under sixty. I hate to make my grandmother cry."

"They'll get over it eventually," I said, not quite believing it.

"Sorry I got you into all this mess. I really did think my cousin just wanted to see me while he was passing through town."

"So what did he really want?"

"We can't talk in here. They don't have nothing on us though. Don't worry. That cop was just talking smack."

"You think so?" I said, pretending I was afraid even though I knew everything was going to be okay, at least for me. I hadn't been in that motel room. Though I knew MJ would never commit a crime intentionally, in our brief friendship I'd learned a couple of things about MJ that could easily land her back in JD—she'd do anything for a friend and she wasn't likely to ever win class valedictorian. A big heart and a not-so-big brain is a dangerous combination.

"Nothing but a thing. That cop though, I didn't like her. The lady cops are always the worst. They have this game, pretending they can relate to you or something just because they're women. She don't know nothing about me."

"Not all cops are bad." When I said this, MJ had the same look in her eyes that skank had just before she hit me. Rage. But it only lasted a second, and turned into pity, the way you look at a squirrel trying to cross a busy street. You know the poor dumb animal is doomed.

"Believe this, Chanti, There's is no such thing as a good cop. Not if you're us."

She waved her hand back and forth when she said this, connecting us. At that moment, I didn't feel like a traitor to Lana at all. I felt like I'd just made a friend for life.

They let MJ out first, about ten minutes before me. That was the longest, most terrifying ten minutes of my life. Once she was sure MJ wasn't coming back, that girl with the uppercut tried to make good on her promise, until I screamed for the guard. I was almost as relieved to see the guard as I was to know that MJ didn't hear me scream like a baby. Then I spent another hour in Lana's office while she finished her report without saying a single word to me after she got some ice for my bruised and swollen jaw. I guess she saw it as another lesson. That if I was terrified enough of jail, I would never get myself into enough trouble to land there again. Let me tell you—my mother is hard.

"What if MJ is down there waiting for me?" I asked her as we took the elevator to the first floor of the department. "What about your cover?"

"You think she's such a good friend she'd wait around here for you?"

"I know she is. You're passing judgment without even knowing her." That last line I actually said to myself. I'm not brave, but I'm also not stupid. I was pretty sure Lana was still looking for someplace to land her shoe.

"She won't be. I had a cruiser take her home. Didn't want to disturb her grandmother. I checked out her whole situation and that girl did some time in JD. Big Mama took on a handful."

When we stepped off the elevator, there was no MJ. I still expected her to be there even though Lana told me a uniform had taken her home.

"You said yourself we didn't do anything."

"You didn't do anything that will keep you locked up, but you made a lot of bad decisions tonight. Taking my car when you only have a learner's permit—be happy I didn't have you ticketed. But don't worry, I'll be treating you to *my* version of jail. And you know nothing good happens at those motels over there. Have I taught you nothing? Your average person wouldn't have noticed what was going on at the motel, but you aren't average. You notice everything."

It was true. But not tonight, and I still hadn't figured out why. Lana had, though.

"That MJ girl is trying to lead you down the wrong path. Not while you're under my roof, Miss Thing."

I was grateful Lana didn't have any more lecturing for me in the car. It turned out she was only waiting until we got home. She picked up where she'd left off the minute we were out of the car.

"There is no way a child of mine is going to be running the streets with all kinds of delinquents. I better not *ever* catch you with that girl again, you hear me?"

She was still talking as she went up on the porch, even though I had turned back to get my bag out of the car, which I will forever think of as my "personal effects." Lana was still lecturing when she opened the front door and went inside the house. I could hear her saying "that girl" at the very moment I noticed MJ come from behind a car parked on the other side of the street.

"I was waiting for you, wanted to make sure those cops didn't hold you when you didn't even do anything, but I see I wasted my time."

"MJ, look, she's vice. I couldn't say anything. She has a cover and I . . ."

"Don't worry, narc. MJ ain't no snitch."

Chapter 24

I thought that was my worst day ever, but no, it actually *can* get worse. It's Tuesday, the day after Lissa spread the story that I robbed Annette's house, and by now everyone at Langdon has probably heard about it. Despite me faking illness, pretending to cry, and for-real begging, Lana makes me go to school today, and I feel like crap. She thinks I'm paranoid, MJ thinks I'm a snitch, Bethanie acts like I don't exist, and I can't find Marco anywhere on campus. Maybe he's like Bethanie, keeping his distance in case anyone thinks he's a crook by association. The rumors are still flying about me. In one version, I'm already in jail, even though I'm sitting right here in the library during my study period, checking e-mail, hoping Lana felt some pity for me and at least looked at the police report on the burglary at Annette's house. Just when I'm looking at my empty in-box and thinking my life could not get any worse, I prove myself wrong. Someone has just deposited their soda in my lap. I look up to find it's one of the clones.

"Oh my God, I'm so sorry. I'm such a klutz."

"You have got to be kidding me," I say, feeling the cold liquid go through my skirt. Great, I have to walk around school for the rest of the day with wet underwear, on top of everything else.

"I'll clean this up. You'd better get to the girls' room and try to dry off. I might have a pair of yoga pants in my gym locker if you want me to bring them." She doesn't mention they're probably two sizes too small for me, like Lissa would have. This clone is nice enough that I might think the soda incident was accidental . . . if I weren't me and didn't suspect everyone of everything, especially one of Lissa's minions.

"No thanks. I have some shorts in my gym bag," I say, walking out of the library amid stares, whispers, and laughs that make me think it was all staged for their entertainment.

After I grab my shorts from my bag and put them on, I hide out in the bathroom of the empty locker room for way too long, pretending to rinse out my skirt. Then I manage to burn through French class by spending an hour holding my skirt under the hand dryer. I can't think of any excuse to skip my last two classes, so I fake like I don't care that the whole school thinks I'm a loser, and finally leave the locker room to accept the fact that I'm in hell. When I get to my locker, I find someone has stuck a note through the slots. I expect it to be some joke about me being an ex-con but it's from Marco. That's so romantic—he's going old school like they probably did in Lana's day. I guess I shouldn't have missed French because he was here at school after all, and seeing him was just what I needed today.

> Sorry I missed you in French. Hope you aren't letting these people get to you. I want to talk, but not around Langdon. Can you meet me at 7:00 at the park on Lexington? There's a picnic table near the fountain. I'll bring dinner and a smile in case you need cheering up. I'll be there whether you come or not. Hope you come.

And just like that, the day from hell turns into the best day I could hope for.

* * *

Marco is right where he said he'd be, but there's no dinner, and he looks a little tired. I may be the one who has to cheer *him* up.

"So what's the emergency?" Marco says, not sounding all that pleased to see me. And hearing him hack up a lung is not quite the romantic reception I'd imagined on the walk over.

"I wouldn't exactly call it an emergency, but you were right. I definitely needed cheering up. Are we going to go somewhere for dinner? I guess I misunderstood—I thought we were having a picnic."

"Chanti, I have no idea what you're talking about. Your message said you absolutely had to see me, that it was urgent. I really hope it is because I had to spend an hour convincing my mom to let me out of the house since I'm running a temperature of one hundred and one. Do you know how hard it is to chill a thermometer just so it says ninety-eight point six? I don't like lying to my mother."

First, I'm incredibly touched that he was willing to lie to his dear old mom just to meet me when I have an emergency. Not only is he gorgeous, but he's sweet, too. But I only get to swim in that delicious thought for a minute, because it's clear someone has set us up. Do I tell him this now, or play along and milk this for all I can? I mean, we're here, even if under false pretenses. We gotta eat. Why not together? But no, it's never a good idea to start a new relationship based on lies. Believe me, I've tried. It doesn't work.

"Sorry, Marco, but I think we've been punked. I'm guessing you didn't put that note in my locker?"

"A note? No way—I would have texted you."

So much for Marco being an old-school romantic.

"Besides, I haven't been to school since last Friday. Fever of one hundred and one, remember?"

"So I guess you don't know what's going on at school, all the rumors about me and Annette's house being burgled."

He starts laughing at this, making him seem a little crazy. But still cute.

"What's so funny?"

"*Burgled.* Is that even a word?"

"It *is* a word, but that's not really the issue. I thought you called me out here to cheer me up from all the accusations flying that I broke into Annette's house and stole some stuff."

"Hey, you may have a lot in common with Malcolm. He went to jail. Wait, I wasn't supposed to talk about that."

So I was right about Malcolm's time off. Note to self: Marco can't be trusted to keep a secret when he's sick and doped up on cold medicine. I want to know more about Malcolm's time, but we're talking about me right now.

"Marco, I'm trying to tell you how my world is falling apart."

"I'm paying attention. You broke into someone's house— Annette whose party you went to. Why would you steal stuff from a friend?"

"First, she's not a friend and second, I wouldn't steal from anyone. All I know is I got into it with Lissa, and stormed out. They left for pizza or something, and while they were gone, the house was robbed."

"What did you get into it with Lissa about?"

Oh yeah, he hasn't been at school the last two days and knows nothing about my criminal record, which is not really a record. I'm thinking this isn't the best point in our relationship to lay this on him. Between his being sick, me being a suspected burglar, and his mother waiting at home for him, victim of her son's first lie, I figure that can wait.

"Oh, something stupid, not important."

"But why do they think it's you? Anyone could have done it, someone who *burgles* professionally." He cracks himself up with this, which makes him hack up the other lung. I ignore his question because he's probably already forgotten he asked it.

"If you haven't been at school, how did you get a message from me?"

"You sent an e-mail to my school account."

"Around 1:30 today?" I ask.

"Yeah, I think so. I was kind of delirious with fever and Sudafed."

"Well, now I know who punked us. But I don't know why, other than I'm apparently the entertainment of the week, not just the day."

The nice clone wasn't so much, and must have used my open e-mail account to send Marco that message. Now I'm looking around the park for signs of a clone. But the park is empty, at least the section we're in. Dusk has fallen, but it's still light enough for me to see that the place is a ghost town. That's when I notice all the little plastic yellow flags stuck in the grass. I guess I missed them before because I was too busy thinking about Marco waiting for me with a picnic basket, all ready to cheer me up. I go up to the closest one for a read, and find a skull and crossbones. No wonder we're the only ones here. They just sprayed pesticide this afternoon. Marco is about to fall over from the flu, so I'm thinking toxic fumes could not be good for him. The love of my life is going to die before we even get to the love part.

"Marco, we have to get out of here."

"Why? You promised me dinner. I'd really love to have dinner with you."

While this makes me uncontrollably giddy, I'm skeptical since it could be the meds talking. Now I wonder just how much Sudafed he's had and whether he should be driving. But we do have to eat, right?

"No dinner," I end up saying, because he's really sick and I'm not quite that selfish. "You need to get home and take care of yourself. We've given them enough of a laugh tonight."

"Who?"

"Our punkers. Whoever thought this would be hilarious, getting you and me out here in a toxic park."

"Maybe they were trying to fix us up. Sort of like a blind date."

"Do you want us to be fixed up?" I ask, hoping his delirium will make him reveal secrets.

"No."

"Oh."

"We don't need fixing up. We're already up, right?"

I hope tomorrow when he recalls this conversation—if he can after his cold-medicine high—that he won't remember the idiotic grin I'm wearing as we walk back to his car. I hope he remembers that I drove him home just to make sure he got there okay. I even hope he noticed that before I walked home, I stood in front of his house for a minute after he went inside, wishing I was in there with him.

Chapter 25

"You know this is crazy, right?" Lana is saying into the phone the next morning.

I'm already running late for my bus and can't find the cereal bars so I guess I'm gonna go hungry because whatever is going on in Lana's world, it's probably not the best time to ask if we have any cereal bars. I wave at her as I head for the door, but she shakes her head and motions for me to stay. That's when I start getting the uneasy feeling that the craziness might be about me.

"This is my kid we're talking about. There's no way this is possible."

No way *what's* possible? Smythe just won't get off my back, will she? Now what's she saying I stole?

"I understand procedure, Sergeant, but . . ."

Okay, that ain't Smythe on the other end of the line.

"Well, can I at least be the one who brings her in?"

WTF?!

"Thanks. We'll be there in half an hour."

When Lana gets off the phone, she doesn't have to say a thing because it's written all over her face. Only thing I don't know is what I'm being charged with.

★   ★   ★

Let me tell you that it feels a lot different when you're sitting in an interrogation room and you know everything's just a big misunderstanding than when you've been arrested for burglary, theft by taking, breaking and entering, and whatever other charges they can come up with. This time Lana isn't the one questioning me. She's on my side of the table, sitting on my right, and on my left is her lawyer friend from the firm where she actually used to be a paralegal back in the day. Across the table is Detective Bertram from the Burglary Unit. I can't believe any of this is happening.

"It all points back to you, Miss Evans," says the detective, summing up his story as though I haven't been there listening to it for the last two hours. "So we've got these Mitchell Moving clients' home burglaries last night. We've got the break-in the night of your friend's pajama-party, when you claim you were walking around looking for a bus stop."

"Which crime are you charging her for?" my lawyer asks. "This warrant says nothing about a pajama-party burglary."

"That's because he's got no evidence. And it wasn't a pajama party. It was just an all-night party and I didn't want to be there all night. When did that become a crime?"

Lana clears her throat and I know I need to pull back on the smart remarks. But I can't help it. That's how I respond to stress. Being interrogated by the police for a crime you didn't commit is right up there on the stress-o-meter, if you ask me.

"So tell me again where you were yesterday, between nineteen hundred hours and twenty hundred hours. That means—"

"She knows what it means," Lana says, more than a little annoyed. "She already told you."

"It's okay, Mom. I was at the park on Lexington meeting a friend." I'm glad Lana is beside me and I don't have to see her face when I say this, because I know she's thinking, *when you were supposed to be home doing schoolwork.*

"Did anyone see you at this park?"

"Yeah, my friend."

"Anyone *besides* your friend see you at this park?"

"No, because whoever punked us—I mean, set up this fake meeting between us, like I told you before—had us meet in this area that had been sprayed with insecticides and was supposed to be off-limits."

"And you missed all the signs that said not to go into the area."

"Because I was, um . . . a little distracted."

What am I supposed to say? I don't believe telling Detective Bertram that I couldn't see straight because I was in lust about Marco would go over well with him or Lana. Or my lawyer for that matter. I can't even believe I *have* a lawyer. To say this day is majorly sucking is an understatement.

"Look, Miss Evans, none of this looks good. You have no alibi at the time of the thefts. You'd been in both of the houses prior to the burglary and had an inventory of all the valuables that were stolen from the houses. You knew the owners of the homes would be out of town. Your fingerprints were all over the place."

"Because I'd been in the house! It's part of my job. I already told you, when we do the assessments, we walk around the house and figure out what needs to be packed, and what—"

"I know. We've heard all that before."

"And you're going to hear it again until you get it that my daughter didn't do this," Lana says, and I'm pretty sure she's finally found a home for her size nine, which is why my lawyer suggests she take a break and get some air. Now I feel a little more free to talk.

"Just call Marco, that's my friend, he'll tell you where I was. Well, sort of more than my friend . . ."

"Is that right?" the detective says, smirking in a way that suggests he just got some dirt on me, and makes my lawyer stiffen.

"Why is that an issue?" my lawyer asks.

"Because Miss Evans's boyfriend is in another interrogation room at this very minute."

"What?" Because I'm sure I didn't hear him right.

"He's been charged, too. So you can see that he doesn't provide the best alibi."

"What's he have to do with this?"

"I'm glad you asked, although you already know." Detective Bertram is having way too much fun ruining my life. What's he got against me? I mean besides some incriminating evidence and a felony charge. "He helped you rob those homes. He drove the van—"

"He doesn't even own a van."

"It was a Mitchell Moving and Storage van that he has the keys to. That's why you were able to get past the gate guard and why the neighbors didn't call the police right away. They'd seen the van there before, you'd just been there last weekend. They knew the owners always use Mitchell to move their stuff every year. It wasn't until you were long gone that they realized moving companies don't usually do night moves."

"This is crazy. We were at the park!"

"Say the two of you."

"So you have eyewitnesses who can place me at the scene between nineteen hundred and twenty hundred hours?" I ask, surprising Detective Bertram. Yeah, I know a little somethin'-somethin' about this game, too.

"Well, we don't have an ID on you. But the description they gave sounds too much like your boyfriend."

"At eight o'clock? It was dark by then. Couldn't have been that good of a look."

"Whoa, save something for me and the courtroom," my lawyer says. He laughs, though I don't think the situation is a bit funny. I don't plan to ever see the inside of a courtroom, at least not from the defendant's table.

"You're definitely your mother's kid," says Detective Bertram, and not like it's a compliment, either. "In which case, you'll understand how bad this looks for you."

That's when he pulls a plastic bag from a box under the table. Inside is my wallet. That stupid no-zipper-having bag of mine.

"Recognize it? It was found on the scene. And it wasn't from your previous visit. It was in the middle of the floor where the residents would have seen it if you'd left it there last weekend."

"This interview is over," says my lawyer, but I already knew before he opened his mouth that it was a really good time to shut mine.

Chapter 26

This time it's the real deal. I've been charged with a felony, and I've been given a court date. Just two weeks to figure out who really did this. But at least I'm out on bail and able to investigate.

"You won't be doing anything close to investigating this case," Lana says over dinner. "My C.O. doesn't even want *me* near this case. Thinks I'm too 'emotionally invested.' "

"So neither one of us will know what's going on?"

"I said my C.O. doesn't want me near this case. I didn't say anything about obeying him."

"You always follow orders."

"Well, no one's ever tried to send my kid up for a class-two felony, either."

"So you believe me *now.*"

"I may have underestimated what you were telling me was going on at school, but I always believed you were innocent. The only thing you're guilty of, the only thing you're *always* guilty of, is being in the wrong place at the wrong time, and usually with the wrong people. That's why I don't want you doing any investigating, observing, detecting, or whatever you want to call it because it will just get you into more trouble."

"But I have access that you don't."

"What kind of access?"

"I don't know . . . possible witnesses, likely suspects."

"Who? Give me names."

I don't think I'm ready to show my hand just yet. Lana's a great detective—I mean, she taught me everything I know—but if I give her names, she might scare off the people I most need to catch in the act to prove my innocence.

"Okay, so I don't have anything, but I just thought . . ."

"Well, stop thinking. I'm not going to let you go to jail for something you didn't do. I know it's hard, but try to focus on schoolwork and let the professionals handle this."

Right now I need to talk to someone other than Lana. Even though she worked in burglary and was probably the best detective they ever had, she can't look at this case in full-on cop mode because she can't see past it being about her kid. Funny how things change in an instant—the day before my arrest, I wanted her to act more like a mom than a cop. Now it's the other way around.

I find Tasha in her driveway handing tools to her father, whose legs are sticking out from underneath his Whole World, as Tasha calls it. The rest of us call it a Corvette—a really old one from the seventies. Tasha figured out a long time ago if she had any chance of competing with the Corvette for her father's time, she'd better learn the difference between a manifold and a carburetor. Her dad is a mechanic who comes home everyday from working on other people's cars to work on his own. I always thought that was strange. I only do homework after being in school all day because I have to. But I guess it's the same way Lana comes home and watches cop shows on TV. Except now she gets to work on the real-life case involving her daughter, thanks to whoever is setting me up.

"What's up?" Tasha greets me.

"You have a second?"

"Dad, I'm going inside with Chanti now," Tasha yells loudly like being under a car is like being down in a well. "I'll make you some iced tea and bring it out."

"Thanks for helping me out, baby girl," her dad says, sounding a little like he *is* down a well. Pretty much the only time I think about what it would be like to have a father is when Mr. Morgan calls Tasha *baby girl*. It makes me think I may have missed out on something.

I haven't been in Tasha's house for a while, not since I started hanging with MJ and Tasha made friends with Michelle. But now it's just like coming home, it's so familiar. Her mom is really into the Southwestern motif, so everything in the house is the color of an Arizona desert at sunset: sage, copper, blue, and clay.

"You still have problems at school?" Tasha asks as she puts the teakettle on to boil.

"Worse. How'd you know?"

"We don't talk like we used to. I figured it must be something bad for you to come over."

I feel a little guilty because she's right.

"You can't tell a soul about this, Tasha. Not Michelle, not even your parents."

"Have I ever?" she asks.

"I got arrested last night for a burglary at the home of one of my boss's clients."

"Wow."

"Exactly. Whoever is setting me up did a great job—they planted my wallet at the crime scene."

"Man, somebody must really hate you, Chanti."

"Somebody really wants to avoid getting arrested so they're framing me. But it could be anyone who has been around me and my sorry excuse for a drawstring purse."

"When's the last time you remember having the wallet?" Tasha asks, putting a bag of Chips Ahoy cookies on the table.

A true friend knows I need chocolate when I'm stressed, and that's what Tasha is. I was worse than Bethanie when I brushed her aside so easily for MJ. Bethanie has known me only a couple of weeks; I've known Tasha since third grade. If I were Tasha, I'd let me suffer without cookies.

"Thursday when I put a couple of dollars in Ms. Reeves's donation jar. I noticed it missing Saturday morning before I went to work."

Talking to Tasha helps me think. It might be anyone in study hall—or at Langdon, for that matter. It could have been Annette or anyone at her party. I may have lost it while I walked all over Cherry Creek Friday night looking for a bus stop, or even on the walk home from the bus once I finally made it to the Heights. But it still had cash in it when I identified it for Bertram, and no one around here would have left the cash, even a few dollars.

Tasha breaks me from my thoughts when she asks, "You didn't need your wallet all day Friday?"

"I keep my bus pass in a separate holder, and Bethanie—this girl from school—bought everything when we went out Friday night."

Now I feel guilty all over again about neglecting my friendship with Tasha—first for MJ, now Bethanie. But Tasha lets it slide.

"So who is Ms. Reeves?"

"She's the crazy teacher I thought was doing all the stealing at school, but apparently not. She confessed to stealing some stuff, but not everything, so the school's still watching me, too."

"You're a mess, Chanti."

She pours me a glass of milk and joins me at the table.

"I busted Ms. Reeves and got her fired. I can figure this out, too."

"Maybe it's the teacher setting you up. You probably aren't

her favorite person right now. Can you really trust a crook's confession?"

"No, the connection has to be Mitchell's Moving. Whoever did it drove a Mitchell van. They had access to my wallet and the clients' keys."

"How do you know they didn't just break in?"

"No signs of forced entry."

"You watch way too many cop shows, Chanti. You're starting to sound like one," Tasha says. It's a testament to my storytelling skills that I've kept my best friend from knowing what my mother really does for a living, and I can't ruin it now.

"That's what the cops said when they questioned me."

"Okay, so name all the people who could have gotten your wallet and a key to those houses."

"There's Marco, but that can't be possible."

"Why?"

"Because he's . . . Marco."

Tasha looks at me for a second like she doesn't understand, then smiles.

"Oh. I guess there's a lot we haven't talked about lately. You'll have to fill me in after we keep you out of jail. Who else is on the list?"

"Malcolm—he's the supervisor of my moving team. Lissa Mitchell, queen witch at school. Annette Park, one of her minions. Annette's house was burglarized the same night she gave this lame party I went to, and Lissa was there."

"Wait—is it a coincidence this chick's name is Mitchell?"

"Not a coincidence. She's my boss's daughter. I guess I haven't told you all the facts," I say, sounding like Lana. I lay it all out for Tasha, after which she just shakes her head.

"You should have gone to North High," she says just as the teakettle begins to whistle.

After I get back home from Tasha's and have dinner with Lana, I tell her I need to do homework, but really I'm going over my list of suspects. The only motive I can give Annette is that she's afraid I'd bust her on the shoplifting charge. But it would make more sense to butter me up than to set me up. Malcolm stays on the list. Marco might think he's an okay guy, but Marco would probably see the best in anyone. So not my style.

Maybe my phone wasn't the only thing that fell out of my bag when I was at Mitchell's on Friday, acting out the lie I told Bethanie. But why would Malcolm do it? Could he dislike working with Marco and I so much that he'd set us up? Tasha said somebody must really hate me. Maybe Malcolm does, though it would be easier just to tell Paulette we suck as movers and get us fired. But he stays on my suspect list until I can find out where he was when the house was burglarized. I'm pretty sure Smythe hates me, and she must have some kind of shady background for her to owe Lana a favor, but she wasn't driving that van and she didn't leave my wallet in that house.

You need three things to make a good suspect: a reason to commit the crime, a way to do it, and the opportunity to get it done. Right now, no one on my list has all three ingredients. Only one person in this mess has all the ingredients, and that would be broke, lost-wallet, stolen-goods-knowing, alibi-challenged me. Basically, I'm screwed.

Chapter 27

Okay, so there's one other person as screwed as I am right now, and I wish I'd had the nerve to call him yesterday when I got out on bail, but I figured it was harder to hate someone in person than it is over the phone, so I decided to wait and see him at school. Really he has nothing to hate me for—I mean, I didn't do anything wrong other than want desperately to be his girlfriend, which made me such an easy target to punk. But then so was he. He showed up at the park because he was just as desperate to have me. And really, is love a crime?

That's what I'm thinking as I walk up the tree-lined drive to Langdon, because there's no way I could face these kids if I didn't know this was my chance to see Marco and make sure we were okay. We have to be okay because it's us against them and because, well, I'm mad about him. But as soon as I get to the circular driveway in front of the quad, I see Smythe standing there with Marco, and neither of them look happy too see me.

"No need to hurry, Miss Evans. As I was just explaining to Mr. Ruiz, you will not be attending classes today. You're both suspended until you're no longer under suspicion by the police."

"What happened to innocent until proven guilty?" I ask.

The last thing on earth I want to do is walk into Langdon Prep, but that's where all the clues are.

"We aren't locking you up."

"But you're locking us out," Marco says. "We worked hard to get our scholarships. If we miss classes, we'll jeopardize our grades. And I'm supposed to start in the next game."

"While I appreciate your concern for your studies, I would think you'd have more on your mind at the moment. We'll arrange for you to keep pace in class. Your teachers will e-mail your assignments to you. Your parents can bring in your completed work. It's the same process we use for students with long-term illness. And the game is the least of your worries."

"We didn't do this, Mrs. Smythe, and I'm going to prove it," I say.

"I wish you luck. But given the circumstances—the thefts that have occurred on campus—the board thought it best that we wait until the police have completed their investigations."

Mildred is coming toward us, looking sad and holding a cardboard box.

"Here's Mildred with your things," Smythe says. "I had her clear out your lockers."

"You didn't even trust us to be inside Langdon long enough to clean out our own lockers?" Marco asks.

"The board made a decision . . ."

"Congratulations, Mrs. Smythe," I say.

"Excuse me?"

"It must be a great day for you, finally getting rid of the scholarship kids you never wanted here in the first place. Two out of three of us, anyway."

"That is not true."

"Neither are the charges against Marco and me."

She stares at me for a second like she might be human,

like she might actually want to know the truth and maybe give me the benefit of the doubt. But she quickly reverts back to Headmistress from Hell, turns around, and heads for Main Hall. Marco and I have been dismissed.

"I'm sorry this happened to you kids," Mildred says, handing over the box to Marco. "It's the same thing that happened to my Reginald. I guess you couldn't help him or yourselves, Chanti."

"I'm not done yet."

"Who's Reginald?" Marco asks.

"Mildred, is this the sign Smythe claims she caught your son defacing?" I ask, pointing to the marble LANGDON PREPARATORY SCHOOL sign inside the grassy circle.

"That's the one. Well, that's the replacement. They had to get a new one carved—part of which Smythe docked from my pay. I'm still paying for it. The art teacher said she saw Reginald in the art room just before Smythe claimed she caught him out here. Some spray-paint cans turned up missing. Reginald told Smythe he was just in that room looking for his sketchbook, but she wouldn't hear it."

"So how did she make the leap from missing spray-paint cans to Reginald being guilty?"

"Said she caught him red-handed with that paint spraying up the sign, even though it was getting dark and the real culprit ran off when she walked up on him."

"They put the replacement sign in the same spot?"

"Yes, why?"

"Did anyone look at the surveillance tape? That camera is angled right at the sign."

"Smythe did."

"Did you?"

"I tried to, but she claimed it was part of police evidence."

That sounds like BS to me. I can't imagine Smythe called the police for such a small-time offense. It wouldn't be worth sullying the Langdon name with any negative publicity. Too many kids of Denver's glitterati attend Langdon and she'd never jeopardize those fat tuition and endowment checks.

"What did the kid spray on the sign, anyway?" Marco asks. "Was it about Smythe?"

"How she's a word that rhymes with witch. In big red letters."

"No wonder she's so mad," I say, though I can't really blame the perp. "Mildred, did you ever hire that lawyer?"

"Just did. I meet with her today."

"First thing you ask her to do is subpoena that tape from the surveillance company. They'll have the master. I don't think the tapes went into state's evidence."

"You think she lied about Reginald?"

"No, but it was dark and I think she *wanted* to see Reginald, so she did. It's amazing what witnesses think they see."

She gives me a big hug and hurries off to call her lawyer.

"Talked to a lot of witnesses, have you?" Marco asks, looking at me like he might be onto me. Or maybe I'm just paranoid.

"Uh, no. That always happens on *Perry Mason*. The classic cable channel plays the reruns."

"So you and Perry Mason save Mildred's kid, but what about us?"

"I guess we have a free day," I say, trying to lighten the mood.

"This is no joke, Chanti. Remember when I got upset with you the other day? My cousin is the reason I jumped off like that."

"Your cousin?"

"Yeah, David. His parents brought him here from Mexico when he was a baby. They were here illegally and got deported last week, but they brought him to stay with us before the feds came. He's fifteen and this is all he knows—the States."

"After all these years they got deported?"

"I don't know—the whole illegal-immigrant thing is getting intense. They had jobs, paid taxes, weren't living off anyone, but they're cracking down I guess. But David shouldn't have to leave everything he knows because of a decision his parents made fifteen years ago."

"Won't he miss his parents?" I say, realizing I sound a lot like a suspicious detective with all the questions, and I don't want to go there again.

"My aunt and uncle just want him to finish high school. It's only three more years."

I don't ask any more questions, just try to imagine what it would feel like if I was told today that I must move to, I don't know . . . Bangladesh, and never return.

"We're going to figure out a way to make him legal, but in the meantime I don't want the police looking too closely at my family. I don't want him kicked out because of my problems with the cops."

"I'm sorry," I say, touched that he would trust me with his cousin's secret. "This must be so scary for your family. But we're going to get out of it. We were set up. I just have to figure out who it was, and then prove it before the cops start digging into your family. Like in the next day or two."

"You know something the cops don't?"

"I know a lot the cops don't. That's why I really need to get inside Langdon. That's where the answers are."

"Is Perry Mason helping you figure this out, too?"

"Something like that," I say, distracted by the sight of Bethanie's car, convertible top down, driving past Langdon Prep on her way to her secret parking spot. I take off down the drive, planning to intercept her before she can walk to the school entrance.

She's still checking out her hair and reapplying her lip gloss when I reach her car. You'd have thought I was about to jack her BMW given the look on her face. It's amazing how quickly your so-called friends can turn on you.

"What are you doing here? I heard you were suspended."

"How'd you hear that? I just found out myself," I say as I make myself comfortable in the passenger seat.

"I just heard, that's all."

"From Lissa right? Because she's all up under Smythe and Smythe can't keep her mouth shut," I say, wondering how much other information Lissa has about me thanks to Smythe. Somehow she found out about my arrest, even though Lana says the record was expunged. That must be how Lissa was able to tell all my business at Annette's party, and to all of Langdon the next day.

"Look, Chanti. I know you didn't do this, but I also know I'm not trying to mess up my thing here, right? Sorry, but bad news follows you, girl."

"Does that bad news include you?"

"What?"

"Did you set me up, Bethanie? Why did you take me to Annette's house when you knew it was the last place on earth I'd ever want to be?"

"Okay, so I should have told you where we were going, but I didn't set you up. I was surprised to find out it wasn't really a party. Remember? I was expecting to meet some guys and get to know all the power people at Langdon."

True, and I don't think she was faking that.

"You said you got a last-minute invite from Lissa," I say. "How last-minute?"

"Right before you walked up to me at my locker that morning. She'd just invited me, and suggested I bring you and Marco. Which is why I was kind of surprised when we got there and she said she'd planned a girls' night out."

So maybe Lissa was planning to set up both Marco and me that night, and when he didn't show, she went to plan B.

"I can't believe you would think I'd ambush you."

"Well, you wanted in with Lissa and Langdon so much, I wasn't sure how far you'd go."

"I'd never go that far. Look, I have to go," she says, looking at the clock on her dash. I guess getting to class on time is more important than helping me beat a false arrest charge. "I can't get caught up in your drama, Chanti."

"I'm not asking you to. All I want to know is what happened that night at Annette's. Can you give me that? No one from Langdon has to know you told me anything."

"You already know what happened. Someone broke in and took all her stuff."

"Not all of it. What did they take? And was there really a break-in?"

"What does it matter? Stuff was taken."

"Please, just replay it for me."

"Okay, the two-minute version and then I'm going to class,"

"That's all I'm asking."

"All right already," she says, adding a final touch to her lip gloss before snapping the visor mirror closed. "We got back to the house a couple of hours later. . . ."

"It took that long to get something to eat?"

"First Lissa wanted burgers, then she wanted to go to Dairy Queen for a sundae. After that, she made me stop at Safeway to get some snacks to take back to the house."

"You wouldn't think someone as skinny as Lissa would have such an appetite."

"She could be a model, right?" Bethanie says, still enraptured with Lissa. "So when we get back, the front door was open a few inches."

"No broken glass, no busted doorjambs?"

I'm thinking whoever did it almost wanted to show that there were no signs of forced entry. I mean, could they have not taken two seconds to make sure the door was closed?

"No, the door was just open. We didn't think much of it

because we figured in the excitement of you storming out and us following you, whoever was last out the door didn't close it all the way."

"Do you remember who that was?"

"I know it wasn't me because I felt bad for you and I was the first one out. I was gonna try and stop you."

I want to ask her why she doesn't feel bad for me now, but I only have about ninety seconds left.

"So it could have been any of the other four?"

"Man, you sound like Five-O. I know it couldn't have been Annette, because she came out behind me jangling that ridiculous keychain she has, you know the one with about fifty charms that make all that noise. Drives me crazy."

"I guess that leaves Lissa and the clones."

"The who?" she asks. She pushes a button on the dash and the top starts closing, my cue that the interview is almost over.

"Never mind. So when you went inside, it looked like the place was ransacked, right? You knew right off the place had been robbed."

"No, that was the weird thing. Everything looked the way we left it, as far as I remember. We didn't know anything was missing until we went to turn on the TV. That was the most obvious thing gone. Then Lissa helped Annette look around the house, and Annette started crying about the missing figurines and how her parents were going to kill her."

"The figurines?"

"Yeah. Remember Lissa showed them to us during that boring tour of Annette's house? Come to think of it, everything missing we saw on that tour. Unless they found more stuff after I left. They called the cops then."

"Whose idea was it to call the police?" I ask as I follow her lead and get out of the car.

"That was definitely Lissa's suggestion. Annette didn't want to. She said her parents wouldn't be back until Sunday night and she'd just try to replace everything so they'd never know there was a party or a break-in. But Lissa convinced her to call the cops. You know how those girls are—they'd follow Lissa off a cliff if she asked."

"So why do you want to even hang out with them?"

"Two minutes are up, Chanti. I'll be late for class."

"I appreciate the information."

"Yeah. Good luck," she says as she walks toward Langdon, and I believe she means it.

Chapter 28

When I get back to the Langdon driveway, Marco is there waiting in his car.

"Need a ride?"

"You don't mind being seen with me?" I say as I get into his car.

"We're both jailbirds, right? Birds of a feather and all that."

"We'd *better* stick together. All we have are us."

Right away I feel like I shouldn't have said that, since it not only sounds like something on a Hallmark card, but it also smacks of wannabe-your-girlfriend desperation.

"What gets me is that they tagged us only because we're scholarship kids." Marco is always so laid-back, but right now he sounds angry. I guess being suspended for something he didn't do is enough to unnerve even Marco.

"Apparently being broke is a motive these days," I say. "When you think about it, that's the motive for most break-ins. People need the money."

"I suppose, but it still seems like a kind of prejudice. Like fiscal profiling. I mean, in this economy, who isn't broke?"

"Everybody else at school. Langdon has to be a connec-

tion, if not for the Mitchell client thefts, definitely for the Annette Park burglary."

"But they didn't charge us for that one," Marco says,
merging into morning rush hour traffic on Alameda.

"Yeah, but it's only a matter of time, at least for me. They
can tie me to that one, too. They'll probably say you were an
accessory."

"Accessory?"

"Yeah, that you were in on that one, too. How else could
I have stolen a TV without a car? Besides, they have us on
more than being broke. There's also means and opportunity."

"Which means . . . ?" Marco asks.

"We had a way to do it, because working for Mitchell, we
knew the homeowners would be gone. Since no one believes
we were together in the park that evening, we had a chance
to do it. Sometimes it doesn't matter what really happened,
only what you can prove happened. There are a lot of innocent people in jail."

"You sound like you know what you're talking about."

"Because I do." I have zero faith in my ability to seduce a
boy, or even walk across a room in heels without falling on
my behind, but you won't find a detective out there with
more confidence than I have in my ability to solve a crime.
Especially when it's my fate on the line. "Do you mind if we
go back to the park?"

"You mean the scene of the crime?"

"No, that's the scene of the alibi no one believes. We're
the only people who know the truth, which means we're our
best chance of figuring out what really happened. If we go
back there, I can think better, maybe find a clue that I
missed."

"Why would there be clues at the park if that isn't where
the crime happened?"

"No, I mean clues in my head. I know it sounds crazy, but

it's the way I think. It's how I solve crimes. I mean, you know, the mysteries of life."

"I have this feeling there's a whole side of you I don't know about," Marco says, turning to look at me while we wait at a red light. "This isn't like that show from back in the day where cops posed as high school kids, is it?"

"Me, a cop? That'll never happen. A good cop needs a certain personality, like not being afraid of your own shadow for starters. But being a good detective? That's mostly in your head—more brains than bravery."

"You know way too much about police stuff."

"I watch a lot of TV."

"I hope that's all it is. I'd hate to be really into you . . . well, as a friend I mean, and then you break the news you're actually a thirty-year-old cop with a husband and kid at home."

Just when I was getting comfortable talking to him one-on-one, he goes and lets it slip that he's really into me and now I'm all tongue-tied. We ride in silence all the way to the park, although in my head I've come up with a thousand things to say. As we walk to the picnic table, the little flags are gone from the grass, but this section of the park is still empty. That probably has more to do with it being nine o'clock on a weekday morning than with pesticides. I really have no idea what I hope to find here, except that whoever set us up has probably been here before and knows how isolated it is, and being here might trigger a clue of who that person is. And it's where Marco first suggested that we were something more than friends, even if his confession was drug-induced, and even if he's claiming today that he's only into me as a friend.

But right now, it's all about the business, the most serious case I've ever had to work. Love comes later.

"Whoever the perp is, he knew about those two homes being empty, and that the owners were Mitchell clients," I say, taking a seat at the table. "How about Malcolm?"

"Wouldn't the perp also have to know about Annette's party and be watching the house so he'd know when to burglarize it? How would Malcolm know all that?"

"I don't know—maybe Lissa was at her dad's office and Malcolm overheard her planning the party and staked it out."

"Why would Malcolm do any of this?"

"Because he's stealing from Mitchell's clients and doesn't want to get arrested again. Maybe he's a second-striker. Did he ever tell you what he was in jail for?"

"No, but Malcolm didn't do it."

"What makes you so sure?"

"Because he's a good guy, for one. Accusing him would be the same thing everyone else is doing to us. He's been to jail, so he must have stolen that stuff. How's that different from, you're broke, so you must have stolen stuff?"

"I didn't say he did it." I'm completely surprised by Marco's allegiance to Malcolm, who, I'm sorry, is just one strange dude. "But we have to look at everyone, and rule people out. That's all I'm doing."

"Well, you can rule him out. He didn't steal so he doesn't need to blame anything on us."

I remember what Tasha said about someone hating me. That's another possible motive.

"Marco, what if he didn't frame us to cover up his crime? What if he did it because he hates working with us? He's always asking to go back to his old team."

"That's a stretch, Chanti. He could get Paulette to reassign him more easily than setting up a burglary. Besides, he has an alibi—his probation officer. He told me he has to meet with him on Friday evenings."

"That's an odd time to meet a probation officer."

"Not when your probation officer is also your AA sponsor and he meets you following your meeting with a whole room full of people who can vouch for your whereabouts."

"Okay, so he's out. And he has a lot of issues."

We're quiet for a minute; then I say what I've wanted to say ever since I found out Marco was in the other interrogation room.

"Do you hate me for getting us into this mess?"

"How did you get us into it? I thought you said someone set us up."

"Yeah, but I think I was the target and you just happened to get caught up in it."

"What makes you think I wasn't the target? Or that whoever it is wasn't trying to get us both?"

He has a good point. Lana is forever telling me how it isn't always about me. Could she be right?

"Is there anyone that angry with you that they'd set you up to go to jail?" It was hard for me to imagine, but of course, I'm biased.

"I don't know if you've heard, but I was supposed to start in the season opener. Hard to do when you've been suspended from school."

"Justin Mitchell?"

"Who did you think it was if not him?"

"Now that you've ruled out Malcolm, my next guess is his sister."

"What did you do to piss her off so much she'd want you in jail?"

"Nothing, really. I mean, she's evil, but I can't think of anything that I did."

Maybe it really isn't all about me. I did know about her best friend's little shoplifting habit, but there's nothing about Lissa that makes me think she'd go this far to protect a friend. Herself—no doubt. But a friend? Unlikely. That's the kind of thing MJ Cooper would do, or maybe even Tasha. Not at all Lissa's style. Marco might be on to something.

"Is football really *that* important to a guy?"

"Not to me, but to some guys, it's everything. There was a college kicker who broke his replacement's leg and tried to make it look like a random attack. Just like Tonya Harding."

"Who?"

"The Olympic skater?" He must be able to read the cluelessness on my face because he moves on. "Justin's grades suck. If his father wasn't such a big booster to the team, and if he didn't have an amazing arm, he wouldn't still be at Langdon. All he had was his football rep, which used to be legit. I mean, when I was at North High, I wanted to *be* him. Always in the prep section of the sports page. You'd see him around town with the hottest honeys."

I think he just noticed another look on my face, as much as I tried to act like I didn't care, because he starts backpedaling as fast as his mouth will take him.

"But the girls didn't matter to me. He had crazy skills, awesome stats. He was on his way to All-American. Then he got so deep into the weed that he couldn't keep his plays straight toward the end of last season. Since practice started, he's late every day, and even missed a couple of days."

"Well, it makes the most sense. Whoever it was knew exactly what to steal—everything I'd written up on that assessment sheet. That's why I thought it was Malcolm. But Justin has access to his father's office."

I almost say my next thought aloud, which would bust me as an eavesdropper. Whoever set us up knew we'd believe those messages telling us to meet at the park. I thought maybe my crush was so transparent that anyone who'd ever seen us together might know. And she did. Lissa questioned me about Marco at Annette's party. She must have told Justin how I was into Marco, maybe that was the text she sent just before I stormed out. That's probably when she told Justin Annette's house would be empty for a couple of hours, then made Bethanie drive around on a food treasure hunt just to make sure.

But it might not have worked if Marco wasn't just as willing to meet me, and Justin knew from that conversation at Mitchell's last weekend that he was. Now I don't know which discovery makes me more excited—that I have my man, or that *I have my man*. But I'm a girl with focus when it comes to solving a crime, especially when my name's on it. Like I said. Love comes later.

Marco drops me off at home and as much as I hate to see him go, I need some alone time to go over what I've learned. Even with a court date looming, a guy that fine can still be a distraction. I check the messages and the first is Lana, saying she's got a late stakeout tonight. The next message is Smythe telling my "foster parents" that I've been suspended until further notice. *Delete*. I figure this information won't help Lana, and will only hurt me. If she knew, she might take some time off and start hanging around the house to keep an eye on me.

What I need right now is room to figure out how I'm going to prove Lissa and Justin set us up. Not that I've completely ruled out Malcolm. He told Marco that story about his probation officer and AA meeting, but until I verify it myself, he's still on the suspect list. If I'm the target, it could be Malcolm working with Lissa instead of Justin. If Tasha was right about someone's motive being hate for me, that's a long list. And I'm not including all the other people who don't have a connection to Mitchell's but wouldn't mind seeing me fall: Donnell, MJ, that big, scary girl poor Robert Tice was going out with. After I exonerate myself, I really should work on my people skills.

Lana would be my first choice in helping me, but seeing as how she'd lose it if she knew I was running my own investigation and not "letting the professionals do their job," that's not an option. So she'll have to stay in the dark about my school suspension for as long as I can keep it hidden from her, which means I only have a long weekend at best. If I make sure I'm in bed before she gets home, that's one less chance for her to question me and figure out something's up.

Hanging out at the park didn't really give me any clues, except that I remembered Lissa saying her maid lived nearby, off Lexington. That must be how she knew that section of the park was fairly quiet and witnesses would be unlikely. That's helpful information, but it isn't anything I can take to Lana. There are only two places where I might find the proof I need, and one of those places has suspended me until further notice. The other is Mitchell's, and tomorrow is payday. I'm sure I'm the last person they want to see, but they have to give me my final paycheck and fire me properly. I just have to come up with a story that'll get me the information I need.

Chapter 29

The next morning, I go through the routine of getting dressed and heading for school. Lana only emerged from her bedroom long enough to tell me good-bye and that everything will work out okay, and then I was out. I headed straight for Mitchell's, knowing Paulette would be there early to open up shop. Paulette loves to talk and hates the Mitchell kids, so it shouldn't be too hard to get the 411 from her.

When I walk into her office, I'm surprised to find Mr. Mitchell there, and immediately think this wasn't the best idea. I mean, I'm not guilty of anything, but I feel like I've caused him a lot of trouble anyway, and he's a nice guy despite his demon children. They both look up at me, and seem very surprised I'm there, and I just want to run. But I remind myself this is business.

"What are you doing here?" Paulette asks.

"I know I'm the last person you expect to see."

"You know how I feel about school and work," Mr. Mitchell says. "Weekend jobs only. Justin and Lissa are out in the car—I just stopped in to talk to Paulette for a second, but I can give you a ride to school."

"Weekend jobs? I just came to get my last paycheck."

"Are you leaving us?" Mr. Mitchell asks. "It's only professional to give two weeks' notice."

"You do know about the, um, incident, right?"

"Of course, I know about it. I also know you didn't do it."

"But it was your clients' homes and . . ."

"I know all about it. Believe me, I've talked to enough cops to learn all the details. And I don't care if all the details point to you and Marco, I know people. I know you didn't do this."

I want to throw my arms around Mr. Mitchell, but I'm pretty sure that wouldn't be professional, so I just walk over and shake his hand and hope he gets how grateful I am.

"I wish Langdon was as open-minded as you, Mr. Mitchell. We've been suspended."

"I'm on the board and I didn't hear anything about a suspension. You'd think given it's my business that's going to lose the most from this, they'd let me know."

"Old lady Smythe, I mean, Headmistress Smythe, met Marco and me at the front gate yesterday and told us we were suspended. She wouldn't even let us into the school to get our stuff from our lockers."

"I'll be having a talk with her. Expect to be back in school Monday morning."

"Yes, sir."

"Tell your boyfriend I expect to see you both here tomorrow."

"Marco isn't . . . I mean, yes, sir." I'm so pleased that he thinks Marco is my boyfriend that I almost forget why I'm here. His kids also thought Marco and I were hooked up, which is how I got into this mess in the first place. Focus, Chanti.

"So about the job . . ."

"Paulette, do you have something they can do here in the office, or out in the storage warehouse?"

"Oh, I can definitely put them to work tomorrow."

"I want you and Marco here," Mr. Mitchell explains, "but unfortunately my clients might feel differently. Until the police get this thing cleared up, you won't be working on home assignments."

"I completely understand, Mr. Mitchell. Thanks for letting us keep our jobs. I know this is going to affect your business."

"When I was a kid, I was in a similar jam. My life would have taken a whole different turn if someone didn't believe in me. Someone did, and it all worked out. Just like I know it will for you."

"I can't believe this. You're letting them work here, even after the police arrested them for ruining your business?"

Justin must have grown tired of waiting in the car. The minute I hear his voice I want to kill him, or at least kick him in the spot Lana taught me would take down a male assailant long enough for me to get away. But I can't get away from this. I have to run right up on it if I don't want to spend the next two years in juvie. So I keep my cool, and only imagine I've just kicked him into submission.

"No one's ruined my business. Keep that in mind, would you? It's *my* business and I'll run it the way I see fit."

"Yeah, but one day it'll be mine, and I'd like to make sure there will be something left of it for me to run."

"Keep going the way you are, messing around with drugs, and you won't be here to run your life, much less my business."

"You don't ever give me a break," Justin says, and I'm not sure whether he's about to go postal or break down in tears, but either way, he's in some kind of hurt and I didn't even have to inflict it. I'm enjoying it, too, even though I think this should be a private moment and it's making me a little uncomfortable.

"All I ever give you is a break, and that's the problem. Both you and your sister don't appreciate anything. I cut off the money and the credit cards and you still don't get it. Maybe taking your car will teach you to value something. To accept responsibility for yourself."

"But you'd let these thieves walk right up in here," Justin says, talking more slowly than an angry person should, almost slurring his words. "You treat them better than you treat us. You like them better than you like your own kids."

"I love my kids, but I don't like who you're turning into. It's my job to set you straight. That's what I'm doing."

"But Dad . . ."

"Come on. Let's get to school," Mr. Mitchell says, and I'm sure he's forgotten all about me standing there, because why else would he put all his family business out there for me to see? If Justin wasn't evil and trying to set me up for a crime he committed against his own father's business, and if he wasn't obviously geeked at eight in the morning, I'd almost feel sorry for him. But he's all those things, so the minute he and his father are gone, I try to get some information out of Paulette.

"That was a little intense."

"You ain't seen nothing. Those two have had some blowups that would shock Jerry Springer. Only thing different is they seem to be more frequent and Stephen—Mr. Mitchell—is getting less inclined to put up with it. It's about time, if you ask me."

"What do you think increased the arguments? Was it recent?"

"You know, I think it's been since he met you and Marco. When he told me you were going to start working here, I was expecting you to come in here and walk on water. You both made some impression on him."

"Really? I mean, we hardly know the guy."

"I guess after years of dealing with his kids, you and Marco don't have to do much to look like model citizens. You're just the kind of kids he'd want," she says, and her face changes from angry to wistful. "He's a good man and deserves better than what they give him, which is nothing but a hard time."

Well, Paulette is full of useful information. We thought Justin had a motive—hating Marco for taking his starting quarterback job. Or maybe Lissa hated me out of loyalty to her brother since Marco and I are a thing. Sort of. It turns out they hate us both because their dad likes us. It probably didn't hurt that he cut off the money and took the credit cards. Now he's taking the car? I'm pretty sure Lissa will be more than embarrassed to be driven to school by her father, especially since he drives a no-frills five-year-old sedan and not the brand-new Escalade she and Justin share.

"I can't believe he's letting Marco and me keep our jobs."

"That's the kind of person he is. He was so happy when he came in here this morning, thinking things were finally turning around."

"How do you mean?"

"Justin and Lissa never want anything to do with him unless they want something from him. He tried to take them camping a couple of years ago and you'd have thought he asked them to go serve in the Siberian army. Took them to New York last summer and they only saw him long enough to ask him for money. Then he tried a cruise, because he figured they'd have to hang out with him—where else are they gonna go? But no, they still managed to spend a total of ten hours with him on a seven-day cruise. I tell you . . ."

"But why was he happy this morning?" I say, trying to get Paulette back on track or I'd never get this out of her.

"Oh right, well, like I was saying, they never spend any more time with him than necessary. But Tuesday evening, they both come in here and tell their father how he works too hard and how they want to take him to dinner at his favorite restaurant. You know, that place up in the mountains that serves weird food like ostrich and boar. I don't see who'd want to eat that when you've got a perfectly good steak on the menu or maybe a pork chop. . . ."

"Wait, did you say Tuesday evening?"

"Yeah, Tuesday. I remember because I was preparing payroll and thought, what are these no-good children up to, because I didn't believe for a minute . . ."

"But that's impossible. That was the night of the burglaries," I say, my whole theory falling apart with just a few words.

"You're right, it was. What's that got to do with anything?"

"Nothing, Paulette. I've gotta go. I'll see you tomorrow."

"Hey, Chanti," she says when I'm halfway out the door.

"Yes?"

"For the record, I know y'all didn't have a thing to do with those thefts."

I'm excited she might have some hard evidence that will clear me until she says, "I just have a good feeling about you kids, and my feelings are never wrong."

Yeah, I got feelings too, but they don't hold up in court.

Chapter 30

When I get back home, I'm hoping Lana is there. I'm ready to tell her about my suspension, tell her everything I know because I'm in too deep and I need help. But she's already left for work, probably on some stakeout, and she isn't answering her phone. Now what? My prime suspects were forty miles from the scene of the crime and have a restaurant full of witnesses. There's something missing to all this. I just need to sort through everything I learned this morning and I'll find it. I do my best thinking outside on the front porch, so I go out there, grateful it's a school day and quiet. No interruptions.

That's when I see the only other person in the world I know might help me figure this out, and not just because she has—had—the mind of a criminal, but because she knows what it's like to be falsely accused. MJ drives by in her grandmother's car and looks at my house. I know she sees me, but she acts like she didn't and turns away. I start heading for her house, and reach it just as she's getting out of the car.

"I ain't got nothing to say to you, Chanti."

"MJ, I need some help. There's no one I can go to."

"How about your mother? Isn't that what the cops do, serve and protect? You got your own personal Five-O right there in your house. Oh wait, should I be whispering? It's a secret, right?"

I consider MJ a friend and all, but I won't have her putting my mother's job and life in jeopardy.

"Never mind," I say and turn to go back home.

"Wait a minute. I heard about what went down."

"And?"

"And I know you didn't do it."

"Why? Don't tell me you got a good feeling. I need some hard evidence."

A look crosses MJ's face that tells me she does have more than a good feeling.

"You know something, don't you?"

"How would I know anything about some job that went down in a neighborhood I never been to, couldn't even tell you where it is on a map? What do I know about some rich people?"

I just stare at her, knowing she's full of it, trying to will her to break.

"Besides, like I told you the last time we talked—I ain't no snitch."

"Yeah, but you know what it's like to go to jail for something you didn't do. I'd help *you*."

"Help me go to jail."

"How do you know it wasn't me who helped us get out that night? How do you know I didn't use my connections?" It's a leap, but I figure I'll take it because I've got nothing to lose.

"I didn't get arrested that night 'cause they didn't have anything on me. Stop trying to perpetrate like you're my friend. You narced on me and got my cousin sent to jail."

"MJ, you know that's a lie. Your cousin got himself sent up. I didn't know anything about your cousin."

"So your mother just happened to be there, just happened

to be the one who broke into that room just when he was measuring out some product for his customer."

"Think about it, MJ. All you told me that night was that you wanted to go visit your cousin. Before that, I'd never even heard of him. The cops were watching him long before you asked me for that ride. Unless you left something out when you asked for that small favor, you didn't even know he was dealing."

She doesn't have a response for this, and just starts taking groceries out of the trunk.

"Wait. You knew? And you asked me to drive you to a drug deal?"

"I was just going to visit while he was passing through. I didn't know he'd be doing business while I was there."

"So how do you expect *I* knew anything if you didn't? Never mind. I've got my own problems to deal with. I don't have time for this," I say, turning to leave.

"Hold on. What did you need my help with?"

"You can't help me. Well, actually you can, but I get it. *MJ ain't no snitch.*"

I walk away because if anyone should be mad, it's me. She knew by asking me to give her that ride she was getting me into some potential trouble, and she let me. She got Lana mad at me all summer, not trusting me—making me quit my job and have to go to Langdon. She has information that might help me and she's holding out on me because of some stupid street code. Lana was right. For someone who thinks so much like a cop, I've got bad judgment. But I never thought that was true about people. I always thought I knew people. Now MJ has shot my confidence to hell.

I'm on the porch at three o'clock, still trying to work things out. Since my conversation with MJ, I'm back to Justin and Lissa being the best suspects, even if they were eating ostrich and boar forty miles away. It only means they had a partner. My first thought was Annette. I've seen her steal myself. But I've ruled her out. She has a shoplifting habit, but I don't think she's smart enough for Justin and Lissa to trust her to be in on their scheme at a deep level. Besides, witnesses say they saw a black or Hispanic male loading the Mitchell van, who the cops assumed was Marco helping me.

But they never actually saw a girl. The cops picked me up because the merchandise stolen matched the exact items on my inventory list, my prints were all over the house, and they found my wallet. I had access to the keys. That takes me back to Malcolm, who also had access to the keys, the list, and possibly my wallet. He's a brown-skinned male. But he has an alibi, so he claims. I should have asked Paulette about him while she was so generous with the gossip. Now I'm just going in circles, coming up with nothing, so I distract myself with the arrival of Ada Crawford, who lives across the street, three doors down from Tasha. She pulls up in her recently acquired Lexus SUV, custom metallic gold paint with gold twenty-two-inch spinners and gold medallions. If you can't *be* gold, drive it.

When Tasha and I first noticed how large Ada was living without a job and then saw all the strange men who come and go out of her house at all hours, we thought she was running a crack house. But Donnell would never allow competition on the block and none of the men looked like crackheads. They were well-dressed, drove nice cars. That's when we deduced Ada was a professional, if you know what I mean. When I asked Lana about her a year ago, she confirmed it.

"So why don't you arrest her?"

"She's small time. What we want are her customers. We'll let her build up her clientele first. It'll be the easiest bust I ever make—run the stakeout from the house, then have some uniforms knock on the door."

"What's up with them? Who are they?"

"Nothing you need to know. I already said too much. Ada's harmless, but you keep away from her house."

Right, like I'd ever want anything to do with Ada. But I'm not hating that car she's driving. That's when I remember something. Mr. Mitchell cut off the bank flow to Lissa and Justin about the time school started, and she's still carrying a brand-new Fendi bag and buying Il Mare face cream. She could have used the five-finger discount to get it like her girl Annette, but Justin can't shoplift pot. Or whatever he's on. And they both act like getting a job would be the equivalent of being a scholarship kid. Unthinkable. So how are they living so large? They must be stealing stuff and selling it.

But they can't be in two places at one time, so they must be tipping off a partner on what to steal, and then giving them access to the goods. That way Lissa could buy Bethanie and the clones dinner the night of Annette's party, while the partner could rob Annette's place. That way they can out-of-the-blue take their father for an ostrich steak while those two client homes were being hit. That way they always have the perfect alibis.

Chapter 31

I don't know who might be working with Justin and Lissa, but I know it isn't someone from Langdon. If the stolen goods are being converted to cash, Langdon kids would have no idea how to do it. There are always pawn shops, but once you start moving a lot of goods, that becomes risky. A legitimate pawn shop, and even the more shady shops when you're dealing in serious volume, are going to run the serial numbers, and won't take anything with the numbers scratched or burned off. That means somewhere down the line, there's a fence involved, someone who knows how to move stolen goods in volume, and I'm pretty sure that isn't a Langdonite. Sorry to be profiling on you, Malcolm, but you're the only connection I can come up with. Marco is hot, but what does he know about getting the truth out of a con, or whether Malcolm's alibi is legit?

I need a break out of my own head, away from this case, so I went across the street to Tasha's. I'm also hungry, and wouldn't mind seeing what goodies Michelle's mother cooked up today, but seeing as how Michelle and I aren't what you'd call best friends, I'll need Tasha to get me into her refrigerator.

"You're here so I guess they haven't arrested you again," Tasha says when she opens her front door.

"That's not even funny. You haven't told anyone, have you?"

"All these years being friends, you'd ask me that?"

Tasha was right. It didn't matter if I bailed on her because I thought hanging with MJ would make my summer more exciting. Just because she started going to tamales happy hour with Michelle on Fridays doesn't mean we won't be friends forever.

"My bad." I was never good with *I'm sorry*. The great thing about Tasha is she already knows that. "You want to go see Michelle?"

"You mean go and eat some of her mom's cooking. Don't your mama *ever* cook?"

"She works long hours down there at the law office. Even when she is home to cook, it never tastes like the food at Michelle's."

"True that. I've had your mom's cooking."

I knew it wouldn't take much to convince Tasha, and a few minutes later, I'm sitting at Michelle's kitchen table eating the best spaghetti and meatballs on the planet. Minus the usual commentary from Michelle about how I'm a freeloader and how her mother's chicken and biscuits have taken up permanent residence on my hips.

"Second helping, Chanti?" Michelle asks.

"Okay, what's up?" I ask, handing her my plate for that second helping. "You don't *ever* want me over here."

"That's not true. I enjoy your company."

"Seriously, what's up?" Now it's Tasha's turn not to believe Michelle's act.

"I'm just in a good mood, that's all."

"Because . . . ?"

"Because Donnell and I are back together."

"No, Michelle." Tasha and I say it at the same time, both of us sounding too done with her.

"Y'all just hating because I got a man. One who cares enough to buy the very best, too. I'll show you."

When Michelle leaves the kitchen, Tasha says, "You know anything DTS buys her he bought with drug money."

Michelle returns, holding her arm in front of her.

"Wow," Tasha says, taking Michelle's hand. "Drugs have been very, very good to Donnell. There must have been a run on crack this weekend."

"Don't hate the player, hate the game," Michelle says, smiling and unfazed by Tasha's snarky, if accurate, assessment of how Donnell could possibly afford this kind of jewelry. I have to admit Donnell has some good taste, even if he did buy it with drug money. I know the diamonds are real because Donnell is trying to build a rep around the neighborhood that he's a real G, so he wouldn't give his girl cubic zirconia.

"Y'all don't know Donnell like I do. He has a sweet side, you know."

"Tell that to the guy whose arm he broke when he didn't pay him for some rock," Tasha says.

"He's sweet, but he's also a businessman."

"Is that what he calls it?" I ask, thinking Michelle is about as deluded as a girl can get over a guy.

She ignores me and tells us just how sweet Donnell is. "Since I wouldn't take his calls, he texted me to meet him at the park. When I got there, he had flowers. I tried to tell him no, I didn't want him back, but then he started kissing on me and I kissed back and next thing you know . . ."

"In the *park*, Michelle?" Tasha says.

"It was very discreet. No one could see us."

"Which park did you say this was?" I ask.

"I didn't. But it was the one on Lexington. And don't go

thinking you might take some boy over there, if you can ever get one. That's me and Donnell's spot now."

"Yeah, your spot and all his buyers'. Oh, I'm sorry. His *clients*. Since he's a businessman and all," Tasha said.

"What you trying to say, Tasha?" Michelle asks, her squeaky voice growing higher-pitched.

"Please, girl. Everybody knows that's where Donnell handles his *business* transactions. Well, everyone but you, apparently."

And me. But now it's all coming together.

"Can I have another look at your bracelet?" I ask Michelle.

"Jealous, aren't you?" she says, taking off the bracelet and passing it to me. "Go ahead, have a good look. Next time you come telling me some rumors about Donnell and Rhonda Hodges, you remember how my man treats me."

I don't know what I'm looking for since I've never seen the bracelet before, but I'm hoping it will jog some memory, some clue. Then I notice something etched in the gold band holding all the diamonds together.

"There's an inscription. It's so tiny I can barely read it."

"I never noticed any inscription," Michelle says. "That's so sweet. Let me see."

I keep the bracelet and check it out with my flashlight key chain.

"It says 'To Z.B., with love. Daddy.'"

"As in, 'who's your daddy?' Is that your pet name for him?" Tasha says, knowing it isn't.

"No, and those aren't my initials. What do you think it means?"

Tasha has a laugh over Michelle's, um, innocence, and then breaks it down for her. "It means cheap Donnell bought your diamonds from a pawn shop."

But Tasha has it wrong. It means Donnell DTS is Justin's dealer, which is why Justin knew that area of the park is usually empty. He'd probably seen the postings that pesticides would be sprayed the day he sent Marco and me there to meet, just extra insurance that no one would be in the park to corroborate our alibi. I bet Lissa doesn't even have a maid, much less one who lives off Lexington.

I jump up from the table and hug Squeak. I'm sure she and Tasha both think I've completely lost my mind. "Thanks for the meal and the lead, but I gotta bounce."

Much as I want that second plate of spaghetti, I have an ex-con to see.

Chapter 32

M_J opens her front door, finds it's me, and tries to close it. I raise my hand to keep it open, surprising myself as much as MJ. We both know she could break every bone in my hand without developing a sweat.

"I'm busy. Got homework to do."

She has a pen tucked behind her ear and by now I recognize it is a Montblanc. Not exactly MJ's style.

"Nice pen," I say, pointing to it.

"It was a gift."

Right, from her rich Uncle Donnell.

"I need some information."

"I thought you said I can't help you. So why you here?"

MJ won't even let me in her house, but steps out on the porch and closes the door behind her. I wish I'd thought of a way to approach her on the short walk to her house, but I was just so excited to solve the crime that now I'm here, empty-handed and with no plan. So I just come out with it.

"How did you know about my arrest, MJ?"

"What?"

"When we talked earlier, you knew all about me getting picked up. How'd you know?"

"Everyone knows."

"Tasha and Michelle don't," I say, because she doesn't know I told Tasha. "They know every time someone sneezes on this street. You don't talk to a soul around here, and you got the story."

"I must have read it in the papers."

"Never made the paper or the news."

She doesn't say anything, so I fill her in.

"There's only one way you heard about this. Donnell DTS. And he heard it from the kids at my school who set me up to take the fall. Because he's working with them. It was Donnell those witnesses saw loading that van. Those same kids learned about our arrest at the motel through Donnell because you told him."

MJ stares at me, still silent.

"Tell me I'm wrong, MJ."

"I got nothing to say to you."

"Only thing I haven't figured out is why Donnell would be talking to you? I mean, it isn't like either of you are the most outgoing people on the street. Someone might think you're in on it with him."

"What do *you* think?"

"I don't think anything. I know you aren't. I know you're serious about leaving all that stuff behind, getting your GED, and going to college, the whole nine. What I don't know is your connection to Donnell. Why would he talk to you?"

She doesn't answer.

"MJ, you might have information that will save me."

"Chanti, I told you . . ."

"So you're going to let some BS street code send me to jail for something I didn't do?"

"If you're innocent, you won't go to jail."

"Yeah, 'cause that's how it worked out for you, right?"

"Your mom's got connections."

"Connections got nothing on evidence, MJ. Forget it. I can take care of myself."

I'm already off her porch when she calls after me.

"One thing I will tell you, Chanti. Don't cross Donnell. He ain't the same kid from down the street you grew up with. He ain't just a small-time corner hustler, either. Stay away from him."

Chapter 33

I could still hear MJ's warning in my head when I left for work this morning. Even though my neighborhood is one where you'd better watch your back, I've never been afraid to walk down The Ave. But let me tell you, that walk to the bus stop on Center felt a lot longer than a block. The whole time I was expecting Donnell DTS to jump out from behind some bushes or run into me as I turned the corner onto Center. When the bus drove past the park on Lexington, I got chills. But when I spoke to Lana before I left home, I didn't let on a thing. If she knew what I'd learned so far, she'd put me on lockdown and get Donnell picked up before I had the proof I need. I can already tell Lana isn't thinking like a cop now that I'm the one with a court date. She's acting strictly like a mother, and that won't help me right now.

Marco is already at Mitchell's when I arrive. Last night when I called him to tell him we still had jobs, I asked him to wait for me if he got there first. I planned to tell him that I knew who was setting us up and that all we had to do was figure out how to prove it. But I don't get the chance because just as I walk up to his car, Mr. Mitchell pulls into the parking lot. Sadly, both of his evil spawn are with him and threaten to ruin the best mood I've been in since Marco and I were arrested. They get out of the car, too, but hang back, leaning against it.

"Good," Mr. Mitchell says, walking over to Marco and me. "I'm glad to see you're both here."

"Thank you, sir, for giving us the benefit of the doubt," Marco says in that polite way that makes Mr. Mitchell wish his own son had turned out differently. "Not many people would have let us keep our jobs."

"There's no benefit of the doubt. I know you didn't do it."

Behind him, Justin is seething. If looks could kill, all of us—including his father—would need every doctor on *ER*, *Grey's Anatomy*, and *House* to save us.

"Paulette's going to put you to work this morning on some projects in the office, but later on I have a storage job that I'd like you to take care of."

"Are you sure this is a good idea?" I ask. I mean, I'm glad he believes in us and all, but I don't want him risking his business for us any more than he has to.

"The customer is fine with it. Asked for you specifically. It's *my* house."

I think Justin just popped a major artery. He starts to walk over to us, but thinks better of it and instead paces alongside the car. Lissa just rolls her eyes at me.

"We're doing some remodeling, and I want a few things put into storage. No heavy lifting—the two of you can manage everything. Here's a list of items and keys to the house. Paulette can get you the address."

"You won't be there?" Marco asks.

"No, I'm afraid not. We've got some family business we need to take care of today down in Colorado Springs. We're looking into military school for Justin. Maybe the Air Force Academy can make a man of him. You should have things packed up and gone by the time we get back this evening."

"You can trust us to take care of it, sir."

Every time Marco speaks, I'm pretty sure Justin wants to punch out a window of the car. His whole body tenses up, and the crazy thing I saw in his eyes that first day at football practice just flares. When he puts his hand in his pocket, I almost want to duck and run, and I'm relieved when he only produces his phone.

"One other thing," Mr. Mitchell is saying, "it's probably best you wait until after two o'clock. It's the housekeeper's cleaning day, and she hates it when people are there and getting in her way."

So they do have a maid. I think I have enough other evidence for my theory about Justin, Lissa, and Donnell to hold up, but this does put a little crack in it.

"Your housekeeper. Lissa mentioned her once. Said she lives in my neighborhood, off Lexington."

"Off Lexington? Lissa's never been good with directions. The woman lives on the other side of town."

Excellent. No more little crack, and it only strengthens my theory. Why would Lissa lie about that unless she didn't want me to know the reason she knew my neighborhood. Her stuck-up phony self would never be anywhere near my 'hood unless she was with her brother when he made his deals with Donnell.

"We'll stay out of her way. We won't get there until three o'clock, just to be sure," Marco says.

"Perfect," Mr. Mitchell says, lingering for a moment, and I'm pretty sure he doesn't want to leave. I get the feeling he'd rather stay with us than go deal with his family business. I mean, just look at his family. "Where did Justin go?"

"I think he left to make a phone call."

Now it's Mr. Mitchell's turn to look like he might go postal.

"If you see him on your way in, please tell him I'm in the car waiting, and that I'll be very angry if I have to come in there and get him."

Now I won't be able to share my theories with Marco because it won't look good if we don't go inside, and I'm certain Mr. Mitchell is hoping we find Justin and pass along his message. Otherwise if he has to go in there looking for him, we might have to call the police down here on a domestic. Inside the warehouse, we not only see Justin, but run smack into him.

"Yeah, you better be in a hurry," I say, feeling tough with Marco there to back me up. "Your dad's waiting for you."

"Just stay out of my business. Come to think of it, stay out of my room while you're at my house. I'd hate for something to come up missing."

He flashes the smile of the devil, and I can't help but think I just made a deal with him without even knowing the terms.

Chapter 34

On the way to the Mitchell house, I fill Marco in on what I know—that Justin and Lissa are behind the thefts at school, and they're Donnell's scouting team on the home thefts. I even tell him that I'm worried about doing the Mitchell job because of what Justin said before he left this morning. Mr. Mitchell might have all the faith in the world in us, but that doesn't mean he won't believe his kid when he claims we stole something out of his room, whether anything is missing or not. I mean, it isn't like Mr. Mitchell has an inventory of his whole house, and even if your kid is Justin, won't you believe him over two people you hardly know?

When Marco pulls up to the house at the address Paulette gave us, I notice a furniture-rental van parked across the street.

"That's weird," I say.

"What specifically? Everything you just told me is unbelievable."

"A furniture-rental van in this neighborhood. Look at these houses. I doubt these people have to pay for their furniture by the month at jacked-up interest rates. That's how we do it on our side of town."

"Nah, I know people just like that. You know those

guys—pushing a Mercedes SLK and can't afford to put more than two gallons of gas in it until payday."

"You think?"

"I bet some people around here are probably faking rich, and really living check to check just like our families do."

Marco is probably right, though I'd expect these folks to be a little more discreet. Even if you *are* faking your wealth, shouldn't you try to keep it on the down low? Not to mention the tacky furniture this company rents, and I ought to know 'cause half my furniture comes from Rooms-4-Cheap. But hey, at least we bought ours. No renting by the month for Lana. At least not after she paid twice what it was worth with the rent-to-own option.

When we walk into the house, it's clear the Mitchells don't know anything about Rooms-4-Cheap. I think everything in the living room alone costs more than a year's mortgage payments on our house.

"This place is amazing," I say, feeling like I just walked into a movie-set living room.

"I don't know how Justin and Lissa could want even more than this."

"That's the problem. They had everything they wanted until their dad cut them off. And rather than Justin giving up his weed . . ."

"That dude is on something stronger than chronic."

"Well, whatever he's on, instead of giving that up and rather than Lissa let on to her clones that she could no longer afford the high life, they came up with this plan to work with Donnell. I think they're planning a whole operation. They started with the school thefts, but that won't buy much. Then after the break-in at Annette's house, with me as the fall girl, they came up with the idea of hitting Mitchell clients."

"But how long could that last?" Marco asks. "I mean, if they keep hitting Mitchell clients, after a while, there would be no clients and eventually the cops would trace it back to someone at Mitchell's. Like us. With us in jail, who takes the fall?"

"I know, that's what I don't get. The operation would fall apart just as soon as it began. But if Justin is the mastermind, we know he's missing a whole lot of brain cells. If Donnell Down-the-Street came up with all of this—well, let's just say he's in no danger of being arrested for being brilliant, that's for sure. When we were kids, he held the record on our street for going the longest without finding anyone in a game of hide-and-seek."

"How you know I *wanted* to find your ugly self?"

Uh, okay, either Marco just changed his voice and got really mean, or we aren't alone. Before I turn around, I already know who it is, along with the terms of that deal with the devil.

"Donnell, where did you come from? How'd you get in here?"

"You oughta know. Didn't you just break it down for your boyfriend, here?"

"I was just talking. . . ."

"Yeah, but you got it right. Mostly right. I ain't half as stupid as you think. You the one going to jail for this, not me."

"Who is this lunatic? Going to jail for what?" Marco asks, looking like he's about to jump bad on Donnell. While I'm sure Marco has game, Donnell has a couple years and some jail time on Marco. He might be a small-time drug dealer, but even they carry. And I know for a fact Donnell DTS does because Michelle told me. So I channel Lana, and think of a way to diffuse a potentially volatile situation.

"Look, Donnell, you want the stuff? We'll help you box it up and put it in your van."

"What van?"

"The Rooms-4-Cheap van out there."

"That ain't none of my van because I'm not here for this small-time crap. See, Chanti, you're almost as smart as I am.

You're right about how the whole thing would have fallen apart before I got any real loot out of it. I mean, it's falling apart now, right? You about to go to jail, Mitchell about to lose his business up his son's nose."

"So what are you here for if not the stuff on the list? Isn't this what Justin called and told you to pick up?"

"It is, but I had a better idea. I'm gonna wait for Mitchell to get home and get a little information from him—like his keys, credit cards, and security codes to all his warehouses."

"You can't hit every warehouse before the cops catch you, Donnell."

"You *are* smart, Chanti. I can't do it by myself, that's right. But see, I got me a whole operation, like a network. I know what you been telling Michelle. You think I'm just a corner hustler, but I got more skills than that."

"Is that what this is all about? Me telling Michelle you're bad news? Everybody on The Ave knows that, Donnell."

"Yeah, but for some reason, she listens to you. I love that girl, and you messed it all up for me."

"Okay, Donnell, this is touching and everything, but I know you. You aren't doing all this just to take me down for breaking up your little relationship."

"Of course not. You got yourself one smart female, amigo."

Marco steps to Donnell, which is when he confirms what I already knew. Donnell is strapped, and now it's unstrapped.

"Back it up, chico. Don't try to act tough for your girl. Let's all just settle in and wait for Daddy Millionaire to come home and make me rich. Both of you, on the couch."

Marco doesn't want to, but I take his arm and drag him to the couch. Heroics will only get us both killed if Donnell gets spooked. Lana always says in this kind of situation, it's best to keep everything calm. I know Donnell. I know his mama. I even know his favorite thing to buy off the ice cream truck on a hot summer day is the Banana Bomb. He won't hurt me. He's only trying to scare me. But then I remember the last thing MJ said to me, and I get queasy. Maybe he isn't the same kid I grew up with.

"You were friends with this freak?" Marco asks.

"I wouldn't call it friends, but we've known each other since we were little."

"That was a long time ago, Chanti," Donnell says, as if I need reminding. I kinda got that point when he pulled his gun.

"Are you going to kill us, Donnell?"

"Not unless you do something stupid. I need you to take the fall for this. It won't help me if you're dead. But I only really need one of you, so keep that in mind."

"What about Mr. Mitchell? He'll know we didn't do this. He'll vouch for us."

"Yeah, that'll be hard for him to do when he's dead. You'll be taking the heat for that too. Cops'll buy that better if he does it," Donnell says, waving his gun at Marco. "They never believe girls will kill somebody."

I know for a fact this isn't true, but I don't interrupt. If I can keep Donnell calm and talking, maybe I can think up some way to keep Mr. Mitchell from getting killed, and Marco and me off death row.

"It'll go down like this: Mitchell catches y'all in here robbing the place, says y'all are going to jail for good once he calls the cops, and amigo here loses it and kills him. I think the cops will believe that. So watch yourself, Chanti—you screw up and you're the one to go. You are expendable." He laughs at this last line. "Sounds like something from the movies, am I right?"

"Donnell, you can't be serious about all of this."

"What part of me holding a nine on you don't you find serious?"

Well, he has a point there. I'm trying to think of a come-back that won't get me killed when we hear the sound of a garage door opening.

"Daddy's home early," Donnell says. "I think I'll meet him at the door. Don't move. Remember, I only need one of you alive."

Of course, I'm glued to the sofa cushion because, as we've already determined, I am a wuss. But the minute Donnell turns his back on us, Marco jumps up and tackles him to the floor. The gun goes flying out of Donnell's hand and for once, I know what to do. I'm afraid of a lot of things, but not a gun, at least not when I'm the one holding it, thanks to all those lessons at the shooting range with Lana.

Just as I turn the gun on Donnell, who is giving Marco a hell of a fight down there on Mr. Mitchell's living-room floor, four guys come through the door and they have guns, too. I'm a pretty good shot, but there's no way I'm taking down four guys and this is one scenario Lana never told me how to handle, because really—when would this kind of thing ever happen to me? But now it has and I think I'm about to lose it, until I realize these aren't friends of Donnell. They have badges hanging from chains around their necks. Undercover cops. You'd think I'd be relieved, but all I can think of is how this scene looks to a cop and how screwed I am.

Chapter 35

"We got this, Chanti," one of the detectives says, almost in a whisper, and that's when I realize I know him. He's grown a beard since the last time I saw him, and I'm pretty sure his dark hair used to be blond, but he works with Lana.

I point the gun to the floor and hand it over, relieved that I no longer had to figure out what came next. I want to ask him how he knew, and where Lana is, but the minute I open my mouth he shakes his head, reminding me that even in this situation, I have to keep Lana's cover. Then he nods in the direction of the door, and I understand that the Rooms-4-Cheap van wasn't Donnell's getaway car. It's a surveillance van and Lana's been out there all this time. Another detective handcuffs Donnell, freeing Marco to wonder what the hell just happened.

"Let's go outside, Marco. They don't need us in here," I say, surprising even myself at how official and businesslike I sound, when really I'm trying hard not to lose my lunch.

"What just went down?" Marco says, still stunned.

"What went down is you took out the bad guy. If you hadn't tackled him, who knows how that would have played out."

"But how did the cops know? I thought you hadn't told anyone your theory."

"That's what I'd like to find out myself."

Two uniformed cops come up to us. One leads Marco away, saying the paramedics want to check him out and make sure he's not hurt. I assure Marco that it's okay, the cops are on his side this time, and he believes me, which makes this day better and not quite the living hell it ought to be. The other cop takes me to the Rooms-4-Cheap van and opens the back door. Lana's in there looking terrified, which nearly knocks me over because I've never seen her afraid of anything. She hugs me so hard that it takes my breath away, and I have to squirm out of her arms before I hyperventilate.

"Why didn't you tell me about all this, Chanti?"

"Because you would have locked me in the house and I'd never have a chance to figure it out. I needed proof. All the evidence pointed to Marco and me. I needed to find a way to prove it wasn't us."

"And almost got yourself killed in the process."

"How did you know I was here?"

"Your new friend told me."

"New friend? Bethanie? She didn't know anything about Donnell."

"The other one. The one I misjudged."

"MJ talked to you?"

I try to imagine MJ willingly going to a cop and it seems impossible.

"Last night when I got home she was sitting on our porch, waiting for me."

"Didn't you get in late?"

"About two in the morning and the porch was dark. I almost had a heart attack, but only after I almost shot her. She isn't the brightest girl, but you could do worse for a friend."

"What did she tell you?"

"She was worried about you. Said you were playing girl

detective with someone who was more dangerous than you realized."

"But I still don't get the connection between her warning you and you finding me here."

"Well, we both had a part in that. At first I didn't believe anything she was telling me because once a con, always a con. But she didn't have to wait on the porch all night for me to come home. And like I said, I did come this close to shooting her and she still wanted to tell me that you were in trouble. So I put a GPS tracker on your cell phone and dropped a bug in your purse."

I want to go off on her about the indignity of being surveilled by your own mother, but it's hard to talk about principles when your mom's snooping saves your life. Instead I say, "Couldn't you guys have come in *before* he pulled the gun."

"We didn't see that coming. I knew Donnell had gone bad, but you guys grew up together. I didn't think he'd really hurt you or anyone else."

"I guess he fooled us both on that count."

"We were hoping the Mitchells would come home and we could get more on tape. But don't worry. We have plenty on tape to clear you and Marco. And by the way? Your *boyfriend?* This is how I have to find out you have a boyfriend? That was kind of embarrassing to listen to with the guys in the truck."

I can see this feel-good moment going places I'd rather it not, so I ask, "What was MJ's part? You said you both had a part in making the connection that Donnell would come here for me."

"Oh. Right. She can give you those details herself. Let's go home."

"Don't I have to make a statement?"

"You can make a statement tomorrow. I want you home with me tonight where I can keep an eye on you."

"But you already got the bad guy."

"Yeah, well. I'd rather be safe than sorry."

That's a little cryptic, but at the moment I'm more concerned with making sure Marco isn't afraid to talk to me ever again for fear I'll get him shot at, extorted, or framed.

"What about Marco? I should probably talk to him. He's probably all stressed out. He's not used to this kind of thing."

"I don't want you getting used to it, either. Let me make sure they've already taken Donnell in, then I'll let you talk to him, but only for two minutes. Then we're out of here."

Lana opens the doors of the van, and the bright glare of the late afternoon sun shocks my eyes. In the few minutes I was inside the van, I'd forgotten it was still light out.

"Wait, Mom. Can I tell Marco about you?"

"Well, he *is* your boyfriend. Go ahead, tell him all about me. That way I can go over and meet him and tell him all about you."

"Never mind. I'll keep your cover."

"Yeah, that's what I thought," she says, and smiles at me before she walks out into the sunlight.

Chapter 36

When we get home, MJ is waiting on the porch again. By now the sun has gone down. Apparently having Lana draw her gun on her didn't scare her off this habit, which makes me think I was right about MJ being the bravest person I know, or that Lana was right and maybe she's not a Mensa society candidate. But Lana was definitely right about the other thing—I could do worse when it came to finding a friend.

Beyond a greeting, MJ doesn't speak until Lana goes inside.

"So you didn't get killed today?"

"Apparently not."

"I told you not to mess with him. People don't ever want to listen to MJ."

"I didn't mess with him. He found me. I had no idea he was coming to that house. Which makes me wonder how you did."

"This is what I wanted to tell you all along, but . . ."

"MJ ain't no snitch—I know, I know."

"Yeah, well, that's not the case after last night."

It's true. MJ must have been really worried about me to come to Lana. This porch must have been like holy water to a vampire for MJ.

"It isn't snitching when it means saving a friend's life, you know."

"Not when you're a gangster."

"But you aren't in a gang anymore."

MJ is silent, which makes my brain start clicking.

"Wait a minute. Did you start running with Donnell? Is he in some kind of gang?"

"Something like that. He was trying to start the Denver operation of the Down Homes. This whole thing was like his initiation. If he pulled it off, then he'd be the head of a new organization here in town."

"How did he even know about the Down Homes? I thought you were leaving all that behind, starting fresh, getting your GED so you could go to college. Or were you just talking?"

"That was the plan until I thought you set my cousin up. You were my only friend out here, and then I wind up in jail. I figured it was true what my old boyfriend said when I was back home. Can't trust nobody but your Homies. That's what we call ourselves in the Down Homes, not just the generic homies."

"Yeah, I get it," I tell her before she gets sidetracked.

"So Donnell comes around and starts asking me to hook him up with some people back home. Everyone around here knows about me. Wasn't like no big secret."

"MJ, do you really think I set your cousin up?"

"I did then. But I got to thinking about it and realized if I didn't know my cousin was dealing out of that motel room, how you gonna know? So I gave Donnell the hookup and told him I was out after that. But some of the Homies called and asked me to help him out, you know, like be a mentor."

I have to work hard not to laugh at this scenario—a Big Brother program to help juvenile delinquents get *into* a life of crime.

"And you said yes? He was setting me up for a murder charge."

"I didn't know anything about a murder or making you take the fall. I thought he was just going to rob your boss."

"Next time, you might want to get all the facts before you help known felons."

"I didn't have any friends out here. One thing I know is you always gotta have someone who has your back. So I told Donnell I'd help him out, and he told me his plan about taking down your boss. Then you come by here asking about him, and even after I told you to stay out of it, I knew you wouldn't."

"It must have been hard to come talk to my mother."

"Yeah, 'cause I still hate the cops. Even now I'm taking a risk sitting here with you."

"Why? No one knows she's a cop."

"You never know where the Down Homes are. They don't know about her, but they know about you. They know you were the one Donnell was setting up. How does it look me being friends with you?"

"That means we're friends again?"

"I don't know about all that. But if you got my back, I got yours."

"Best homies forever," I say, thinking I'm pretty clever.

"That ain't funny, Chanti. Later," MJ says and like that, she's gone, heading home. But it's all good because I know it's true. *Later.*

Chapter 37

The first day back at Langdon is not my idea of a good time. After all I'd been through, Lana said it was okay if I wanted to transfer to North. I told her I'd stay and give it until the end of fall semester. Yes, leaving Langdon is all I've wanted since the beginning. No, I have not completely lost it. But it's only been three weeks, a crazy three weeks that could never possibly happen again. I have to believe Langdon is not such a bad place if I don't have a stoner quarterback setting me up for a felony because he has issues with his father, or his evil twin helping him ruin my life, or a crazy bio teacher running a one-woman theft ring with my name all over it. Yeah, I still have the Headmistress from Hell to deal with, but as soon as I get the dirt on whatever she did to owe Lana a favor, I'm sure I'll find a way to use that information to keep her off my back.

Mildred is my ally for life. When her lawyer got the surveillance tape from Smythe and had it enhanced, the school board easily recognized the boy on the tape—Justin Mitchell, who apparently was wreaking havoc long before I showed up at Langdon. Turns out he looks a lot like Mildred's son Reginald, especially when it's kind of dark out and you really *want* it to be Reginald like Smythe did. That's why he looked familiar when Mildred showed me his photo. When he returns to Langdon next week, I'll find out how much alike they really look.

Bethanie and I danced around each other all day, both of us trying to figure out what to say. It's true she gave me information about the night of the party that helped me solve the crime. She didn't have to do that. On the other hand, I don't even know what her real name is, or the secret she's hiding. There's more to her story than lottery money. People tend to be way more loyal to their secrets than to their friends, and I don't need any friends I can't trust. With the queen of the clones now the one on suspension and awaiting her court date, and Annette lying low in embarrassment (it turns out she has a shoplifting habit, but was otherwise an innocent pawn in Lissa's game), Bethanie is on her own at Langdon.

We may work it out, but not today, and not until I discover why Bethanie and her family are on the run. I have plenty of theories—they stole that winning lottery ticket and now a really pissed-off someone wants their money. Or maybe they created a counterfeit lottery ticket and got away with it until now, and the feds are tracking them down. It could be the life that Bethanie said she was never going back to, no matter what, is trying to reclaim her. Whatever it is, I'm making it my mission to figure it out ASAP and I can't do that if I leave Langdon.

There is one other reason I decided to give Langdon a try. The one who's starting the home opener this weekend against North High and can fake the sexiest French accent outside of France. I get through the day knowing we'll meet after school to rehearse our skit. Since we go onstage tomorrow, it's the last chance we have to get it right. He has his lines down perfectly. It's me who might cost us some points.

After the last bell, I try not to look too eager on my walk over to the library, but it's all I can do not to run. I'm full-on crazy for him, and I promise myself this is the day I'll let him know. You'd think sharing a near-death experience would have brought us close enough for one of us to make a real move, for me to make him the boyfriend the rest of the world thinks he is to me. So this is it. But as soon as I see him sitting on the library steps waiting for me, I turn to lava, hot for him but without form. I have no resolve; everything in me turns soft.

"What's up?" Marco gives me a nod, the way guys greet each other, not the way a guy greets a girl he can turn to lava just by looking at her. What's worse, I give the guy-nod back.

"Ready to rehearse?"

"As I'll ever be."

We go inside and find our usual table in the humanities section, which is thankfully quiet and empty.

"Look, I brought props," Marco says holding up a slice of bread. "We'll pretend it's a *baguette*."

"I think I'll take over responsibility for the props. There's a bakery near my house. I'll pick up a real baguette before school tomorrow."

"You have to use your imagination."

"That's what I'll tell Madame Renault when I mess up my lines. She can imagine I got them right."

Our skit is supposed to be a couple enjoying lunch in a café on a Parisian boulevard. Since we get to make it all up, our story has us sipping Cristal champagne and driving a Bentley to the café. Marco and I figured if we're going to do it, we ought to live large. It's our homage to the Langdon lifestyle. But for some reason, I still can't focus on my lines. All I can think about is how his leg keeps *accidentally* brushing against mine as we sit side by side. I wonder if he's noticed that I've opened an extra button on my shirt, one more than the Langdon dress code allows. Can he smell the perfume I dabbed on my neck this morning while thinking of him?

"Marco, aimes tu mes jambes?" I say in what I hope is a very sexy accent.

So when he breaks out laughing, I'm a little disappointed.

"You're supposed to ask me if I like the ham. *Le jambon.*" He can barely get it out between the laughing.

"That's what I said."

"No, you said 'Do you like my legs?'" More laughing.

I meant to be bold today, but not that bold. A minute ago, everything seemed perfect, and now I want to slide under the table, run out of the library. I try to think of something to say, a witty comeback that won't sound stupid, but Marco saves me from myself.

"Yeah, I do," he says, no longer laughing.

And that's when it happens. He leans toward me and I can feel warmth coming off him in waves and he smells so good and I feel like there is no one else in the world but us and *oh, it's finally happening*! and his lips touch mine and so soft, but not too soft, and yes, it is perfect.

MY OWN WORST FRENEMY

Kimberly Reid

ABOUT THIS GUIDE

The following questions are intended to
enhance your group's reading of
MY OWN WORST FRENEMY.

DISCUSSION QUESTIONS

1. Stereotyping got MJ ostracized on the Ave and Chanti suspended from Langdon by Headmistress Smythe. Have you ever had to deal with being stereotyped or profiled? Have you caught yourself doing it to others?

2. Being a snitch is seen as the lowest of the low. It's one thing to be in people's business and spreading information maliciously; it's another to share information about a person who hurts others or themselves with someone who can help. Have you ever been in a position to help or protect someone by divulging information, but feared being labeled a snitch?

3. Have you ever tried "trading up" friends the way Chanti did when she befriended MJ and neglected Tasha? How did it work out?

4. Even without being arrested like Chanti, being falsely accused is a frustrating experience. It can hurt to be accused of taking your sister's favorite earrings or starting a rumor about someone when you know they're innocent. Has this happened to you, and were you able to clear your name?

5. At first Chanti is worried Marco sees her only as a friend, which kills her because she's so into him. Have you ever liked someone as more than just friends, or been surprised by sudden romantic feelings for a person you always considered just a friend? Were you ever able to tell the person how you really felt? How did it affect your friendship?

6. It's tough being judged simply for being who you are, whether it's for being a book-geek like Chanti, or for the way you dress as Chanti did to Tasha and Michelle, or being the outsider like all the scholarship kids at Langdon. How do you deal with the haters?

7. Do you have friends like Michelle who just can't say no to the "bad boy" type? Or maybe you're like Michelle. The "bad" boys or girls are often just so irresistible—why is that?

8. Childhood friends sometimes grow up to be bad news, like Donnell DTS. We hear about celebrities who make it big but "keep it real" by hanging out with old friends and end up getting into serious trouble. Have you ever remained friends with someone out of loyalty even though you know they're bad for you?

9. We've all had a frenemy at some point—a girl who sabotages your plans to eat healthily by offering you your favorite junk food, or a boy who creeps on the girl he knows is your crush. Why do you think so-called friends do things like that? Have you found a good way to deal with frenemies?

10. Sometimes we can be our own worst frenemy. We love ourselves but still do all kinds of self-destructive things. Chanti always seems to land in the middle of trouble. Maybe you want to get into a good college, but do more partying than studying. How can we stop sabotaging ourselves and become our own best friends?

Coming up next . . .

CREEPING WITH THE ENEMY

A Langdon Prep Novel

Turn the page for a preview of Chanti's next adventure . . .

The line in the bodega is five deep because it's Freebie Friday and the tamales are buy one get one. I don't mind the wait—the scent of green chili reminds me how lucky I am to live on Aurora Avenue, just two blocks from the best tamales on the planet, or at least in a thirty-mile radius. Seeing how it's smack in the middle of Metro's second worst police zone, there isn't a lot to appreciate about The Ave, so that's saying something about these tamales. Since they only let you get one order, I always find someone to go along who doesn't love them like I do so I can get one extra. Today my tamale pimp is Bethanie—we're numbers six and seven in line—and she's calling me some choice words for making her wait for a free tamale when she can afford to buy the whole bodega. I'm trying to explain to her that there's no sport in being rich (not that I would know) when a guy walks in from a Ralph Lauren ad and becomes number eight in line.

I don't know how a person could look so out of place and seem completely at ease at the same time, but this guy is pulling it off. He's also checking out Bethanie so hard that even though he's a complete stranger, he makes me feel like I'm the one who crashed the party.

"What's so good in here that people are willing to wait

for it?" he asks Bethanie. He pretty much ignores me, so I almost laugh when his line goes right over her head.

"Supposedly the tamales are," she says, "but I wouldn't know."

I'm no pro at the flirty thing, but I'm sure he wasn't expecting her answer to be *tamales*. I move forward in the line, ignore their small talk and study the five-item menu as though I don't know what to order. Now there are only two people in front of me. Some Tejano music and the smell of cooking food drifts into the store from somewhere behind the clerk. I imagine somebody's grandmother back there wrapping corn husks around masa harina and pork. Yum.

I check out Preppie Dude like I'm not really looking at him but concentrating on the canned peaches on the shelf behind him. Cute. Not so cute he couldn't at least say hello to me before he starts fawning for my friend. He's still the last person in line even though tamale happy-hour runs from 4 to 5 and the line is usually out the door until 5. Weird, because it's only 4:30. I'm about to mention how weird that is to Bethanie, but she's finally figured out Preppie is flirting with her and has apparently forgotten me, too.

Now there's just one person ahead, Ada Crawford, who lives across the street from me and who I'm pretty sure is a hooker even though I don't have any proof. If we lived in a different neighborhood, I might say she was a call girl since her clients come to her. But we live in Denver Heights, so she doesn't get a fancy title. Luckily she hasn't noticed me behind her because I'm not supposed to be here and I wouldn't want her to tell my mother she saw me. Not that Ada ever has much to say to my mom.

Still no one else has come in. Along with the clerk I don't recognize, maybe they've also changed the cut-off time to 4:30. I suppose the owners would go broke if all people did was come in for the Freebie and not buy anything else. Or worse, get a friend to pimp an extra Freebie. I place my order—feeling slightly guilty—when I hear the bells over the door jangling a new arrival just as Ada walks away with her order. I look back to see a man holding the door open for Ada. He stays by the door once she's gone, and just stands there looking at the three of us still in line. He's jumpy. Nervous. He looks around the bodega but doesn't join the line and doesn't walk down the aisles of overpriced food. His left hand is in the pocket of his jacket, and my gut tells me to get out of the store. Just as I grab Bethanie's arm, the man brings his hand out of his jacket. It's too late.

"Alright, everybody stay cool. Don't start none, won't be none. Just give me what's in the drawer," he says to the clerk, pointing the gun at him.

I'm hoping the clerk won't try to jump back and pull out whatever he has under the counter. Every owner of a little mom-and-pop in my neighborhood has something under the counter. Or maybe it's in the back with the tamale-making grandmother. But no one comes from the back and the clerk isn't the owner. From what I can tell, it's his first day and he doesn't care about the money or the shop, and opens the cash drawer immediately. Bethanie pretends she's from money, but I know she's a lot more like me than she lets on. She knows what to do in a situation like this. Stay quiet and let it play out. We steal a quick glance at one another and I know I'm right. Either she's been through it before, or always expected it to happen one day.

I'm trying to stay calm by thinking ahead to when it will be over. Ninety seconds from now, this will just be a story for us to tell. The perp will be in his car taking the exit onto I-70. Hopefully I will not have puked all over myself by then. Or worse.

But then the cute guy speaks.

"Look man, just calm down."

What the hell? Just *shut up*, I want to scream. The clerk has already put the money into a paper bag and he's handing it over right now. This will all be over in thirty seconds if Preppie will just shut up.

The perp turns the gun in our direction. I lock eyes with him even though I know it's not the smartest thing to do. He realizes I can identify him, I can see him thinking about it, wondering what to do next. Suddenly, the smell of tamales sucker punches me and my stomach lurches. The wannabe-hero turns his back to the perp and shields Bethanie, pushing her to the ground and sending the contents of her bag all over the bodega floor. That move is like a cue for the perp—he breaks our gaze, grabs the paper bag from the clerk and takes off.

I was right—it's over in just about ninety seconds. None of us wants to stick around to give the cops a statement. Preppie, who might have gotten us all killed, helps Bethanie grab the stuff that fell out of her bag while I scan the store for cameras. There aren't any that I can tell. As the three of us leave the store, the clerk is picking up the phone to call either the owner or the police, depending on how good the owner is about obeying employment laws and paying his taxes. I manage not to puke until I reach the parking lot.